By S.A. Stovall

The Dusk Parlor
The Night Sky Festival

MODERN GLADIATOR
Modern Gladiator

RANGER STATION HAVEN
Ranger Station Haven
Thirty-One Days and Legos

Published by Dreamspinner Press
www.dreamspinnerpress.com

MODERN GLADIATOR

S.A. STOVALL

Published by
DREAMSPINNER PRESS

5032 Capital Circle SW, Suite 2, PMB# 279, Tallahassee, FL 32305-7886 USA
www.dreamspinnerpress.com

This is a work of fiction. Names, characters, places, and incidents either are the product of author imagination or are used fictitiously, and any resemblance to actual persons, living or dead, business establishments, events, or locales is entirely coincidental.

Modern Gladiator
© 2019 S.A. Stovall.

Cover Art
© 2019 Kanaxa.
Cover content is for illustrative purposes only and any person depicted on the cover is a model.

Trade Paperback ISBN: 978-1-64405-145-0
Digital ISBN: 978-1-64405-139-9
Library of Congress Control Number: 2018961346
Trade Paperback published March 2019
v. 1.0

Printed in the United States of America
∞
This paper meets the requirements of
ANSI/NISO Z39.48-1992 (Permanence of Paper).

To John, forever and always.
To Nicole, a wonderful editor.
To Marcus,
my half brother who everyone assumed wasn't related to me.
To Ann, for encouraging me to write this.
To other Ann, for all her Australian goodness.
To a relationship lost.
And to everyone else who helped.

Chapter 1
Cage Match

Corbin Friel

MY SISTER, Malala, enjoys sports like she enjoys life, with unrestrained enthusiasm and lots of shouting. Weighing in at one hundred and fifteen pounds, you'd think she wouldn't be all that noisy or aggressive.

"I could have thrown a better punch," Malala yells at the combatants. "C'mon! Get your head in the game!"

I don't usually watch mixed martial arts. The thought of two people attempting to render each other unconscious disturbs me. On the other hand, MMA fighters are at the pinnacle of human physique. I get weak in the knees looking at some of these guys and their six-pack perfect abs. Hell, some of them might have eight-packs, but I feel weird for staring too long, so I don't bother to count. When they throw punches, they're the epitome of masculine brutality.

The fight ends with one man unconscious and the other so bloody and lumpy his head resembles a half-crushed tomato. The winner smiles and revels in the cheers that flood the auditorium. One victory lap around the octagon—an eight-sided fighting stage lined with chain-link fences—and then he's ushered away.

"Next up, we have our light heavyweight match," the announcer says over the microphone. "In the red corner, fighting out of Sacramento, California, with a professional win-loss record of five to three, we have Derek 'the Stinger' Smith!"

Applause explodes all around us, drowning out everything else. A man walks into the octagon. They call it a "cage" for the fighters, and I can see why. The chain link doesn't obscure the fight, but it does make it seem more barbaric than a boxing match. Cameras swivel atop the fence posts, catching the action from above and playing it across large flat-screen TVs for everyone to see.

I hold my hands over my ears, lessening the decibels pounding at my eardrums. The music and applause have reached new levels of torture. I won't be able to hear for a week. Why did I show up to this event?

"I can't wait," Malala says with a squeal.

That's why I'm here. She wouldn't let me say no.

Malala—well, I just call her *Lala*—turns to me with an exuberant smile. "This is it! The final fight before the heavyweight bout, and there's my favorite fighter!"

"Which one is your favorite fighter?" I ask, my voice nowhere near as loud as my sister's.

"The Stinger, Derek Smith! He's right there!"

I squint, trying to get a good look at the guy while he parades around the cage. His white shorts have a million advertisements on the side—even Derek's gloves have the Nike swoosh. But that all pales in comparison to the fine tone of his tanned skin and the pelvic muscle that forms a vee groove, right above the waistband of his shorts. He's got a lion-head tattoo on the side of his ribs, adding another healthy dose of testosterone to his already-too-manly-for-words appearance. Even his beard looks like it could kick half the audience's ass without breaking a sweat.

The announcer, a husky man in a tuxedo, holds up his hands, quieting the audience. "And in the blue corner, fighting out of Stockton, California, with a professional win-loss record of three to zero, we have a fighter on a blazing winning streak! I bring you Keon 'the Watchman' Lynch!"

Half the crowd claps and shouts, but the other half, louder than the rest, boos. Even my sister gets to her feet and thrusts her thumbs down. "Loser," she shouts. "You're going down!"

I grab her shoulder and attempt to pull her back into her chair. "Is that necessary? You're acting like a delinquent."

Lala gives me a wide smile. "C'mon, don't be like that. This is all part of the experience. You have to trash talk the other side. We want Derek to win, right? Get him psyched and get the other guy sweating."

I cover my face with one hand, careful not to smudge my glasses, red from my ears to collarbone. "Do we have to yell?"

"Of course we have to yell. C'mon, Bin-Bin!"

"Don't call me that." Not *here*, of all places.

"I'll keep calling you that until you stand."

I hate my nickname. Corbin is a fine name, but *Bin-Bin* makes me sound like a pet rabbit. I'm sure she started calling me that after I began calling her Lala, but it's not the same. Lala isn't a bad nickname. I'd much rather her call me Friel, my last name. It's what people will call me once I become a doctor. Dr. Friel. She should get used to it.

"Bin-Bin, c'mon! They're about to start! Yell something!"

Keon also struts around the octagon. It must be part of the show for the fighters to rile the crowd. He holds up his hands, and with his fingerless gloves, he flips off the half of the audience that booed him. An explosion of sound rips through the arena. More boos, cheers, and laughter mix together into a cacophony. Despite his vulgar gesture, people love the spectacle. Even my sister insults him again, a smile on her face.

A couple of sexed-up girls in bikinis walk around the outside of the octagon, holding up signs to indicate the match is about to begin.

The booing intensifies. Some shout curse words, others encourage Derek to "rip Keon a new asshole" and other colorful instructions. These must be fan clubs, people here to encourage their favorite fighter.

If we were sitting in the back of the auditorium, maybe I wouldn't feel so self-conscious about trash-talking someone on stage, but Lala got us front-row seats. We're feet away from the action.

Lala elbows me in the shoulder with her boney arm. "Do it. Yell something."

I take a deep breath and stand. I can't ever tell my sister no. But what should I say? I've never trashed-talked someone before—I prefer cutting wit to yo-mama jokes any day—but this isn't the place for repartee. I guess I should go with something to-the-point and generic.

The announcer holds up his hands just as I shout, "You suck, Keon!"

My voice carries over the hushed audience, clear enough to be heard by the people in the cage. Keon turns on his heel and locks his gaze onto me, his eyes narrowed in an intense glare.

I shrink back into my seat and slide down until I'm huddled in the shadows. My stomach and intestines curl into themselves, my whole body wracked by the embarrassment. How did I let Lala talk me into this? I should've stayed home and studied.

3

Lala sits down and laughs under her breath. "That was great! I think Keon heard you."

"Oh, he heard all right." I'll be lucky if he doesn't jump me in the parking lot.

"Why are you so sullen? Maybe now he's shaken."

A harsh ring starts the match, but I can't bring myself to watch.

The savage brutality of the match echoes over the speakers. Each punch, like a frozen steak hit against cold metal, reminds me how frail the human body can be. A broken bone could puncture the skin and poke out the side of the body, organs can be bruised or busted, and some places never fully heal. The nose and ears can become malformed, and they'll stay that way without cosmetic surgery.

This is why I avoid MMA fights.

My sister gasps and flails around in her seat. Then the whole arena collectively holds its breath. Even the announcer shouts, "Brutal!"

Curiosity gets the better of me. I sit back up and watch the match.

Oh Jesus.

Derek might as well have been hit by a car—his blood stains the octagon like a surrealist painting.

But Keon…. He doesn't have a scratch on him. I barely took note of his appearance before, but now it's all I can focus on. Sweat dapples his dark, tanned skin, glistening under the harsh light of the octagon, highlighting his many muscles. And he has beautifully developed muscles. Pronounced deltoids, strong pecs, obvious biceps—and he didn't forget his triceps either—along with some steel quads and edged lats. No tattoos. Not a single one. I figured all fighters were half thug—marking themselves with the ink of all their gang affiliations. Then again, I don't know much about fighters outside of movies.

But not having tattoos allows me to better admire his physical perfection.

This is why I like MMA fights. My pants grow uncomfortable as I study the guy like I'm preparing for a muscle-group quiz in anatomy. Why must fighters be gods among men?

And unlike Derek, who wore loose shorts, Keon has a pair of tight black shorts with the same number of endorsements and advertisements.

Monster Energy Drink is written across the backside of the shorts, which is fitting, because he is a monster fighter.

Keon strikes Derek across the face, bloodying Derek's fine beard. And before Derek can fall, Keon does it again, this time with a left hook worse than the right—a one-two combination to the cabbage that renders Derek unconscious.

Derek hits the floor, his leg twitching. Another harsh bell rings throughout the stunned auditorium.

"Ladies and gentlemen, thirty seconds into round one and we have a winner!"

Everyone jumps to their feet, flaring with either excitement or hate. There is no middle ground. Bits of popcorn and food get thrown into the octagon, but the cheering quickly overtakes any negativity.

Keon pivots on his heel and faces me—definitely *me* and no one else. Frozen in place, I wait. Keon smirks and then gives me the middle finger, like he's saying he won the match fast to prove my trash-talking wrong.

I duck down again, hiding away from his gaze, my heart rate high and my pulse hot. I don't know why, but his cocky confidence has my stomach doing flips. Why am I always attracted to macho bravado? It can't be healthy. Especially because I'm sure he wants nothing more than to beat the pulp out of me.

Lala shakes my shoulder, a deep frown on her face. "I can't believe Derek lost. And to a complete rookie."

"I don't think he's a *complete* rookie."

"Derek is so much better than this. He got overconfident. That's it. He needs to keep his head in the game. Did you see the way he tried to dodge the first punch? He should've ducked to the left."

"I didn't see the first half of the fight."

"What? How could you look away? That was an intense match!"

Medics jump into the octagon and tend to Derek's broken face. He woke half a second after he hit the floor, but he's obviously still disorientated and reeling. The medics snap their fingers in front of his eyes, and he nods. He'll have a balloon for a face tomorrow, no doubt about it.

The announcer takes Keon's left hand and raises it into the air. "We have a winner! Keon Lynch wins by TKO! Do you have anything to say?"

Keon takes the microphone and half smiles. "This win was for all the doubters out there." I swear he gives me another quick glance before turning his attention to the rest of the audience. "Thank you to all my fans. I'm not going to disappoint. I will become a UFC light heavyweight champion!"

More cheering, clapping, and the occasional boo. Again, I hold my hands over my ears, trying to lessen the intensity of the crowd. It goes on for a solid minute before Keon drops the microphone and walks out of the octagon. Then, somehow, the boisterous applause doubles in strength. Everyone likes a showboat, apparently.

Lala shakes me. She says some things, but I can't hear them.

"I'm going to go to the restroom," I say, though I don't know if she heard me either.

I walk through the rowdy crowd of half-drunk fans and enter the men's room to escape the noise. Although still loud outside, I relax and splash my face with some water. I'm the sole occupant of the room. I can handle this. No pressure or anxiety.

With muscle-memory precision, I go through my hand-washing routine. I have my own disinfectant, and I carry a small bottle of it in my pocket at all times. After all the horror stories of contracting deadly diseases from random locations, I've developed an irrational fear of public squalor. I know the chances of catching anything are astronomically small, but I still can't shake my dread of unsanitary surfaces.

I scrub my hands for a solid thirty seconds.

"What am I even doing?" I ask the mirror as I straighten my glasses.

I know why. Someone had to go with Lala to the fights. She suffers from osteogenesis imperfecta. Brittle bone disease. She could fracture any number of her bones from falling, or even cause a major break. It's not as bad as it used to be when she was younger, but if something were to happen, someone would need to be there for her.

After a long exhale, I exit the restroom—careful not to touch the door handle—and duck through the crowd until I reach the snack bar. A few stands are set up, selling all the "best" fight-night foods a guy could want. Hot dogs. Popcorn. Nachos. Beer. Soda. I'm sure they all taste great, but I try to watch what I consume, which means cutting out unnecessary fats and sugars. I order water, get an odd look from the cashier, and then walk away.

A huge rumble of applause shakes the building. The heavyweight fight must have either ended or started. I can't tell which. I stay in the snack bar area, sipping my water in the corner, waiting for the raucous energy to die down.

I watch the clock and think about all the studying I'll need to do to make up for the night. Ninety pages of human anatomy won't read themselves. But I'm not too worried. I'm third in my class, and having parents who are both doctors means I've been exposed to the field of medicine all my life.

When the excitement peters out, I walk back into the main auditorium. Sure enough, the announcer is the sole person in the octagon, finishing up the last of the announcements.

"What a fantastic show tonight, ladies and gentleman," the man says. "Remember to stick around for the raffle and charity event! And remember to get your tickets for the next event!"

I reach my sister, and she smiles up at me.

"There you are, Bin-Bin!"

"Ready to go?" I ask.

"No, we can't leave yet. I have raffle tickets!" She unravels a whole damn wheel of tickets, allowing them to spill to the floor for dramatic emphasis. "C'mon! We have to see if I won!"

I exhale and follow her to the booth for ticket winners. Everything has been drawn in advance, and Lala rushes over to the winning ticket list to see if her myriad of tickets won her anything exciting. They have T-shirts and gift baskets and even tickets to future games, but I'm not interested. I can't wait to get home.

People crowd around, and I keep my arms crossed tight across my chest. I stand out. I know I do. While everyone else has casual jeans and jackets, I'm in a pair of slacks and a button-up shirt. My mother stresses professionalism in the medical field, so I endeavor to maintain her legacy, but perhaps a sporting event wasn't the best place to wear steam-cleaned clothing.

"*Ohmygosh*!" my sister squeals. "I won! Bin-Bin, look! I won!"

I swear my sister doesn't have a medium setting to her volume. She either shouts or whispers. There is no middle option.

"Grab it and let's go," I say.

"No, look! I get to go backstage and meet one of the fighters!"

"Wait, right now?"

She hops over to me, boundless energy flowing from her like an aura. Even her long black hair bounces like an uncoiled slinky. I hold up my hands, trying to calm her.

"Be careful," I say. "You don't want to hurt yourself. Think of your body."

"I'm fine. Stop treating me like I'll break any second. Let's go!"

Although my sister is older than I am—her twenty-eight to my twenty-two—I swear she acts ten years younger than me. I'm not surprised. Lala spent several years in the hospital as a child, and I sometimes think she's making up for lost time by enjoying life like only a kid can.

Lala holds a special pass in hand as we snake our way through the sea of bodies. We make it all the way to the back ring door when a pair of bouncers grabs us both by the shoulders. Their black suits and sunglasses make me think I'm waiting in line at a fancy nightclub, but their bursting-at-the-seams muscles remind me of the reality. They hire badasses to protect the badasses, that's for sure.

"Fighters and their corner guys only," one bouncer says in a gruff tone.

Lala holds up her prize. "I want to see Derek 'the Stinger' Smith!"

The two bouncers exchange a quick look, both frowning. "You sure you want to meet that fighter?" the other bouncer asks. "You don't want to meet someone else?"

"I definitely want to see Derek."

"All right, then. I'll show you to the room."

The one guy leads us through the door. I'm hit with a heavy scent of sweat, mixed with a hint of blood. Weight trainers, dojo owners, and other fighters wait around the water coolers and complimentary snack tables. Each fighting association seems to have its own space, but we aren't taken to any group. I keep my head down and avoid eye contact. Can we trust anyone back here? Professional fighters are only one step up from criminals in my mind—loose cannons with dangerous weapons, ready to hurt someone else at a moment's notice.

And I especially don't want to run into Keon. He's an unpredictable fighter with a reason to throw me against the wall.

The bouncer leads us to a back room with a couch, a few cushioned chairs, and a TV with video feeds to the ring.

"You'll have fifteen minutes," the guy says. "You can ask the fighter to sign your stuff or take selfies but no endorsements, got it?"

"Sure," I say.

He nods and exits, leaving me and my sister alone in the room.

8

"So exciting," she whispers. "I feel like a VIP."

"This room looks like a teachers' lounge."

"But for fighters!"

"I'm a little underwhelmed, to be honest."

"What did you think they do backstage?"

"I don't know. Practice for their match? Wrestle tigers? Something more impressive than sitting around."

Lala laughs. "They don't want to injure themselves right before a fight. They need to relax." She sits on the couch and fidgets with her jeans.

The door opens, and I flinch, way more tense than I thought I was. Two men walk through the door—a bloodied Derek, and none other than his opponent, Keon Lynch.

Derek smiles, but it's hard to tell. His face looks like thirty bees went to town stinging him. I'm surprised he's not drooling on himself. What if he has a concussion? Did the medics sign off on his health?

"Someone asked to see me?" he says, his speech thick with saliva and cotton balls. He must be bleeding from the inside of his mouth.

"I did," Lala says as she stands. "I'm Malala Friel!"

"Whaddaya want signed?"

Derek holds up a Sharpie, his fingers swollen, but he keeps his grip.

Wow, I guess Keon really did a number on this guy. But Derek seems happy. Too upbeat, to be honest. He just lost a fight. What is there to be happy about?

"Hey."

I turn and find Keon glaring at me. Up close, I notice more details about his overall appearance. He has a slight mohawk, his dark hair unkempt, and his chin has a dusting of hair I've always found attractive. His dark tan skin has a bronze hue I find fascinating. Both Keon and Derek are still in their shorts, and they've donned T-shirts since the match. Tight, form-fitting T-shirts. I try not to stare.

I'm on the fence—should I run or should I hit on the guy? The piercing glower Keon gives me says I should probably run. And I have no idea if he's interested in men. Hitting on a fighter who *isn't* gay will definitely get me punched in the face. Why did I have to trash-talk a professional fighter? I should've known life would make sure it came back to haunt me.

Chapter 2
Biggest Fan

Corbin Friel

"WHAT'S WRONG?" Keon asks. "You had all sorts of things to say before the match started."

I glance over to Lala, hoping she'll save me from this. But she and Derek moved to the other side of the room, and now she's in whisper mode. Why did she have to abandon me?

"I think you're mistaking me for someone else," I say.

"Am I? You're the only asshole wearing a suit and glasses."

"I, uh, well... lots of people have glasses. Besides, I wouldn't dare say anything negative about you. You were clearly the superior fighter. Good job. With the fight. It was great." I rub the back of my neck, forcing a laugh, flushed from the toes up.

Keon steps closer to me. I take a step back out of reflex, but there's nowhere to go. There's a single door, and Keon stands in the way. Up close, he smells of powerful deodorant and gym sweat. A pleasant combination, but I shouldn't be thinking about that right now.

"So, it wasn't you?" he drawls. "The one in the front row?"

"No. Not me. I'm, uh, a fan. A huge fan. Your biggest fan."

He's not buying it. Hell, *I'm* not buying it. I couldn't lie to the most gullible person on earth—I've never been good at subterfuge. Then again, lots of people booed him. Why would he care about me? I guess those other people aren't in the back room trying to get stuff signed from him and his buddies. And what if this guy is a rage-o-holic? Aren't all fighters too crazy for words and hyperaggressive? I bet he would punch a dude for looking at him cross-eyed.

"A fan, huh?" Keon says, dragging me from my spiral of terrible hypotheticals. He barks a single laugh and then smirks. "Why don't I sign your shirt, then? That's what every fan wants, right?"

10

My shirt cost fifty dollars. Do I want someone to write all over it with Sharpie? No. Definitely not. Am I going to tell the MMA fighter I'm the one who yelled he sucked? Nope. Not going to do that—never in a million years. So I guess I'm losing out on a shirt.

"O-okay," I say. "That would be great."

Keon holds up a Sharpie, grabs the collar of my shirt, and pulls me close. He chortles under his breath, like he's enjoying every second. My heart beats against my rib cage the moment he pokes his pen into place. I swear he could stab me with it, that's how strong he is.

"This looks expensive," he says. He writes across my chest in big letters. "Nice material. You must be a lawyer or some other fancy Popsicle."

"I'm a med student."

"Is that right?" He finishes another line on my shirt. What is he writing? "I know a med student. You must be an egghead, just like her…."

He gives me the once-over, his eyes trailing at a slow and steady pace. My face heats up, and I look away.

"You work out?" he asks.

"I don't usually have the time," I say. Is he flirting with me?

"Yeah, it doesn't feel like it," he quips.

I grit my teeth and silently berate myself. Of course he wasn't hitting on me! He's just messing with my head.

Keon finishes his signature, and then he offers me a playful smile. My fear and hesitation rapidly boil into irritation. He's not going to beat me up—he's just messing with me.

I glance down at my shirt. He wrote: I LOVE BIG DADDY KEON LYNCH. His signature sits underneath. If embarrassment could kill, I would have stage 3 terminal humiliation. I can't believe I didn't bring a jacket or a sweater. I'm going to have to walk out of here with *this* on my chest—and it isn't small either. Big, bold print. Keon wanted people to see.

I guess this is better than getting punched in the face.

"Come see me in the cage again," Keon says. "I'd hate to have a fight without my biggest fan in the audience."

What a douchebag. Why must everyone with a body like him be so infuriating?

"I knew you'd remember," Lala says with a squeal, her volume shifting to super loud in an instant. "We sat right next to each other, after all."

Derek laughs. "I can't believe it. You recognize me? From second grade?"

"Of course! You were the one who showed me around school when none of the other kids would. And when I saw you on Facebook and that you were a pro fighter now, I had to go to all your matches."

"Wow. I'm flattered. We should get a picture."

"Yes, we should." Lala turns on her heel and waves me over. "Bin-Bin, get a picture!"

Why? Why does she insist on using my nickname? I'm already wearing a ridiculous shirt, but now I'm subject to my sister's pet names being spread around like a cough in elementary school.

I walk around Keon and pull out my phone. She hugs up close to Derek, her arm around his bruised body, and he grimaces. Derek hides it when Lala glances up at him, however, forcing a half smile on his messed-up face.

I snap a few pictures. Derek makes a fist with his free hand, like he's taking a fight photo, and Lala does the same. They laugh and have a good time with it, but I'm ready to go. Heck, I was ready to go a few hours ago, but now I'm secretly hoping for a coma to rescue me from this event.

Lala hugs Derek a second time, and my chest tightens at the sight.

"You two know each other?" I ask.

"He was in my second-grade class," Lala says. "That was the year between hospitals, when I had to use forearm crutches. None of the kids wanted to play with me, but Derek did."

I was way too young to remember any of that. And even if he was an amazing friend in second grade, that doesn't mean he's a good person now.

Derek rubs the back of his neck. "I forgot you had the crutches. It's all coming back now. I beat up the kids who made fun of you."

Lala nods. "I know. I guess it was your destiny to become a fighter, right?"

She beams up at him. I've never seen her look at someone like that. Ever. Derek must feel something too, because he looks away, still chuckling, his face so swollen he can't seem to adequately display any emotion outside of *intense pain.*

The door opens and a bouncer pokes his bald head into the room. "Time's up."

"Aw," Lala groans. She turns to Derek. "I'm so glad I got to meet you in person. I'm definitely coming to all your matches in the future."

"Hey," Derek says. "Why don't you give me your number? I'll hook you up with tickets."

"Really? You can do that?"

"Oh yeah. All the fighters get tickets to give to their friends and family. And I'd love to see you again."

"I'd like that."

I put an arm around my sister and nod to Derek. "Okay, okay. I think we need to go."

"I'll wait for her to write her number down," the bouncer says.

I hold back my objections. Who is this Derek guy, anyway? Already asking for my sister's number? Pretty forward. Too forward.

Lala writes her name and number on a napkin and hands it over. Then she grabs my arm, and we leave the lounge. I give Keon one last glance before exiting. He's stretched out on the couch, watching us go with an amused smile. He's good-looking—more than good—but I still feel a lingering irritation when I catch his gaze. And he's a fighter. They have to be insane at a certain level. They're up in cages beating each other *for fun*. They can't be smart people.

Lala pokes my chest. "Wow. Looks like you made a friend."

I cover Keon's signature with my arm. "Never mention this to anyone."

"You'll come with me to other fights, right?"

"Maybe," I say, flushed all over again. "We'll talk about it later."

Keon Lynch

I FINISH packing my equipment and glance up at the clock. 2300 hours. Damn. It's been a long night.

"You gonna do any celebrating?" Derek asks.

He doesn't have to pack his equipment. He came with a dojo— some place called Rodrick Hu Goju Karate—and the coaches gather everything for their fighters. Must be nice. I'd join a place if I could afford the membership.

"Nah," I say. "No celebrating."

13

Derek holds his napkin close and examines the phone number. "Can you believe it? I lost and still had to fend off the ladies." He attempts to waggle his eyebrows, but I don't think he'll be able to move his face for a week.

"Congrats."

"I remember Malala being nice. Full of energy, ya know? And she was hot, right?"

I give him a sidelong glance as I thrust the last of my towels into my duffel bag. Derek replies with a nervous laugh and tucks the napkin back into his pocket.

"Sorry. I keep forgetting you're not into the ladies."

How can he forget? Then again, Derek forgets a lot of stuff. We've been friends since our time in Afghanistan. We both served two tours together, and he's the most forgetful man I know. People joke it's because he's taken one too many blows to the head, but I know better. He's always been like this.

I check our surroundings, hoping no one heard his comment. We're separated from the others. While most fighters wouldn't care what team I played for, some will make my life a living hell. I don't want to risk getting kicked out of the fighting league over some bullshit homophobia.

Most fighters are friends with each other, even after fighting in the ring. There's a limited amount of fight nights to participate in, so everyone knows everyone else. If my sexuality came out and some guys made an issue of it, my fighting career would become infinitely more difficult. They'd all band together to see me ousted.

I'm friends with Derek, sure, but we were in the Army together, and he's always treated me like a long-lost brother. He treats all his friends like that—like a kindred spirit he's known through a million past lives.

"You gonna join us?" Derek asks. "For food?"

"Nah."

"You sure?"

"I have work tomorrow."

"All the losers get sloshed together," Derek says with a smile. "It's pretty hilarious."

"Hanging around depressed people just gets me depressed."

"Oh, I get it. That's how I am with horny people."

I chuckle as I sling my bag over my shoulder. "You haven't changed a bit since we were in the infantry together."

Derek rests back on a foldout chair, his breathing a little heavy. "You rushin' home to your new squeeze or something?"

"Would you stop talkin' about this? I don't have anyone."

"How? We're in California. I wouldn't be surprised if we changed our state animal to a rainbow. There has to be someone here for you."

"Maybe."

"You have to find someone to kill the loneliness with. Trust me. I went to dark places when I didn't have any friends or family around. Didn't you leave everyone you know in South Carolina?"

Yeah, thanks for reminding me, Derek. I keep the comment to myself and sigh. "Yes."

"You don't want to end up like those drunks who fight to forget, do you?"

"Heh."

It's not hard to find a guy for a night—at least, not for me. When I lived in South Carolina, I knew a lot of gym rats who wanted a workout partner to go home with them after their training. Lots of fun, but I have to be careful now.

"I don't need anyone," I say.

"You haven't seen anybody who interests you?"

I've seen plenty. But my thoughts drift to the coat rack with glasses who insulted me during my match. I knew the moment I started manhandling his shirt that he was into me. No guy blushes that hard or avoids looking at my body unless he's into men. I'd stake my life on it.

And he said he was a med student. Ironic. It makes him stick out in my mind, unlike any of my other admirers.

But I really can't start thinking about bullshit like that. I have too much to do and not enough time to do it.

"What about you?" I ask Derek, trying to clear my thoughts. "You got anyone in mind?"

Derek holds up his napkin and points to the phone number.

"Old elementary school flame, huh?"

"Something like that," he says.

"Who was the guy with her?"

"That was her brother. I don't remember his name. Bun-Bun or something?"

"That's not it. That's not even a real name."

"Dude, I don't remember. She said it was her brother. Why?"

"No reason," I say, trying to remember his name for myself. "I was just curious."

Derek snorts, and a little blood from his broken nose drips onto his upper lip. He wipes it off with a towel. "All right. I'll catch you later."

"See ya."

After a long exhale, I give Derek a quick wave and head for the door. The Sacramento night air stings my sweat-coated skin. I forgot how chilly it can get in California, especially during the winter. South Carolina had a humidity that refused to quit—like living on top of a boiling pot. Anything is good compared to that.

I walk over to my motorcycle. The parking lot is anything but empty. Groups of fighters hang with spectators, discussing the fights or meeting up for dinner. They laugh and chat at volumes inappropriate for 2300 hours, but half of them are drunk and probably don't realize where they are anyway. Beer flows as much as the blood at these events.

"Hey," someone calls out as I tie my bag into the back.

I turn to face another fighter. Clark Suna, I think his name is.

"What's up?" I ask.

Clark saunters over, his thumbs tucked into the waistband of his shorts. He's heavy. Weighs more than my 205, that's for sure. And he keeps his hair braided back in a tight ponytail, revealing the myriad of tattoos on his neck. His shirt tells me he fights with some Gracie jiujitsu place—the Alpha MMA Academy. It's a middling fight club trying to break out onto the scene.

"I see you're making some waves," Clark says.

Three more walk over, each wearing identical T-shirts with the Alpha MMA Academy logo on the chest. That's how most fighting academies work. They have support teams that come out to cheer their fighters, each wearing the uniform of their trade. I don't mind—I'm even a little jealous, since I don't have a team of my own—but it can get intimidating for some newer guys. If someone's support team is bigger than someone else's, the jeering can rattle the weak-willed.

I glance between the four guys. "I'm just here to win fights."

"Yeah," Clark says. "You had a good match, pal."

"Thanks."

"And I heard you say you wanted to join the UFC."

"That's right."

"Look, maybe you should join a dojo or academy fight. Get the lay of the land before you go diving into the big leagues."

"They cost money."

Clark shrugs. "Some academies will take new fighters who show talent. I'm trying to help you out. Lots of guys want a shot in the UFC. Not everyone gets it. And it's better if you have a crew to back you up."

"I'll keep that in mind," I say as I grab my helmet. I don't like Clark's tone, and I know where this is going.

"Maybe you should join our academy," he says. "Maybe, in a couple of years, you could really make a name for yourself."

"Or maybe, in *one* year, I'll make a name for myself by joining the UFC."

"I don't think you're ready for that, pal."

Heh. I knew it. He's trying to scare me away from the UFC qualifier fight. The less competition, the better his academy can do, the more famous they'll become.

It's hard to join the UFC—the Ultimate Fighting Championship. It pays good money, the fighters get tons of exposure, and it's the pinnacle of fighting careers before they retire to be a broadcaster or a personal trainer or own their own gym or fight academy. Every professional fighter wants to join the UFC, which is a shame, because the more popular it becomes, the harder it is to stand out among fellow competitors.

Which is why everyone wants to enter the UFC qualifier coming up twelve months from now. The winners get invited to fight in the UFC, and those who win the overall get UFC contracts.

Clark's thinking long-term. I can see it in the way he narrows his eyes into a glower, irritated with my refusal to join his academy. He wants my glory, or he wants to take me out early.

"I think I've done well on my own," I say, sliding onto my motorcycle.

"Don't say I didn't warn you."

It's the last thing I hear before I rev my engine.

I'm used to assholes trying to get their way through sheer bravado. I'm not the type to roll over and take it. If they want to stop me from getting into the UFC, they'll have to beat me in the cage.

Chapter 3
Tickets

Corbin Friel

I WALK up the stairs of my apartment building, holding my groceries close. My phone buzzes nonstop. I continue on my way, ignoring the vibrations. I've mastered juggling things while walking up steps. And I know it's just my sister. Every text she sends, every voicemail she leaves reminds me that she has tickets to the next fight night. She's practically been doing it for the last two weeks.

I didn't know they had MMA fights once a month. And Derek isn't even fighting, but he gave her tickets anyway. I don't want to go—I really don't want to go—but I hate the idea of my sister being alone with a fighter guy. We don't know much about Derek except for the fact that he punches people for a hobby. Sure, he went to second grade with Lala, and maybe he helped her out, but he was a kid then. And really, how sane can someone be to step into a fighting arena? I'm willing to bet he's not all right in the head.

But thinking about her makes me wish she were here. If I'm not driving her around or taking her to doctor's appointments, I'm not really hanging with anyone else. I go to school, sure, but then I'm attending a lecture or examining cadavers in lab. That isn't the time for socializing.

A small piece of me wants to stop carrying my groceries and answer the phone. I haven't had any company the last two days. My small apartment might as well be an island in the middle of the ocean.

But my phone stops buzzing. If I want company, I'll need to watch the show *Friends*.

When I reach the fourth-story hallway, I freeze.

My ex, Justin Riddle, leans against the wall next to my apartment door, his eyes glued to his cell phone. The lonely corridor and cold draft tell me my neighbors have all gone to bed. Most people who live in these apartments are well over the age of sixty, and although it's only 8:00 p.m., it doesn't surprise me that they're sound asleep.

18

Justin spots me a second later and flashes me a Hollywood smile.

"There you are," Justin says. "I knew you'd be home around this time. They could set clocks to the exactness of your schedule."

A piece of me is happy to see him, because at least my desert island got a visitor, but the rest of me—the logical part—knows this will leave me more depressed than before.

I sigh and amble over to my front door. "What do you want?"

"Ouch. Not even a friendly hello? What would your mother say?"

My mother always scolds me for rude mannerisms. I bite back a sarcastic comment and say, "Hello." Then I shoot him a glare. "Now what do you want?"

Justin pushes away from the wall and brushes himself off. He has a wiry frame that complements his impressive height—a few inches over my 5'10". No matter the time of year, he wears beach outfits. Cargo shorts, T-shirts, sandals. He has an easygoing aura that only Californians can achieve. And his short, spiky blond hair only adds to the overall visual.

"I came by to chat," Justin says.

I hold my bag of groceries in one arm and unlock my door. "Just like when you came by the last two times?"

"What can I say? I get lonely. You understand."

"I've been seeing someone."

"No you haven't."

I grit my teeth, hating how much of my personal life he knows. Justin comes by every week or so, looking to chat or hook up. We broke up because he's a flaker of the worst degree—always disappearing for days on end with no explanation—and I want to be with someone who won't dodge every question or avoid truthful answers. I want someone disciplined and honorable. Someone I wouldn't feel ashamed to associate with.

But as a friends-with-benefits type, I guess Justin's not bad. I wish he would tell me before he comes over, or at least keep a consistent pattern. He acts as though my plans don't matter, even if I need to study.

Justin takes the groceries out of my arms. "I got this. Let's get inside. It's cold out here."

I could send him away and spend the evening on my island, lamenting my lack of company… or I could acquiesce to his arrival and attempt to enjoy his company.

I exhale. "All right. Come in."

We enter my apartment. It's nothing special. One living room–kitchen combo, one bath, and one bed. No pictures. Two plants. White walls. A simple space for studying. That's all I need. Oh, and four bottles of hand sanitizer. I like to have them within easy reach. My aunt made a crude joke about the frequency of my masturbation, but she didn't take a class on the hidden germs lurking on the surface of everyday objects. If she knew the diseases that sat on the keys of an office keyboard, she would have four bottles of hand sanitizer as well.

Justin places my groceries on the kitchen counter, and his gaze falls to the sink.

"What's this?"

He pulls out one of my white button-up shirts—the one Keon signed at the match. I've tried everything to clean it, but nothing works. Tonight I was going to soak it in bleach, but I'm sure it'll ruin the garment completely.

"It's nothing," I say as I unload the bag.

"'I love big daddy Keon Lynch,' huh?" he says, reading it with a smile. "When did this happen?"

"When I spent time with my sister at the fights."

"And this was from one of the fighters?"

"That's right."

I place my fruits and vegetables in the fridge just as Justin steps up behind me and wraps his arms around my torso.

"Are you trying to make me jealous?" he asks, his tone husky.

"You and I aren't a couple. Not anymore."

"Why do you keep saying that?"

"Because we aren't."

I elbow him away and shut the fridge door. I hate when he tries to tell me *we're still dating*. I broke up with him, but he continues to act as though nothing happened. He keeps coming around; he keeps talking about us like a couple. He keeps expecting the same things from me…. It's like he lives in a different reality, and he's slowly wearing me down until he gets what he wants. I mean, we're still having sex, so maybe I'm giving him mixed messages, but sometimes it's just easier to give him what he wants so he leaves me alone rather than fight about it.

Justin rolls his eyes. "Can we not do this? You let me into your place. At a certain level, you want me here. Why can't we enjoy each other's company? Why do you need to bring up a bunch of stuff that doesn't matter?" He gets up close again, all smiles and reeking of lust. "I know something you'll want to hear. I got a job."

He presses me back against the fridge and runs his hands down to the waist of my pants. He's always been good at foreplay. All our past trysts flood my mind. He's a handsome guy. Really nice ass too. This is why I keep seeing him. And why I feel guilty afterward. Shouldn't I be with someone for more than just physical reasons?

But I must admit, hearing he has a job does remove some of my hesitation. He knows me too well—always saying the right things to get me to break.

"What kind of job?" I ask.

"I'm night security guard for a hotel. They gave me a uniform and everything."

"Must be the kind of hotel that doesn't care if its stuff goes missing."

Justin cocks an eyebrow. "Get your jokes out now. I'm being serious."

"Do you actually show up on time? That's why you got fired from your last four jobs. They wanted someone who would adhere to a schedule."

"I've got it, I've got it. Don't worry, Bin-Bin."

"Well, congrats on your job."

Heat courses through my system as he undoes my belt.

Justin stares me right in the eyes, his casual confidence another trait I love about him. And I enjoy the warm touch of his hands on my skin. My tiny apartment might as well be a morgue. Cold, uninviting, devoid of life—the descriptions are interchangeable. I guess Justin's helping me stave off the feeling of loneliness, and I should be grateful, but Justin isn't doing this for me. He's doing it for himself. He came here because he was horny and wanted a quick lay.

Then again, what else was I going to do tonight? Should I really fight this? If I don't, it only adds to his delusion about our relationship.

Justin undoes my zipper when my phone buzzes for the hundredth time. He reaches into my pocket and pulls it out. "Your sister?"

I take the phone and place it on the counter. "She wants me to accompany her to another fight."

"You really liked watching those guys, didn't you?"

The mere mention of the fighters has my mind racing to all sorts of fantasies. It doesn't help that Justin slides his hand into my pants, draining blood from my mind as it rushes to other places.

"I bet you couldn't take your eyes off them," Justin says, stroking me through my boxers. He smirks. "Can you imagine being in the ring with them?"

"Cage," I correct. "It isn't a boxing match."

"Fine, the cage, whatever. Can you imagine? Fighting one?"

"N-no."

Justin gets on his knees, despite the kitchen tiles. He breathes heavy on the front of my boxers, and the warmth of his breath quickens my pulse to extreme levels. Sometimes, when we're like this, I almost forget why I left him in the first place. I enjoy having someone around, even if it's only for limited activities. I'm sure I'll hate myself in the morning.

"I can imagine fighting one," Justin whispers as he drags his teeth along my stiff shaft. The fabric between us is too much. "We get in the cage, not for belts or titles, but because we've got pent-up energy. We both agree: whoever wins gets to do whatever he wants to the other guy."

I swallow hard as Justin pulls down my boxers, exposing me to the chill of the kitchen.

He licks my length, staring up at me with his bright blue eyes. "Would you like to watch?"

"Watch what?" I ask, breathless.

"Me and some other guy fight. Winner gets to take the other guy however he wants."

"Y-yeah. I'd watch."

Justin takes me in his mouth, his tongue doing all the work. I hold my breath and stifle my grunt of relief. I want him to go faster and harder, but his slow method works as well. I haven't done anything sexual in the last five days—not a single thing, not even satisfying myself—and I'm more pent up than I imagined. With a gentle touch, I pet Justin's spiky hair. It's hard and doesn't move much from its position, but I don't care. All I can focus on is the heat from his mouth and the pressure he applies as he sucks.

I brace myself against the fridge and take a few deep breaths. When Justin picks up his speed, I moan, lost to the sensations. But then he stops and stands, rubbing his knees the entire way up.

He pulls me toward the attached living room and pushes me back on the narrow couch I have against the far wall. I stretch out along the length, and Justin gets between my legs. He removes my slacks, his hands running the length of my thighs.

"Hey, so, I have something to ask," Justin says as he kneads my skin.

"Can it wait?"

"It'll only take a second. I need to borrow some money."

Heat drains from my system. I throw my head back and rub my eyes under my glasses. Did he have to do it right now? Of course. This is Justin.

"How much?" I ask.

"Three hundred."

"Why?"

"Does it matter?"

Always dodging questions.

"Three hundred is a lot," I say.

"Well, my car has been acting up. I swear I'll pay you back when I get my first paycheck. It really isn't that big of a deal."

I stare at the ceiling, dwelling on the possibilities. All my money comes from student loans. I take enough out for living expenses, and I manage every penny I spend to make sure nothing goes wrong. My parents have given me enough clothing over the years, in prep for my med school experience, and as long as people don't *write all over them*, I should be good there. They also pay half the rent on my apartment, so I don't have to live on campus.

I gave Justin a hard time in the past about not having a job, but if he went to school full-time, I wouldn't have said anything. Studying and lab time make keeping even a Starbucks position an impossibility.

But I do have three hundred dollars I could spare.

"Fine," I say. "But I expect that you'll pay me back."

Justin smiles. He leans down and kisses me along my length. It doesn't take long for the heat to return to my system. "Thank you," he whispers against my skin. "You're so very good to me."

At least that's over. We argued about money from time to time when we lived together. He never worked, never did chores, and lounged around the apartment with the cleanliness of a rat. After I broke up with him, he kept coming by and sleeping on the couch because he had the key. I had to move here to avoid him, but I swear he can get into my place still. I found things rearranged before, and stuff has gone missing. I have no proof, but I know he can pick locks.

Justin takes me in his mouth again and I moan loud enough to echo throughout the apartment.

I guess I can overlook some of Justin's transgressions.

Keon Lynch

I WALK into my shithole apartment and throw my gym bag down on the futon.

The whole place smells of dust and mold. I can't complain, because it's in my price range, but that doesn't mean I have to like it. I had to take the first place I could get once I left the Army and moved out to California. I didn't have a lot of funds saved up, and now I'm living paycheck to paycheck.

With a sigh, I walk into my kitchen and gather up my dinner. A protein shake and a banana. Tomorrow I'll heat up some plain chicken, but tonight I have to watch my calorie intake. I've got another fight in a week and I need to make weight.

I chew on my banana while the blender mixes my shake into the consistency of baby food. When the whir of the blender stops, silence blankets the area. I don't bother with a cup, so I drink straight from the glass blender top.

Woo. What a night.

My phone buzzes, and I answer without looking at the screen.

"Yeah?"

"Hey, Keon," Derek says, his voice filled with the sound of his smile.

"You're feeling better, I see."

"Oh yeah. Much better. I told you a few good nights' rest and I'd be back to normal."

"What's up?"

"Dude, she said yes."

It takes me a moment to remember what he's talking about. "Malala?" I ask. "That girl who saw you backstage?"

"Yeah. You won't mind if I show her around before the fights, right? I was hoping you could get us access to the back area."

"I already told you I would."

"Good. You're really helpin' me out. She's stoked to see where the sausage comes from, if you get what I mean. Maybe we can meet you at weigh-ins and show her every step of the process a fighter goes through before a fight."

"You sure she would like that?"

"She's totally into it," Derek says with a laugh. "And that way I can spend the whole day with her. It'll be great."

"All right. Whatever."

Derek isn't fighting this upcoming set in Stockton, not after I pummeled him in our last match. I didn't want to hurt him, but I have to give it my all. I've only got so many fights left before the UFC qualifier, and I'll only be allowed to participate in that if I have seven pro wins. Three more wins to go.

"Well, I'll see you then," Derek says.

"Wait," I say before he hangs up.

"Yeah?"

"Well…."

"Everything okay?"

"It's nothing. Forget it."

I hang up. It's just me, my shadow, and the silence between us.

I finish up my protein shake and amble around my apartment. I have thirty minutes to burn before I have to go to bed. Not enough time to go out, not enough time to start something interesting. Instead, I throw myself on my futon, use my gym bag as a pillow, and turn on my tiny television set to watch some bullshit before heading to bed.

While I surf through the channels, I tap my leg on the edge of the armrest and flinch. For a brief moment, pain flares from the middle of my shin. I glance down and glare at the skin. There's no coloration or bumps. What happened?

I rub my leg with my hand. Everything is in order until I get to the same spot. For whatever reason, when I squeeze my shin, I feel agony radiate from deep within.

If this were any other time in my life, I would schedule a doctor's appointment, but I don't want to risk missing out on my fights. Doctors are required to report any medical reasons fighters can't get in the cage, even if the fighter says he wants to participate—even if the fighter is willing to risk serious injury. I don't want an overprotective doctor claiming I'm unfit to fight or saying I need to take it easy to recover from a little bruise.

I'm already thirty. If I want to get into the UFC, I need to do it soon. People talk about women's biological clocks, but all fighters have almost the same thing. Once you get too old, your career is over. And I'm right on the cusp. If a doctor said I needed to take it easy to recover from a stupid leg injury, I might not get another chance at a UFC qualifier ever again.

Plus, I don't like hospitals. Or clinics. Or nurses. Or doctors. Everything about medicine fills me with an uneasy dread.

I exhale and lean back on the futon. If I'm not touching the spot on my leg, nothing is wrong. I didn't even notice anything while I was walking, so it can't be all that bad.

I settle for a movie classic: *Die Hard*.

Man, I love *Die Hard*.

Chapter 4
Weigh-Ins

Corbin Friel

LALA SHAKES my shoulder.

"Stop that," I drawl. "I'm driving."

"Aren't you excited?"

"It's too early to be excited."

Right now I should be studying or listening to a lecture, not gallivanting around town waiting to watch a fight.

I glance down at the clock. 9:00 a.m. The fights don't start until 5:00 p.m. Why are we going to meet Derek? Apparently he's going to show us every step of the MMA process. Fighters weigh in before noon to make sure they're within their weight category. What an odd procedure.

"Why are you so grumpy?" Lala asks with a tilt of her head. "I thought you were a morning person."

I rub my eyes under my glasses and sigh. "Justin has been coming by after work lately. Apparently he has graveyard shifts most nights."

He says he's a security guard at a hotel, but I never see him in uniform, and his schedule has the consistency of pudding. One day he's over at two in the morning, the next it's six, the next it's three. And when I ask him which hotel he works at, he never answers.

Lala gives me a coy little smile. "Oh. A midnight meeting, is that it? So naughty."

Heat floods my face. I don't know why—because we're both adults, and she's never betrayed my trust—but the thought of discussing intimate matters with my sister has never sat right. *She* has no problem discussing such matters, that's for sure. She'll discuss every man she finds attractive until we're both dead. One time she dragged me to a male strip club. I had my face buried in my palm the whole evening. It was fancy, no one actually got full-blown nude, but I could not have been any more uncomfortable even if I were trapped in an iron lung and dying of polio.

"Are you and Justin back together?" Lala asks.

"No."

"Uh-huh. Sure you're not."

"We're not. At least, not yet. He says he's getting his act together, and we'll see, but I'm still wary."

"I think you two look cute together."

"You think any pair of anything looks cute together," I say, rolling my eyes. "A pair of puppies. A pair of shoes. Two homeless people sleep next to each other and suddenly they're soul mates."

"Hey," Lala barks. "They were *cuddling* together. Obviously they were more than just street-corner buddies. I think something beautiful was there."

"Oh jeez."

"We're all searching for a super special someone, no matter what walk of life we come from. I want to imagine everyone will find their one true mate, okay? What's wrong with that?"

"Nothing. I'm just questioning whether Justin is my one true mate."

Lala waves away my comment. "Maybe you should loosen up. You're too anal about stuff."

My phone beeps and I follow the GPS to the designated location. The residential area, while not the wealthiest part of town, has a clean and feel-good vibe about it. Kids play out in the front yards, a man washing his car offers us a wave, and the trees lining the street create patches of pleasant shade.

"What're we doing here?" I ask as I park in front of the designated address.

Lala steps out of my car. "Derek said to meet him here." She jogs toward the front door. "Keep the engine running. I'll be right back!"

She really shouldn't be running. I want to say something, but at the same time, I know she's heard it all a million times before. Lala is an adult. She can make her own choices and take her own risks, but I would hate myself if something happened to her on my watch. Our mother says the new medication has done wonders to strengthen Lala's bones, but they still aren't where they should be. All unnecessary strain should be avoided.

Derek steps out of his house, and I snap my attention to his pronounced pectorals and fine shoulders. I love the way he carries his oversized duffel bag. Then I turn away and scold myself under my breath. I can't *check out* my sister's date. What kind of gentleman am I?

Still. Derek looks much nicer without his face all bloodied. I sneak one last look. His trim beard, tight black shirt, and tan cargo pants are the perfect manly combo. And his smile—expressive and confident—everything I'd imagine from a pro fighter.

They walk together to my car, but Derek freezes with his hand on the passenger handle.

"What're you doing here?" he asks, giving me a sidelong glance.

"You said you had two tickets," Lala says, smiling. "So I brought my brother."

Derek frowns. "Oh, right…."

"You sure it's okay?"

Derek returns to smiling. "It's all good. I know the event manager and I can get as many tickets as I ever need, so don't worry. Bring your brother any time you want."

Lala clasps her hands together, holding back a squeal.

They both pile into the back of my car, leaving me up front with the radio as my sole source of company. Funny how I can feel lonely, even in a car full of people. I drive away from the house and plug the new GPS location into my phone.

Time to go watch some fighters weigh in for their fights. Riveting.

"You guys are related?" Derek asks as we leave the residential area. "You two are… different."

I glance back, using the rearview mirror, and sneer. Derek isn't the first person to notice me and my sister aren't exactly the same. She's darker skinned, with black hair and chestnut eyes—just like her father. I have hazel eyes, a fair complexion that varies with the weather, with thick brown hair—just like my father. Our mother gave us the same full lips and straight jawline, and when people compare us side by side, they can see the similarities, but otherwise no one would guess we're related.

"We have different dads," Lala says, summing up all my thoughts in half a sentence. "It's no biggie."

Derek replies with a slow nod. "Oooh. Cool."

Not the deepest thinker, I see. I guess I was right about fighters. Dumb as rocks. Maybe I should tell Lala this isn't a good idea. She deserves someone intellectually capable.

"Why did you bring your gym bag?" Lala asks. "I thought you weren't fighting tonight."

"I'm not, but Keon asked me to be his corner man, so I brought some towels and water bottles and stuff. Just in case."

"Corner man?" I ask.

"The guy on the side of the octagon. I can give him tactical advice and encouragement."

I stifle a laugh. "Tactical advice? This isn't chess. What kind of advice is there to give? *Hit him harder. Throw more kicks.* Kids playing arcade games could be his corner, man."

Lala drives her knee into the back of my seat. She doesn't say anything, but I can feel her glare on the back of my head. I shouldn't mock this guy's sport, I see.

"There's all sorts of tactics," Derek says, either oblivious to my sarcasm or choosing to ignore it. "Some opponents have good game on their feet, so you might want to grapple them to the ground. Other fighters have a certain go-to move, so it's best to avoid it or disarm them before they get rolling. Or knowing when to press a guy when he's winded."

Hm. Sounds more complicated than I gave it credit for. Maybe the sport has some nuance after all. And maybe Derek isn't as shallow a thinker as I thought.

"Why aren't you fighting tonight?" I ask.

Derek shrugs. "I lost my last match, and the doctor said I should take it easy. Keon didn't get a scratch on him, so there wasn't a long waiting period for him to fight. The event manager signed him up as fast as he could. Keon gets the crowds going. People like that."

"You mean by flipping everyone off? People *like* that?"

"Of course," Lala says. "Everyone loves a big personality. I know I do."

The back of my car gets quiet. I cast a glance back. Derek and Lala whisper things to each other, and I feel like a parent chauffer dropping my teen daughter off at the high school prom. Not how I imagined my Saturday, but I guess it's better than leaving her alone with Derek. I don't care for him, but I'm not going to say anything. Only petulant children whine about someone else's date for no good reason.

I'll let Derek do something stupid first, and then I'll advise my sister to leave him.

I glance at the GPS. The fights take place in a city a little ways south, so I turn on the radio and cruise along toward my destination, admiring the surroundings.

California weather doesn't change much. First it's warm, then it's hot, then it's hot some more, and if we're lucky, it'll rain. For an hour. The coast gets some nice ocean breezes, and the mountains get snow, but from South Sacramento down to Bakersfield, it's a central valley of dryness. Today is no different. A cloudless morning fills the sky with rays of unabated sunshine.

Derek flexes an arm, and Lala squeezes his bicep, giggling. I can no longer admire the scenery.

I grit my teeth and say nothing. At least he isn't coaxing her to touch other parts of his body.

She strokes his beard, and the two of them return to their whispered conversations. I know I'm an overprotective brother, and I shouldn't stew over their flirtations, but another part of me wishes *I* could be the one fawning over the muscles and masculinity of a rocked-out fighter. Not that Derek would even be interested in a man giving him any attention—he hasn't looked in my direction since he got in the back seat—but it would be nice to flirt with someone besides Justin.

I haven't dated anyone other than Justin since eleventh grade.

Eh. I shouldn't dwell. I need to remain pleasant for this all-day event. That's what Lala deserves—a well-behaved brother so she can enjoy her time out.

The drive takes us down the highway and little else. Fields of agriculture rush by the windows, broken by the occasional farmhouse or factory. I grow bored and restless while the pleasant tunes on the radio play at a low volume. Derek and Lala remain all smiles until we get into town. I don't bother inserting myself into their conversation, so I instead think back to my anatomy lecture. Our next test is on the brachial plexus, a cluster of nerves that affect the arm. Important stuff.

"Bin-Bin, there it is," Lala says as she taps my shoulder.

Sure enough, I spot a gym and dojo on the outskirts of town. The parking lot, packed to the brim, has people standing in groups from one end to the other. Everyone must be here to back up their designated fighters.

I pull the car into the lot and take the last open spot. Derek and Lala jump out, and I join them, though I wish I could wait in the vehicle. A lot of guys look on edge. Muscular guys. Some look a little redneck. How sure are we they won't break out into a fight? There's enough testosterone in the air to choke on it.

Then again, most of them are buff and fit. I'm surrounded by more perfect tens than Hugh Jackman in a mirror maze.

"Hey, Derek," someone calls out. "What're you doing here?"

"Supporting Keon," Derek shouts back. "Good luck with your fight."

"Thanks!"

A few more guys offer Derek a quick welcome as we walk toward the gym. He must have a lot of friends. People give me odd looks when I walk by, however. No over-the-top greetings for me. I understand. I'm not one of them.

We enter the gym and get hit with a blast of cold air. Fighters are lined up in front of a medical scale, each taking their turn to get weighed by a professional and then have their photo taken. Each guy strips down to his fighting shorts before it happens. I avoid staring too long, for fear one of them might take offense. Some guys get defensive—or insulted—when another guy admires them. I've tried to explain it's nothing more than a compliment, but they don't want to hear it. Best to avoid the situation and keep my admiration to myself.

"Hey, baby," one guy says when he catches Lala staring. "How're you?"

Derek throws his arm around her. "She's doin' great, thanks." Lala leans into his body and smiles, happy with the answer.

"Oh, Derek, I didn't know you had a girl. Sorry about that. What's her name?"

"Malala." He holds my sister close and then gives me a quick motion with his hand. "And this is her brother. Uh...." He leans over to me. "What's your name again?"

Oh, hurray. I'm the afterthought. "Corbin Friel," I say.

"Right. And this is Corbin, her brother."

Two fighters walk over to me after the introduction. They slap my shoulder, and I stumble a bit, but I don't think they're trying to be hostile. Both smile and motion to my outfit.

"What's this?" one asks. "Are you a lawyer, Corbin?"

I straighten my vest and brush off my slacks. "I'm in med school."

"Oh, that's, like, *college* college, right? For PhDs and stuff? Impressive."

Hm. I'm guessing this guy's IQ is squarely around room temperature.

The other fighter nods along. "If you have free time, you should join our gym. We can teach you Gracie jiujitsu, get you some fighter training. Karate. The whole nine yards. Ever heard of Nate and Nick Diaz? I know where they train."

"I'm honored, but I'm not looking for a gym right now."

"Think about it. You'll be a hit with the ladies."

"Lucky me."

Both fighters laugh. Then they hit my shoulder again, and I struggle to keep my footing. They're more powerful than I think they realize. "You're okay, Corbin," the first one says. "I hope to see you around more."

"Thank you?" I reply.

Lala grabs my arm and pulls me over toward the weigh-ins. I allow her to drag me, even though we look silly, but I dig my heel into the ground before we get too close. The fighters all have serious expressions, bordering on somber. I don't know if we should get near.

"They're about to weigh Keon," Derek says, standing close to the line of fighters. He points to the front, right when Keon steps up to the scales.

"What weight should he be?" I ask.

"Two hundred and five."

"What if he's overweight?"

"He could get penalized, or his fight could be thrown out."

"Really? I had no idea. Do other sports make you weigh a certain weight?"

Derek bursts out laughing. Lala chortles alongside him.

I cross my arms and wait. I don't understand what's so funny, so I assume he's laughing at my ignorance on the matter.

"You're hilarious," Derek says between straggled laughs. He throws his arm back around Lala. "Did you hear him? I had no idea your brother had a sense of humor."

She forces a smile. "That's my brother. A jokester."

Oh, they thought it was a joke? I guess weight doesn't matter much for other sports, then.

Keon finishes and grabs his duffel bag off the floor. He pulls on a tight-fitting T-shirt before joining me, Lala, and Derek. The first thing he does is stare straight at me. For a moment, neither of us says anything. Then Keon smirks.

"Well, if it isn't my biggest fan, Bun-Bun."

I frown. "It's Bin-Bin. Er, I mean—" Why am I correcting him to my terrible nickname? "My name is Corbin Friel."

"Corbin, huh? How'd you get a nickname like Bun-Bun?"

"*Bin-Bin*," I say through clenched teeth.

Lala laughs. "He's my little brother. I would call him all sorts of things when we were younger. Bro-Bro. Bin-Bin. Thee-Thee."

I hide my red face with my hand, hating every moment my sister reminisces. I know it's not the biggest deal in the world, but standing next to a group of manly men and being reminded of the nickname *Thee-Thee* makes me feel… childish.

"So, did you make weight?" Lala asks.

Keon rubs the length of his smooth jawline and nods.

"What do you do now?"

"I usually get something to eat and wait until the fights start."

"Oh! Fun. Let's go. I'm starving." She turns to me and motions to the door. "You'll drive, right?"

"Sure," I say with a groan. "Let's go."

This day can't end fast enough.

WE SIT around an IHOP booth and I stare at the varieties of syrups on display. Somehow, because life hates me, I'm seated next to Keon, while Derek and Lala sit on the opposite side, their shoulders touching the entire time, laughing it up like we were at a comedy club. Does Derek even know how to treat a lady? He should give her some space.

But I'm not going to say anything. It's her choice who to date. Even if I hate him.

The waitress drops off our food, and I breathe a sigh of relief.

I have an egg-white omelet with a single piece of toast. Lala ordered two pancakes with a side of fruit.

And I guess Derek and Keon ordered everything else on the whole damn menu because they both get three plates each. All-meat omelets, a stack of waffles, four squares of french toast, a mountain of hash browns, three pigs' worth of bacon and sausage—their food could feed a small village of starving children.

"Aren't you worried about your weight?" I ask Keon as he scarfs down half an omelet in a few bites.

"I made weight," he says between chewing. "Now I don't have to worry about it."

Derek nods. "Yeah. Now he needs them calories. He can't be depleted for his match. Eat up."

The two of them hoover their food like they were part vacuum.

I take my time to cut bite-sized pieces of my omelet, but by the time I'm a fourth of the way through my meal, both Keon and Derek are chugging their orange juice and burping loud enough to be victory roars.

Lala laughs. "You guys are awesome!"

"You should see me eat pizza," Derek says. "I once ate two large pepperonis all by myself."

"I'd love to see that."

"Don't worry, babe. I'll show you any time you want."

Babe? Since when did he start calling her *babe*? I narrow my gaze and give the guy a squint, but he doesn't pay any attention. Keon lifts an eyebrow, however.

"Something wrong?" he asks me under his breath.

"No," I mutter.

"Looking forward to the fights?"

"Oh yeah. Can't wait to watch two idiots beat each other senseless."

"Idiots?"

I open my mouth to explain but stop before any words escape my lips. Lala and Derek haven't heard a word I said and probably won't until someone says their names, so I'll have to climb my way out of the hole I'm digging.

"Why did it have to be fighting?" I ask Keon. "I mean, of all the sports you could've done. There are safer options. Tennis. Golf. But getting hit in the face repeatedly seems like a dumb decision all around."

Keon leans back on the booth. "Is that right? You sound like you have *all* the answers, then."

"Well, I don't have—"

"Why aren't you studying to become an astronaut? Or a marine biologist?"

I roll my eyes. "You're only proving my point. All my options are legitimate careers that don't place me in danger. You picked one of the worst sports in history, second only to the gladiators in ancient Rome."

"Some of us have passion," Keon says.

"Passion? For hurting people?"

"Not that. We want the primal rush that comes from life-or-death situations. We want raw power and unmatched physical capabilities. Obviously we can't go around wresting crocodiles to the death, so participating in judged MMA matches is the next-best thing." He shrugs. "And I've always had a knack for fighting. I was on the wrestling team in high school, and I learned to grapple in the military. But I guess everyone who isn't a doctor is an idiot to you, am I right?"

"Well—"

"Guys," Lala says. "We still have a few hours before the fights. Why don't we go check out the octagon? Derek says the event manager will let us in!" She shakes her hands around like she doesn't know what to do with her excess energy.

Keon slides out of the booth, obviously done with our conversation.

I'm not making a good impression with the man, that's for sure. But I guess it doesn't matter—it's not like my sister is dating Keon. We don't have to get along for much longer.

I hope.

Chapter 5
Rear Naked Choke

Corbin Friel

SECURITY AROUND the arena is tighter than before. Bouncers and rent-a-cops watch every door. Early fans create lines and wait around in the afternoon sunlight. I want to join the people waiting in line, but Derek ushers us straight to the building. I don't like breaking the rules… and the odd glances we're given add to my guilt.

"Hey, guys," Derek says to the bouncers. Before they can send us away, Derek pulls out a lanyard with a photo ID. "These two are with me."

Keon flashes the same lanyard, and the bouncers let us in, no questions asked.

We enter an empty arena, and the door shuts behind us with a long whoosh akin to a sigh. Lala bounds forward, golf-clapping the entire way.

"These are our arena's fine features," Derek says as he points to the VIP seats, the snack bar, and then the octagon in the center of the room, acting like a glorified tour guide.

Lala follows his gestures like a cat follows a dot of light on the wall. I trail behind, unimpressed with a room devoid of people. Keon walks beside me the entire time, and I wonder if he's going to mess with me like he did with my shirt.

"What year of med school are you in?" Keon asks, much to my surprise.

I clear my throat. "First year."

"So you haven't taken the USMLE yet?"

I catch my breath and stop dead in my tracks. "You know about the USMLE?"

Keon turns to me with a lifted eyebrow. "All med students have to take the first part at the end of their second year, right?"

"Y-yes. But…."

The USMLE—United States Medical Licensing Examination—has three parts administered to med students over the course of their

37

education. It's a huge exam, but only med students ever know or talk about it. Why would Keon, some ex-military fighter jock, know anything about the USMLE? Maybe I really am underestimating fighters.

Keon turns away and continues toward the octagon.

"I know someone in med school, remember?" he says. "She posted about it on Facebook a lot when it was happening."

I jog to catch up to Keon. "Your girlfriend?"

"No. She's a… family member."

Ah. That explains it. "Are you planning on attending med school?" I ask.

Keon laughs. "No. I don't like school, to be frank. I'm not good at standardized testing."

"Well, what do you plan on doing in the future?"

"I plan on becoming a UFC fighter," Keon says, curt. "All I need is three more wins and I can enter the qualifier at the end of the year. The winners get UFC contracts, and I'm going to be one of them."

"What if it doesn't happen?"

Keon wheels around on me and glares. "It *will* happen."

I reply with a slow nod, taken aback by his level of intensity. I guess he's serious about making it in the UFC. "Is this that passion you were talking about?"

Keon looks away and continues toward the octagon. "Something like that."

"Hey," I say, rubbing my neck. "I'm sorry for my behavior back in the IHOP."

"Don't mention it. I don't care."

Ah. I guess I should've known better. Fighters get made fun of and yelled at each time they enter the octagon. They must have skin as thick as a brick wall.

Half the lights are off, shrouding half the arena in darkness. Derek and Lala shuffle through the stands until they're on the other side of the room. Before I can discourage them from separating, they enter the backstage rooms, leaving me and Keon alone near the octagon. I want to follow them, but I know I'd be acting like a pest, then. Maybe I should let them have a private moment before I crowd them again with my third-wheel presence. And it's more likely Derek will make a fool of himself if I'm not around. Lala will see right through him.

The fighting stage looks like a trampoline, three feet off the ground, but instead of a jumping area, it has a flat white mat covered in advertisements. The sides were a six-foot-tall chain-link fence, and I stare up at the cage for a prolonged moment, wondering how long we'll be here.

Keon walks up the stairs to the octagon gate and swings it open. "Wanna check it out from the inside?"

"Uh...."

"You'll like it. Come here."

I walk up the stairs, my hands tucked tight under my armpits. The inside of the cage is larger than I expected. Wide enough for two grown men to fight, and then some. I jump when Keon shuts the gate, trapping us inside.

"How many fights have you been in?" Keon asks as he throws his duffel bag into one of the corners.

"None," I say.

"Not even in elementary school?"

"No. I'm a civilized person, thank you very much."

I led a boring childhood, honestly. My parents were more concerned with Lala—as they should have been, so I'm not complaining—and I was content to read and study in my room most nights. I have friends, but not many, and most went out of state for college. It's hard to get in fights when my interactions with others are so limited.

No lights shine over the arena seating. I can only imagine what it's like to hear the crowd and the announcer while trying to fight a guy at the same time. The pressure must be intense. Too intense. I don't think I could do it.

Keon stretches and twists. Then he gives me a sidelong glance. "Fighting requires a lot of skill and training. Not unlike med school."

"You think they're the same?"

"No. But I know I have to learn and execute hundreds of moves."

"How hard could that be?" I ask.

"Let me show you a few."

I mull over the rest for a moment. "Okay."

"Stand in the middle."

I comply with his demand, but I watch him closely. What's he planning? Is he actually going to show me a few moves? Or is he going to mess with me, like he did when he signed my shirt?

Keon walks up behind me, and I glance over my shoulder, trying to keep him in sight at all times.

"I'll show you how to do a rear naked choke," he says.

I jump away, my shoulders bunched at my neck. "Okay, knock it off. Let me out of here."

"What's wrong?"

"I'm not stupid. I can see a prank coming from a mile away. There's no move called the *rear naked choke*. Well, maybe a sex move, but no way it's a fighting move. You're just making fun of me."

Keon laughs long and hard. Then he wipes away water from his eyes and shakes his head. "That's what it's really called. I'm not making it up."

"Stop it."

"I'm telling you the truth. It's a pretty common jiujitsu move. You have a phone, don't you? Look it up."

I bust out my phone and google the term, half expecting a flood of porn to assault my screen. To my surprise, a whole host of Brazilian jiujitsu articles show up, demonstrating the proper technique for the rear naked choke. I lift both eyebrows, stunned. I didn't know the world of MMA could be so… colorful.

"Believe me now?" Keon asks.

"Yeah, I guess."

"So stand in the middle. I'll show you how it's done."

I put my phone away and stand in the middle of the cage. Keon walks up behind me and slides his arm around my neck, until the crook of his elbow is below my chin. I grab his forearm with both hands, my whole body stiff. I didn't think he would get this close, I just figured he would motion or mock perform it himself.

I love the scent of his spring-fresh deodorant. It messes with my thoughts, along with his well-muscled arm and warm touch.

"Wait," I say.

"I'm not going to hurt you," he says, his hot breath on my ear.

"No, I'm not—er, well—I date men, okay? I'm into men."

Not the most eloquent way to put it, but I have to get it out there. Some guys get weird about knowing my sexuality. They don't want to get near me, like homosexuality is a contagious plague they could contract if they got too close. I don't want Keon to think I was secretly trying to touch him in any way—best to be upfront.

Keon doesn't release me. "Was that a warning or something? I'm pretty sure if you try to force yourself on me, I can fend you off."

"I'm not going to force myself on you!"

"Then why bring it up?"

"I, well...."

"Let me tell you a secret," he whispers, his gruff voice sending a shiver down my spine.

"O-okay."

"I don't care where you stick your dick."

I hold back a laugh. Not caring is a fantastic response, considering I'm trapped with him in a fighting arena. Better than him being offended.

"Ready to learn this move?" he asks.

I nod.

He tightens his hold around my neck and pulls me into his chest, so that my shoulder blades press up against his pecs. He locks his other arm around the back of my neck, forcing my head forward and choking me in an instant. My face and brow feel engorged, and I know he's cut off the blood flow to my head. With a choke like this—a blood choke—I'll pass out in a matter of seconds. I grab at his arm and attempt to pull it away from my neck, but his grip is solid and reinforced with his other arm.

Before I black out, Keon releases me.

I stumble forward, rubbing at my throat, relieved to feel everything returning to normal.

"Okay, now you try it on me," he says. "And then I'll show you how to counter it."

"You want me to use it on you?"

"Yeah. Wrap one arm around my neck."

"You're a little tall," I say, motioning to our difference in height. It's not much, but it's enough to become a problem.

Keon kneels down, his back to me. "Okay. Go ahead."

41

The novelty of learning MMA moves with a pro fighter invigorates me. I step up behind him and slowly wrap my arm around his neck. His whole body is solid rock wrapped in a thin layer of skin. His bulging shoulders, his tight neck, his perfectly sculpted back—I swear his body-fat percentage has to be less than ten. It's hard for me to focus on anything else.

"Use your other arm to torque the first," Keon says. "Make sure your grip is tight. Really pull back."

I do as he says, but I know I must look like a fool doing it. I'm nowhere near his level of athleticism, and all I can think about is Justin's weird fantasy, the one about two fighters duking it out, the winner getting his way with the loser. Just imagining such an event, me and Keon here in the cage, has my mind going to all sorts of crazy places. Sweat dapples my skin, and I'm not even straining, I can't seem to keep the heat from my body.

"Pull harder," Keon says.

When taken out of context, his command only adds to my daydream.

I torque back, and Keon taps my arm. I release and jump away, worried I actually hurt him.

He brushes his shirt off. "Not bad. See? Wasn't that hard. You had a good stranglehold then."

"Y-yeah."

"Now let me show you how to counter it." Keon motions me back over with a jerk of his head. "Wrap your arm around me again."

I go to comply, but Keon dips his chin close to his body, preventing me from wrapping his neck. Then he brings one hand up to his shoulder and pushes my arm aside. "See that?" he asks. "Simple. Try to choke me again."

Hoping to be clever, or at least impress him, I throw my arm around his neck as fast as I can. Keon gets his chin down before I can secure anything, and then he rips my arm away in the next instant. He stands and whips around, facing me in the matter of a split second.

"You're skilled," I say. "You must have studied these moves and practiced a lot. I'm impressed. Genuinely."

Keon pats me on the shoulder. "And I'm impressed you tried your damnedest to get me in a choke hold." Then he chortles. "Maybe next time try to concentrate. I could feel just how much you *like to date men* that entire lesson."

Icy dread and red-hot embarrassment mix in equal parts throughout my system. I turn away, bright red in the face, and shuffle to the gate of the octagon, adjusting my pants the entire way.

"I am so sorry," I say, unable to look at the guy. "That was, I mean, just—unprofessional. Ungentlemanly."

I grab the gate and shake, but it doesn't open. I shake harder. Nothing. How does this thing work? I need to get out of here. I slam my shoulder onto the fence, but it doesn't budge. I want to leave and avoid this awkward moment before it kills me.

"How do you open this?" I ask, half a shout, half a demand.

Keon laughs. It grates on my patience, but what can I do? I grit my teeth, straining my jaw to hold back some choice words.

I cross my arms. "Just open the damn gate!"

Keon saunters over, like he's going to take his sweet time about everything, but the slam of the arena door draws both our attention. A group of men walk in, each wearing a black T-shirt and pants. Keon straightens his posture, his expression shifting to something unreadable, and I hold back any questions to avoid making any noise.

The men circle around the octagon like a group of sharks watching an idle diver.

"Hey," one says. "If it isn't everyone's favorite fighter. The one too good for a dojo."

"Hello, Clark," Keon says, his voice terse.

Clark pulls out a protein bar and smiles. He has the physique of a bear and the hair to match. The tattoos on his neck crowd together, so I can't make anything out, and they're thick enough to be another shirt underneath the first. Although he doesn't have perfectly defined muscles visible from half a mile away, I can tell he's stacked enough to give a bull a run for his money.

And he eats his protein bar like he's punishing it for disappointing him.

The guy gets me nervous.

"Have you met Anderson?" Clark asks between bites. "He's the one fighting you tonight."

A man about Keon's size leaps onto the outside of the octagon and pulls himself over the fence in a sheer display of athleticism. He hops

43

down and strides over to Keon with his head up and his shoulders back. I step away, certain there will be a fight.

Anderson plants himself right in front of Keon, their faces so close I swear they could make out.

"I look forward to kicking your ass tonight," Anderson says as he holds out a hand to shake.

Keon smirks, ignoring the offer. "I've seen videos of your past fights. You're not the worst fighter in your academy, but you better hope he doesn't retire."

"You think you're clever, huh? You better not get hurt too bad tonight, or else you might not recover in time for that qualifier."

The thinly veiled threat isn't lost on anyone.

I clear my throat.

Everyone turns to face me, some with confused expressions, like they had forgotten I existed.

"Who are you?" Clark asks.

"The safety inspector," I say. "I came to check out the cage, and here I find unsportsmanlike comments. I might have to report this."

The group of black-shirted men exchange looks and back away from the octagon. Anderson steps away, both hands raised.

"We were just being competitive," he says. "We're all friends here. Right, Keon?"

Keon offers a slow nod. "Yeah. Friends."

"Good. Then I'll see you in the cage tonight."

"I look forward to it."

Anderson hops over the fence as effortlessly as before. Once the group of men is together, they make their way to the backstage area, and my thoughts return to Lala and Derek. I doubt anything will happen, but I can't stand the thought of my sister getting hurt.

"Come on," I say, motioning to the gate. "We should get out of here."

"Safety inspector, huh?" Keon asks with a smirk.

"It's nothing. If those guys were any dumber, someone would have to water them twice a week."

Keon snorts back a laugh. "Still. They've been out to scare me into joining their fighting academy for some time. Tonight I think they were done with that route and ready to get rid of me."

"Are you… sure you'll beat Anderson in the ring?"

"As long as he fights fair, yeah."

"What if he doesn't?"

Keon shrugs. "We'll have to see, won't we?"

"To be safe, we should stick together with Derek. Maybe they'll leave you alone."

"Here's hoping."

Keon opens the gate to the cage—a simple latch on the side was all it took. What kind of idiot am I?—and I try to hide my flushed face as I walk out of the octagon. Keon follows after me, but I stop a few feet away.

"I hope you kick Anderson's ass," I say.

Keon lifts an eyebrow. "Oh yeah?"

I hadn't cared if Keon won or lost until now. The fact some people are trying to bully him into quitting gets under my skin.

"Well, I'm your biggest fan," I say, offering him a half smile. "So of course I want you to win."

Keon relaxes a bit and chuckles. "That's right. It's a good thing you're here, then. I definitely need at least one person cheering for me to win."

Chapter 6
Fight Night

Keon Lynch

THE DEEP rumble of rock 'n' roll pulses through my veins.

Heat scorches every inch of my muscles, making me want the fight even more. I hop in place, hyped on anxious energy. They haven't opened the doors yet, but the announcer calls out my opponent. It won't be long now. Then I'll walk out to the octagon and the fight will begin.

One of us is going down.

"Ready?" Derek asks.

I reply with a curt nod.

The doors open. I'm bombarded by a wall of sound from the crowd. Cheering. Booing. Food gets tossed my way. I ignore it. Nothing will shatter my focus tonight. Anderson thinks he can break me? He's got another thing coming.

Derek walks to the side of the octagon and stands at the corner closest to my side. I stride into the cage and tap my gloved hands together, enjoying the feel of my body straining to contain my excitement. Anderson dances around the opposite side of the mat, his sweat glistening under the harsh spotlight overhead. He glowers at me. Adrenaline steels my heart. I won't be shaken by the likes of him.

There's a bell ring. The match has started.

Anderson holds out his hand. He wants to tap gloves. It's a show of respect—of brotherhood camaraderie. Not every fighter wants to do it, especially not with me, a guy they barely know, but I always appreciate it when someone offers.

I hold out my hand and step forward.

And then Anderson throws a punch inches before we tap gloves. I step back, dodging the blow.

A roar of excitement washes through the crowd. The announcer says something, no doubt about the treachery, but the pounding of my heart deafens me to everything.

Anderson steps forward for a follow-up strike, but he has a predictable fighting style. I saw it in all the videos. I rush in and punch him across his face, my knuckles cushioned by the gloves, though I still feel the undeniable sensation of hitting bone square on. He stumbles back, and I go to throw a left hook. Anderson lifts his arm, blocking his face. I strike his elbow and jump away, satisfied with the blow I landed.

His eyes take a second to focus. I rattled him good.

I take in a deep breath, and it's like swallowing raw power.

This is it. The intensity. The bloodlust.

I *want* to destroy my opponent. I want to prove I have the potency—the strength—to stand among the greats of the world. If our lives are fleeting, if we're nothing more than stars in an endless ocean of darkness, I want to flicker just once before fading away. I want to feel as though I've made an impact on the world. I've made a name for myself. I've accomplished. I won where others failed. I succeeded where others gave up.

Nothing tastes as gratifying as victory.

Anderson throws a kick. I sidestep away. He throws a second kick, too fast and too reckless. I catch his leg, getting him off-balance, and then I toss him to the mat. The slam rocks the octagon and the audience. Cheering cuts through my focus for a brief second as I stand over Anderson and punch downward, pile-drilling home a heavy blow. I bust his nose, and blood explodes across his chin.

I punch again, splitting open his eyebrow. I go to punch a third time, ready to end this fight, when he strikes my right shin.

Fire flares to life under my muscles, flooding my leg with agony.

Anderson didn't punch hard—it's the same pain from the other night.

I leap away from Anderson and stagger backward, my adrenaline waning. The crowd and announcer seem louder than before. People scream and yell. My name. Anderson's name.

"Why'd you stop?" Derek shouts. "You had him on the ropes. Push! Push!"

Derek doesn't know about my leg. And why would he? There's no mark or bruise. I had almost forgotten it hurt. Even now, the pain has subsided, but the brief graze almost had me tapping out. I can't let Anderson hit me there again. I need to end this fight fast.

Anderson gets to his feet. His face looks like a mudslide, blood weeping into one eye.

But he doesn't look confused. He might have seen my grimace when he struck my leg.

Anderson rushes forward and sweeps with a low kick, straight for my shin. I dance away, my breathing heavy. He knows.

Fuck.

When he comes in for another low kick, I punish him for it. I punch straight into his gut, making sure to keep my right leg back. He hits my left leg, sure, but I can take some abuse before I need to back off. Anderson kicks again. I punch him in the jaw. His lip splits, and blood splatters across my forearm, but he doesn't go down. He's got fortitude. I'll give him that much.

Anderson throws a fast punch, no doubt fueled by desperation. I lean away, my heart pounding hard enough to drown out all other distractions once again. I charge forward and slam us both to the mat. I can't risk him kicking forever. Instead, I hold my breath, flip him over, take in a controlled gulp of air, and then mount him from behind. He bucks—he's strong—but I'm better.

I wrap my arm around his neck in one quick snakelike motion. I lock my other arm behind his throat and torque. Anderson flails and thrashes. I keep to my left side, protecting my shin as much as possible, counting down the seconds.

One Mississippi. Two Mississippi. Three Mississippi.

Anderson arches his back, all muscles straining to dislodge me.

Five Mississippi.

I torque harder, like I'm trying to pop his head straight off his body.

Give up, asshole. You've lost.

Seven Mississippi.

Then his body goes lax, and he taps my arm with a feverish energy. That's it. I won.

The ref grabs me. I let go of Anderson and hear his raspy cough as I'm dragged to my feet.

Corbin Friel

I SHAKE my sister's shoulder. "That's a rear naked choke! He used a rear naked choke."

Lala cocks an eyebrow. "Yeah, I know. Everyone knows. Yeesh."

"But *I* know what that is now!"

"Just shut up and cheer, Bin-Bin. This is the time for celebrating."

She returns to jumping and cheering with the rest of the crowd shouting Keon's name.

Anxiety drains from my system now that the fight's over. I hated watching. It was worse than before. The thought of Keon losing caused my stomach to screw up into knots. And then imagining him in the hospital almost made the fight unbearable, especially if it was the result of a bunch of gym bullies. Thankfully Keon was in control the entire time. Well, except when he ran from Anderson. I saw Keon's expression change—from vicious confidence to pensive confusion. I know something went wrong. I'm not sure what, but for a fraction of a second, I honestly thought he might lose, just from shaken nerves.

Maybe I imagined things. Keon looks fine now.

The announcer grabs Keon's arm and thrusts it over his head, getting another round of cheers from the crowd. The only people who *aren't* celebrating are the thugs from Anderson's fighting academy. They remain seated, not a smile among the group.

I guess I wouldn't be smiling either. Anderson needs help cleaning his face—the blood won't stop pouring from his busted eyebrow. Head wounds are notorious for bleeding copious amounts, but it seems worse when his nose is swollen and his eyes refuse to open.

Maybe now they've learned to leave Keon alone.

LALA AND I wait outside of the arena. While most audience members funnel their way to the parking lot, we stand with the coaches and dojo members by the back door. The fighters and their corner men exit out the back once they're done collecting their things, but Derek and Keon have yet to emerge. It's already 11:30 p.m.

Anderson and the rest of the Alpha MMA Academy people shuffle out a good hour after the end of the fights.

"You put up a good fight," Lala says as Anderson passes by.

"Thanks," he says, his spittle pink with blood.

I grab my sister and move her away from the crowd of muscle-bound meatheads. "Why are you talking to him?" I whisper. "That guy threatened Keon before the fight."

Lala waves away the comment. "They didn't mean it. All guys talk smack to each other. It's part of the game. They're all good friends. Look at Derek. They fought, but tonight Derek was Keon's corner man."

"This was different. You weren't there."

"I think you're overreacting, like you always do. We have to be cordial to all the fighters once the matches are over, okay? Try to smile."

I grumble under my breath, but I don't bother arguing anymore. Lala won't change her mind until she sees their aggression for herself. Hopefully it never happens, but Anderson and his crew glance over their shoulders a few times, giving me quick glowers. They must've realized by now that I'm no safety inspector.

Lala pulls out her phone and checks the time. "Where are they?"

"Did you try calling Derek?"

"Yeah. He's not answering."

"I don't know what to do, then."

"Let's go inside," she says as she marches toward the back door.

"No, no, no," I stammer as I rush to get in front of her. "Remember all those bouncers and security guards? We should wait here. Or maybe in the car."

"Stop being such a wimp. Look. Most of them went home."

She motions to our surroundings. Sure enough, most of the doors have been deserted, and the security guards have dwindled down to a single patrol car circling the front parking lot.

"Following the rules isn't tantamount to *being a wimp*," I say matter-of-factly. "I don't want to get us, or Keon and Derek, in trouble."

"It'll be fine. C'mon. Follow me."

Before I can get another word in edgewise, Lala walks up to the back door and pulls on the handle. Locked. She taps her foot and waits until someone on the other side exits. She smiles at the fighter and his buddies—some lightweight guy I don't know the name of—and holds the door open until they've all gone. Then she slips inside, almost leaving me behind.

"Hey," I bark.

I grab the door at the last possible second and scurry in.

"Try to keep up," Lala says.

What's wrong with people these days? When did it become *uncool* to follow the rules? Well, I guess it's always been uncool to be a rule follower, but still. We have rules for a reason. If people listened to safety regulations and general ordinances, I'm sure there would be a lot less 911 calls. Is it really that unreasonable to ask?

The back area has half the lights and less than ten people milling about, picking up the trash. It takes me a moment to spot Derek and Keon, all the way in the far corner of the room. They're sitting on their gym bags, Keon's gaze drilling a hole in the floor.

Lala bounds straight up to them. "What's going on?"

"Uh, hey, babe," Derek says as he stands. He rubs the back of his neck. "Give us a minute? Keon needs to rest."

"He does? But he wasn't hurt at all during his fight."

"His shin has been hurting on and off for a few days. He wants to take it easy for a bit before we go get something to eat."

"It's been hurting for a few days?" I ask, interjecting myself into the conversation.

Derek nods. "Yeah. That's what he said."

"Do you mind if I look at it?"

I know I'm not a doctor yet, but I have a deep desire to examine everyone's ailment, no matter what they're complaining of, even a toothache. I walk over to Keon and kneel in front of him. He motions to his right shin. I straighten my glasses, squinting at the skin, but there's no discoloration or marks. I place my hands on his ankle.

"Tell me when it hurts," I say. "And give it a number. One for *not very painful* and ten for *the most painful thing you've ever felt*."

I run both my hands up his rock-solid shin, impressed with his calves, squeezing the entire way. Halfway up and Keon flinches. Before I can open my mouth to ask, he grabs the collar of my shirt and jerks me close, his fingers twisting into the fabric and half choking me.

"It fucking hurt," he says through clenched teeth, his tone so cold I shiver.

"O-okay. How much?"

"An eight. Maybe a nine."

"And what kind of pain do you feel when I'm not touching the shin?"

"Nothing."

"What about when you walk?"

"No pain."

Wow. It must be deep. And odd he wouldn't notice it unless I'm squeezing. That eliminates my first few thoughts, but the remaining options are terrible. "You might have an injury on your tibia or fibula."

"What?" Keon asks, lifting an eyebrow.

"Those are the bones in your shin. One might be cracked. Or you could have an infection."

The information gets Keon pensive. He releases his grip on my collar and returns his gaze to the floor. My chest tightens when I get a good look at his face. But this can be fixed.

Lala has had more bone-related injuries than I can count. Broken bones, infections, bruising, shrinking—every possible mishap. I'm confident Keon has something wrong with either his tibia or fibula, but only X-rays would reveal the real cause of his pain.

"You need to see the doctor," I say.

Keon glares. "No."

"What? Why not?"

"He'll miss his next fight," Derek says. "Dude, doctors don't allow you to fight if you have bone injuries. They'll say he's unfit, and he'll miss his chance for the qualifiers."

"Who cares? That's a terrible reason to avoid the doctor. If he really does have a crack or a break or an infection, he should get it treated immediately. There could be permanent repercussions for not tending to injuries in the quickest manner possible."

Keon stands. He grabs his bag and tosses it over his shoulder. "Let's go."

"To the hospital?" I say.

"No. To get something to eat."

"But—"

"I don't care about the long-term consequences, okay?" Keon says, curt. "I can deal with the injury after I get a contract with the UFC. Anything that puts that in jeopardy just has to wait."

"Doctors have ethical obligations," I say as I stand and straighten my posture. "I can't ignore this. Problems in the bone can spread to the surrounding soft tissue. If you wait too long, you could lose your leg, and then it won't matter what kind of fight contract you have."

"Uh, Corbin," Lala says under her breath. "Maybe we should drop this."

"Are you threatening to expose my injury unless I go see a doctor?" Keon asks. He turns to face me, his expressions set into a hard-lined resolve, like it's the start of one of his fights.

My mouth gets dry. "This could be serious."

"I'll handle it myself."

"You're not handling it at all."

"That's my goddamn choice."

His volume is three times what is was before, and his words echo throughout the room. The last of the cleaning crew glances over, gets one look at Keon, and then shuffles away as fast as he can without breaking out into a full-blown run.

Derek and Lala have their lips sealed tight, like neither of them want Keon's wrath. I don't blame them. I almost wish I could back out of my stance, but at the same time, I really don't want Keon to suffer a terrible fate because he was worried a doctor wouldn't approve him to fight in the octagon.

"W-well," I begin, "what if we compromise?"

Keon grits his teeth and says nothing.

I rub my hands together, wishing I had sanitizer, just to clear my thoughts. "My mother owns a private clinic. Maybe we—"

"Ohmygosh," Lala interjects. "We could go there and use her equipment! That's a fantastic idea, Bin-Bin."

"What? No. I was going to say—"

"You know how to use it, right? If you don't, I do. My mom has taken so many X-rays of me over the years, I could work the equipment blindfolded. We have every tool known to man to examine bone injuries, trust me." She pats Derek on the shoulder. "Remember how I said I had osteogenesis imperfecta? Yeah, of course you do."

Derek nods, but it's clear by his expression he isn't 100 percent following along with the conversation.

"I don't want to be examined," Keon says.

Lala holds up a finger. "But Bin-Bin is right. It could be terrible. Then again, it could be something you can ignore until after the fights. Why not figure it out? We can be in and out of my mom's clinic in no time. And I bet you don't want to lose your leg, right? C'mon. I think this is a brilliant compromise."

This wasn't my plan at all. I was thinking of asking my mother to perform the examination—and not to call up Keon's record or report her findings. Breaking into her clinic to use her equipment without her permission is a far cry from anything I think prudent.

"Fine," Keon says, glaring.

"Really?" I ask. He'll agree to this?

"If you can do the examination quick, and I can decide what to do about it afterward, I don't care. And if it turns out it's a *minor* problem, I don't want to hear shit about this again, got it?" He gives me the same piercing stare he gave me when I insulted him at the first fight.

Is he really upset that I'm concerned for him?

"I'm not trying to prevent you from fighting," I say. "I'm just concerned."

"Why?" he snaps. "What does it matter to you what I do?"

I straighten my posture. "I'm your biggest fan."

For a moment, no one says anything. Then, to my relief, Keon chuckles. He rotates his shoulders, loosening his tense muscles, and even Derek relaxes a bit after that. I'm glad he's not as upset. I really don't want him to miss out on his fight. Not when people like Anderson are trying to chase him away.

Lala grabs my arm. "C'mon, Bin-Bin! You're driving, remember?"

Keon and Derek turn to me, ready to follow my lead.

I guess we're actually doing this.

Chapter 7
Clinic Visit

Keon Lynch

GOD, I hate hospitals.

Hate might be too strong a word. I get uneasy when I'm around them. When I was younger, my mother was in a terrible car accident. Her liver got shredded, and she needed a new one to live. We were in and out of hospitals. Specialist doctors were called in to keep her alive. When she finally got a donor, it was another twelve months of examinations and tests. Doctor after doctor said she wouldn't make it—that her body was attempting to reject the transplant.

I went to every hospital visit thinking my mother would be dead. It gave me nightmares as a kid. People dying for no reason or doctors hunting us down to kill us. Insane stuff.

And that's not even taking into account my fear of illness. Getting sick means I won't be able to train. Staying combat-ready is like swimming up river—the moment I take a break will be the moment I fall behind.

We walk up to Corbin's mother's clinic, and I'm already regretting my decision. Corbin's hypothetical situation where I lose my leg disturbed me enough to agree to come, but how likely is that outcome? It's probably rare.

I take a deep breath.

I should leave.

"You have keys to this place?" Derek asks.

Malala shakes her key ring. "Of course. My mother keeps extra medication for me, just in case. Like I said, I was *really* fragile at one point." She opens the front door, and a harsh beep sounds off at regular intervals.

"What's that?"

"The alarm. We need to put in the code before it calls the police. We've got sixty seconds."

"The police?" I balk. "Will they show up here?"

If I get arrested, it'll be just as bad as having a doctor prevent me from fighting. Fighters with criminal charges get suspended from the league, sometimes for up to a year.

"It's fine," Malala says as she walks inside. "Just stay close."

Before I can protest, Derek, Malala, and Corbin funnel into the clinic. I trail behind and cross the threshold into a shadowy seating room. Chairs and tables blend into the darkness, creating odd shapes at the corner of my perception. Malala strides through the environment with confidence. It's obvious she's been here before—many times.

She taps at a number pad on the wall and the beeping stops.

Corbin flips a light switch, illuminating a small portion of the clinic. The dim lighting is almost worse than the dark void—I can see things, but not all the way, allowing my mind to play tricks on me. I squint and stay close to Derek.

"In here," Corbin says.

He opens a door in the back office and flips on another few lights.

This place has all the comfort of a horror movie. Derek must feel the same way because he gives me a nervous glance every couple seconds.

We walk into a room with two parts. One section has an X-ray machine and the other half of the room, the side with the X-ray controls, is separated by a glass wall. Corbin points to the chair inside the glass section.

"Take a seat," he says. "I'll make sure you're situated."

Take a seat, he says. Like it's easy.

I stare at the warning posters plastered to the walls. Radiation. Cancer. These aren't helping my stress levels. And to make matters worse, there's another sign reminding me that only certified personnel should be operating the equipment. I never should've agreed to this.

"I said, *sit down*," Corbin says. "It's a simple instruction, really. I need to point this at your leg."

I take a seat—I'm already here, body practically operating on autopilot—and Corbin moves a long, armlike piece of the machinery over to my shin. It has a fat end, like a camera, and he positions it a few inches from my leg. Then he wraps me in a heavy apron. It hangs like dead weight. Maybe it's filled with lead? I don't fucking know.

"You okay?" Corbin asks.

I take in a deep breath. My heart beats against my ribs, like it's trying to escape. I don't blame it. Maybe they can put me to sleep to do this. I'd prefer that. Hell, I'd prefer that for every random checkup. Anything to escape the horrors of this doctor's office.

"Hey," Corbin says. "I asked, are you okay?"

Corbin Friel

KEON DOESN'T answer me. He just stares at his lap, his brow furrowed. His hands tremble, and his breathing has become shallow. Color drains from his face, and a piece of me wonders if he'll puke.

I step up close to him and offer half a smile. "You're not afraid, are you?"

He shoots me a glare. "And what if I am?"

"I just watched you walk into a caged octagon, stand off against a professional fighter, and then proceed to break his face. You're the bravest guy I've ever met, yet here you are, shaking like a leaf. What's wrong?"

"I can't *punch* X-rays," he says, sardonic in every regard. "If you fuck this up, what am I supposed to do then?"

"You'll be fine."

"Will I? You said I might lose my leg."

"Well, that's a possibility. But you can still lead a normal life, even with one leg."

He scoffs. Then Keon runs a sweaty palm through his mohawk hair, his hand still shaking. "Listen," he says, his voice low. "I don't have anything else, okay? I don't have any savings. I never got a degree. I've only ever been good at physical shit. If I… if I lose my leg, or get cancer from this machine, I don't know what I'll do with my life. I'll have nothing. I might not even have a reason to live anymore." Keon takes a deep breath.

I hadn't thought about it like that before. Keon really doesn't want to lose what he has going. I thought he was avoiding the doctor because he was making impulsive and terrible decisions, but I guess he might have a deep-seated phobia of losing his chance to be a fighter. I've made a lot of negative assumptions about him, and fighters in general, and I'm feeling like an ass for being so judgmental. He's dedicated to the craft of fighting, like I am to my understanding of medicine.

My father said the mark of a good doctor was to make the patient feel comfortable with the treatment. To make them feel confident that everything will turn out fine in the end. And just being a good doctor won't cut it—I want to be the best damn doctor ever. I have to instill confidence in my patients. I have to make Keon feel comfortable and reassured.

I place my hand on his solid shoulder. "This isn't a rare case or occurrence."

Keon narrows his eyes.

"What I'm trying to say is, this problem has been dealt with a million times in the past. I've come from a long line of doctors, and I've heard more medical stories than bedtime fairy tales. Even if this is a marrow infection, ninety-nine times out of a hundred, nothing even remotely complicated happens in the healing process."

"What if I'm that one hundredth case?"

"Lala is the hundredth case," I say. "Her genetic disorder results in the worst bone condition a human can have without dying. And look— she hasn't lost any limbs." I squeeze his arm. "It's because my parents are fantastic doctors. Modern medicine made them that way."

"But they aren't here. You think you can handle this?"

"Well, you *could* have seen them. You're the one who made this whole awkward examination happen." I cross my arms and frown. "I would have had you see my mother in an instant, but reading a few X-rays is indeed within my wheelhouse. If anything happens I don't think I can handle, I'm going to call my parents right away so they can deal with it."

It almost sounds childish to threaten to call my mother and father, but it's exactly what I would do. If Keon's condition is something terrible and life-changing, I wouldn't want to risk his well-being for my ego. He needs proper treatment.

"I want to help others," I say. "It'll be one of my oaths as a doctor, and I already take it seriously. People can only be their best self when they're healthy. That's why I admire the medical field like I do. I know you'll be fine. One way or another."

Keon places his hand on top of mine. He's still clammy, but his trembling has stopped. "I need to be a UFC fighter, no matter what."

"Why?" I ask. Surely he can be anything else he wants.

"It's all I have. It's all I am. You might think it's a hobby, but I consider it my budding career. If I can't do this…. If I fail…. What will I have? Nothing. I'll have wasted my life. Literally."

The gravity of his words weighs heavy on my thoughts. I don't think I've known anyone with this level of dedication or passion. Even my love of medicine doesn't consume me like fighting does Keon. It's unnerving and inspiring at the same time. It means so much to him—I don't want to see him fail either. I rub his shoulder, wishing we were close enough that I could express my thoughts without restraint.

He exudes passion enough to fill the air around him. Keon is amazing.

"I'm going to help you," I say. "You're not going to fail under my watch."

Keon forces a smile. "Thank you."

"All right. Let's get this X-ray done."

"Please. Just make this quick."

"It'll be over before you know it."

I get the X-ray shields in place. Keon doesn't protest or comment. Once everything is secure, I step out of the room and walk over to Lala and Derek.

"Isn't this expensive to use?" Derek asks.

Lala shakes her head. "Like ten years ago, we used photos to take X-rays. That could get expensive because you had to develop those, but now everything is digital. Look right here." She points to the screen as she pushes a button. Keon's X-ray images snap center screen. "See? All done. No photo development. Not a thing."

"Wow. Cool."

Cool indeed.

I love hospitals and medical equipment. A few hundred years ago, people would have to cut their arms off if something became too infected. Now we have antibiotics, salves, and therapy programs to recover from any injury, no matter how severe. Treatments range from oral medication to intravenous infusions. Sure, some amputations still exist, but not for minor ailments, not anymore.

And hospitals are so clean. It's a common misconception that they're filled with sickness and disease. People with illnesses go to a hospital, of course, but the precautions the nurses and doctors take prevent flippant spreading of diseases from one patient to another. Everything is kept so sterile, people could eat off it. Most keyboards are dumpster fires when compared to the cleanliness of a hospital room.

Even my mother's clinic has a wonderful lemon-fresh scent that only cleaning supplies could create. I love this place. If I could, I'd live in a space similar to this.

"Bin-Bin," Lala says. "Look at this."

"What is it?"

"This black spot."

I glance through the X-rays, checking each angle. Lala points to Keon's right fibula, and no matter which angle the picture was taken, I can see the black spot. Fortunately, the spot is tiny, and centralized. If I had to guess, I would say it's the worst outcome from my hypothetical— an infection of the marrow—but Keon's is small and easily manageable.

Derek takes a step back. "Oh shit. It's cancer, isn't it? I knew it."

"There are lots of ailments that aren't cancer," I say.

"Fuck. Are you saying it's a tumor?"

"What? No! It's nothing of the sort. This is an infection."

"Huh? How did it get infected?"

"Most likely from blunt force trauma."

Lala opens the glass door and motions with a jerk of her head. "Come on out, Keon. Bin-Bin thinks it's an infection."

Keon leaps off the chair, throws off all the X-ray guards, and half jogs out of the screening room as fast as he can go without full-on running. He walks straight to me and stares down with a hard look, his dark eyes filled with an intense focus.

"Well?" he asks.

I point to the X-rays. "It's definitely not a break. We'd be able to see a crack or any splintering. This dark spot here indicates you have an infection. Osteomyelitis, most likely. See how small it is? And see how the edges of the spot are defined? It means it hasn't spread anywhere. It's still localized."

"And... that's good?"

"Yes."

"How do I... fix this?"

I straighten my glasses. "Well, you can ingest antibiotics. Anything that treats staphylococcus aureus. If that doesn't work, you'll have to see a doctor who will take a sample of the infection and create a culture in the lab. This culture can be used to create a specific targeted antibiotic. And if that doesn't work—"

"Stop," Keon says. He exhales. "I don't want to think about all this. Just tell me what to do. Where do I get antibiotics? How many should I take? When?"

Lala claps her hands once and moves toward the door. "Don't worry! I had to take antibiotics for staphylococcus aureus not too long ago. My mom still has some—I'll go get them." She disappears before I can say anything.

"I'm going to go with her," Derek says as he slips out the door to follow her.

It's against most regulations and standard protocol to share medications. The reasons are easy to understand. Most medications are tailored to the individual, including dosage and frequency of use, and the chance someone will hurt themselves from overdose is too high to justify sharing. Antibiotics aren't pain medications, however. It's damn near impossible to overdose on antibiotics, and as long as they aren't expired, they should do the trick.

I glance over at Keon. He's still staring at me. It takes me by surprise, and I rub the back of my neck, avoiding eye contact with him.

"You'll be fine," I say. "Osteomyelitis in the shin is the easiest place to cure. Some people have an infection there for years and never notice. That's how low-impact it is."

"Thank you," Keon says. His earnest tone is a little more vulnerable than I ever could have imagined.

I chuckle to hide my sheepishness. "Don't mention it."

"I really appreciate this."

"Like I said. It's nothing."

"You've only had one year of med school and already you can do all this? I'm impressed. Really impressed."

"I'm impressed with your ability to fight," I quip. "So, I guess we're even."

"You said you dated men?"

I catch my breath. "Y-yeah."

"Are you dating anyone right now?"

"Well, not really." Justin and I have been in limbo for longer than I care to admit. "Why?"

Keon takes a step closer to me. Our proximity gets my heart rate up. Is he going to mock me for my choices? Or being alone? Is he… hitting on me? I really don't know. He continues his silence, staring down at me like I should say something more.

"What?" is all I manage to say. Not the best way to start this conversation, but he's not giving me anything to go on. I stare into his eyes, searching for the answer, but he's too focused and hard-edged to read.

"I—" Keon begins, but he stops himself. "Look, I just want to thank you. You did a good job."

That seems like a non sequitur. What is he trying to say? I wish he would just say it. Why can't people say what they mean? And why is he so close? He didn't need to be this close to tell me that. But I do enjoy the warm flow of his breath on my cheeks. Probably too much. I take a step back and stare at the floor.

Keon shifts his weight from one foot to the other. "Listen. I admire people like you. People who do things I could never do." He takes another step closer, returning to our close proximity. "And this is beyond helping me out. You did me a solid. I can't… express that enough."

His close proximity, the husky timbre of his voice. My legs almost buckle. Why the praise? A simple thank-you would've done. He has adoration and… something else… laced in his tone. Is he being sarcastic and I don't even realize? Maybe he's making fun of me? I don't know. But I like it.

I clear my throat. "I—"

Keon leans closer, and I stop myself from continuing. Heat sluices through my system at the thought of locking lips with him. He can't possibly be leaning forward to do that. Wait—is there a chance he's hitting on me?

My desire to taste him overrides all other thoughts.

Chapter 8
Medication

Keon Lynch

THE DOOR opens, and Corbin jumps back like a startled animal. I almost grab him and keep him close, but I restrain myself. I should've just asked him on a date—that's more my style—but the words never came.

"Did I interrupt something?" Malala asks with a tilt of her head. She places both her hands over her mouth. "Were you two getting along? Ohmygosh. I'll come back later."

She goes to exit the room, but Corbin holds out his hand. "Wait! It's okay. Stay. Did you bring the antibiotics?"

"Yeah, but…." She holds up two bottles—one plastic, one glass. Something about the containers gets Corbin jumpy because he rushes over and examines them both with a critical eye.

"Mom gave you this too?" he asks.

Malala nods. "Yeah. Those two shots, remember?"

"I forgot about that."

"She said they were to stop the spread of infection."

"Well, not entirely, but it should be okay." Corbin walks back over to me and holds up the medication. "These are oral antibiotics"—he shakes the plastic bottle—"and this is meant to be injected behind the knee."

"A shot?" I ask.

"Only two. It helps with the pain and healing process."

I hate shots. Again, not for any logical reason or a phobia, like most people, but because of all the memories I have associated with hospitals. The doctors barely cared when they administered shots or when my mother would complain about the pain. Maybe they hated patients, I don't know, but their bedside manner never won me over.

Corbin, on the other hand, did make some points. I appreciate his earnest logic. Reminds me of my sister. She must be in her fourth year of med school by now.

And Corbin impresses me. I don't know many people who have a firm grasp on the knowledge of their career long before they start it, and although Corbin's on the arrogant side, he has skills to back it up. Arrogant assholes who have no business stroking their own egos are the worst, but I must admit, I find confidence—and a bit of hubris—to be a turn-on. Corbin might not be able to fight me in the octagon, but I bet he wouldn't hesitate to match wits with anyone in the room.

I glance around.

"Where's Derek?" I ask.

"He's in the boy's room," Malala replies. "He's a little jumpy. I wouldn't be surprised to hear he crawled out the window."

Corbin scoffs. "Are you serious?"

"No, no. I'm sure he's fine."

"Good. There's no reason to be scared of a hospital. This is one of the best places in the world."

He says it so matter-of-factly, it almost tempts me to challenge him. I let it slide, though. No sense in arguing, especially since it's all subjective.

Malala yawns, and she pats her brother's shoulder. "Okay, you have this settled? It's almost one in the morning."

Corbin gives me a sidelong glance. "Can you give yourself two shots?"

"I don't know what I'd be doing," I say with a huff.

"It was a joke, obviously. I'll be doing it."

"Here?"

"Well, no… I think it would be best if you come home with me tonight. You need one shot first, then another in six hours, and then you can continue the antibiotic treatment until the infection is gone." He straightens his glasses and holds his head high. "And we'll have all the time, and privacy, to answer your medical questions."

"All right."

The way he emphasizes the word *privacy* tells me he wasn't offended by my close proximity earlier. Which is good, because all I can think about is what he's done for me. I want to thank him—I want to keep him close—I want him flushed and excited, panting underneath me. Would he like that? I just need to stone up and ask him if he's interested.

Maybe he wants something more than a hookup.

I must admit, I'm not the greatest at dating. While in the military, I didn't want to cause any trouble by being "the gay one" in our barracks, and I didn't have a lot of free time anyway. I lived on base, which made things even more difficult, and I'm certain my old drill sergeant was homophobic at his core. Now I'm a pro fighter, and getting outed could harm my career in the sport. Both situations dampen my desire to hang in a gay bar or set up any online profiles that could easily be found by any schmoe with a phone.

While I've had hookups and a few dates, they've been fleeting.

I *know* Corbin finds me physically attractive, but he's made it clear he thinks he'll need to explain everything to me using a box of crayons. Then again, he did apologize for the comments and has genuinely come around.

"We need to drop Derek off first," Malala says. "And then you two can have some *alone time*." She giggles and nudges her brother with an elbow.

Corbin gets red from the ears down. He flails at his sister and says something harsh under his breath. She just laughs and slaps his shoulder. I swear he turns a shade of crimson. Which I'll take as a good sign. If he wants me, I'm more than willing to perform, especially after everything he's done.

"Let's go get Derek," Corbin says, pointing to the door. "He's probably lost, and we should get going regardless."

CORBIN PULLS his car in front of Derek's house around 0200 in the morning. Fog hangs low on the cold Sacramento air, obscuring most of the neighborhood, but Derek's simple one-story home is easy to see. He steps out of the vehicle, and Malala follows him. Out of the corner of my eye, I spot Corbin fidget in his seat, almost like he'll protest. It never happens.

At the front door, Derek and Malala speak for a moment. They're too far away, and I'm in a vehicle, so it's not like I can hear anything. Corbin watches the entire time, his eyes narrowed. To my surprise, Derek leans down and gives Malala a kiss—one that lasts a few seconds and clearly involves tongue, even at our distance.

"Unbelievable," Corbin mutters. "So forward. What if she didn't want to kiss on the first date?"

Malala wraps her arms around Derek's neck and pulls him close.

I chuckle. "I think she wanted it."

"W-well, we don't know that for sure."

"There's a good chance she tells you to leave her here, that's how much she obviously wants it."

Corbin groans and then looks in the opposite direction. "Tell me when it's over."

"You don't like kissing on the first date?" I ask, ready to take mental notes.

"I don't mind, but I would be upset if anyone made an inappropriate move on my sister. She's led a rough life. I know it doesn't look that way now, but she was bedridden for years and not allowed to leave the house. She deserves to be happy every second she can be."

I rub my face, concealing my half smile. Again, I'm reminded of my own sister back in North Carolina. I feel the same way about her happiness—she's five years younger than I am, and I've always been protective of her. She was never bedridden, but our father drank a lot. When he hit her, I fought back. First real fight I was ever in. I'll never forget the rush—the adrenaline—of stopping his beer-fueled tirade with my bare fists.

That kind of power is hard to describe. It was like I wasn't helpless anymore—that I had the ability to right all the wrongs in the world. I didn't have to be afraid, and no one could force their hate on me or my sister ever again.

I wasn't a child after that.

It's fair to say that if Corbin had been an ass to his sister, we wouldn't have a chance together. I can't stand people who would treat their family like a punching bag, either physically or emotionally, not even a slight amount. I wish I could visit my sister—see her in person rather than hearing about her accomplishments from others, or watching her life unfold on Facebook—but I doubt that will ever happen. We've been estranged for years now.

Malala hops into the back seat of Corbin's four-door vehicle, smiling enough that it can be seen from space.

"Derek is the same sweet kid I knew in second grade," she says in a singsong voice.

Corbin rolls his eyes and drives forward. "No one is the same person they were in second grade."

"He's not completely the same, of course. Still soft on the inside, though. I can't believe he's a fighter! He wouldn't hurt a fly outside of the octagon."

"Hm."

"Derek was always the nicest guy in our barracks," I say. "He made time for everyone, was ready for any task, and helpful to all the new recruits. It was Derek who helped me find an apartment in California." A shitty apartment, but still. He's a good guy.

"Swell," Corbin says. "I'm sure he's a candidate for the Nobel Peace Prize."

"Have a problem with Derek?"

"No," he snaps. Under his breath he says, "Never mind. I'm fine."

"I am ready to hit the sack," Malala says as she throws herself back against the seat. "Take me home, Jeeves."

Corbin forces a smile. "Of course, Miss Daisy."

I don't press the issue.

I GLANCE at the clock on the dashboard. It's 0300 by the time we reach Corbin's apartment building. The shabby structure has seen better days, but an older maintenance worker shuffles around the outside, his tool belt jingling in the quiet of an early morning—way too early for any maintenance worker I've ever known. He offers Corbin a wave and a smile before turning his attention to the peeling paint on the outside of the building. He takes out a notebook and makes a couple quick marks before carrying on.

"I live on the fourth story," Corbin says without looking at me. "I, uh, live alone."

"All right," I say.

We hadn't talked the whole ride here. I tried a couple of times, but Corbin had less than three words per reply, so silence kept us company instead. He reeks of anxiety, and he's been that way since I got a little too close.

Maybe he doesn't want me to hit on him. He said he wasn't in a relationship, so maybe he doesn't want *me* and he's worried about turning me down. This guessing game gets under my skin, however. I shouldn't have been ambiguous, because then I would know.

Corbin rubs his pant legs. "Would you like to come up?"

Odd question, considering that's why we're here. I lift an eyebrow, and Corbin gives me a nervous chuckle.

"Sorry," he says. "Er, let's go."

We exit his vehicle. I grab my duffel bag and then head to the front door. Corbin punches in a security code, and a waft of smells washes over us. It reminds me of an old folks' home. Doesn't bother me, and once the night air rushes in, the scents dissipate. I stay close to Corbin's side as he heads for the stairs. To my surprise, he springs up the steps with little problem or hesitation. Most people dread several flights of stairs, but I suspect Corbin—who isn't rocked—at least keeps his health at the forefront.

Stairs don't bother me. I dash up with little problem, barely breathing heavy by the time I reach the fourth floor. I do conditioning training to keep my breath intake at a steady pace. Prevents gassing out or wheezing.

Silence fills the hallway. I glance around, wondering if most of the apartments are empty.

Corbin unlocks a door and ushers me in without a word.

Soup cans have more room than his apartment, but I can't complain. His place is bigger than mine.

I throw my bag down on his narrow couch and stare at the perfect countertops of his sterile kitchen. No dishes out of place. No silverware to wash. Even the paper towels are kept on a spindle mounted next to the window. Neat and tidy.

It reminds me that I haven't bathed since my fight.

"Do you mind if I take a shower?" I ask.

Corbin looks me up and down, a hint of pink about him. "No. Of course not. It's through my bedroom." He points to the only other door.

I remove my shirt and throw it on top of my bag. Corbin holds his breath, his attention straight on me. The thought of stripping right in front of him gets me smiling. Would he like that? Might be too forward for a guy like him. He seems more into classy affairs, considering his button-up shirt, tucked neat into his slacks, and little vest. I like that. He has standards.

"Would you rather I stay?" I ask.

Corbin looks away. "Uh, n-no. You should get yourself decent."

Decent, huh? "All right."

I grab a new shirt and shorts and head for the bathroom.

Corbin's bedroom, cramped like a coffin, has space enough for a bed and a dresser. I shuffle past them and enter the matchbox-sized bathroom.

Corbin Friel

THE STRAIN of the pipes tells me Keon has started his shower.

What am I going to do? I can't believe he's here, in my apartment, talking to me and... taking off his clothes. I figured I'd never be this close to a guy of his physique without shelling out copious amounts of money. My palms sweat thinking about it.

I remove Keon's medication from my pocket and go to the medical kit I have in my kitchen. I keep a few epinephrine injections and syringes, just in case. I can give Keon his shot and antibiotics, and then again in six hours.

None of that worries me, yet my hands still shake and my heart beats hard against my ribs.

Keon surprises me. He knows about things I didn't think a fighter would ever know, and every time I see him without a shirt, I swear I can identify another muscle group I missed before. And now I think he was flirting with me. Of course, I've never been competent at flirting, so I could be miscalling this. But every gesture he makes gets my pulse racing. Standing close to me. Staring straight into my eyes. Removing his shirt in my living room? I saw his tight little smirk. Did he know I would enjoy the show?

But what should I do about this? After all, Keon didn't say anything when I admitted I dated only men. He could have mentioned his own proclivities then. It would have been a perfect opportunity, yet he said nothing, so he's probably not into men. Right? That must be the explanation.

But what if he *is* into men? He could be bisexual, which would be the reason he didn't bring it up.

What should I do to indicate I want this to happen? When I flirted with Justin, it was a different story. We were both in high school, and he was the other gay boy I knew. Curiosity made us a couple, and complacency kept us together.

I should tell Keon I'm interested. That would be the quickest and easiest way. But what if he gets offended? Some straight men take a proposal to date as an affront to their manliness. And I would prefer to avoid another "relationship" like I currently have with Justin. I don't feel good about how Justin and I interact, and I'd rather have a healthy relationship. I've read tons of medical reports that support the medical and mental benefits of a stable, loving partner.

Maybe I'm overthinking this. I'm fretting. I should relax and have a simple conversation with him. I should be professional and straightforward.

Keon turns off the shower, and I know my time to think is limited.

I'm not confused about my wants. I *want* to flirt with Keon. I *want* to see where it goes. He's handsome, confident, and filled with an unrivaled drive. I should try to make this happen.

I walk to the kitchen and wash my hands. I don't know why, but it does help me calm my anxiety.

Keon walks out of my bedroom, wiping his damp hair with a towel. His new shirt and shorts, both black and tight against his body, do wonders for his appearance. The man should always wear such fitted outfits. Or nothing at all, but I'll never actually suggest that.

He crosses the living room and stands next to me in the kitchen. "Ready to do this?"

"I, uh, need to wash my hands first." I grab the soap and wash my hands a second time, still uncertain of what I should say.

"You seem nervous."

"Maybe you should get your eyes checked," I snap, my anxiety bleeding into irritation. "I'm perfectly composed."

"You sure?"

I don't say anything.

The real problem is, I want to say the right things, but the words aren't coming. I'm sure if I was more suave or debonair, I would know exactly how to phrase my attraction. But uncertainty eats at my composure.

Keon steps close to me. "We don't have to talk, ya know. Not if it's going to make you uncomfortable."

I turn around and face him, my mouth dry and my breath shallow. "It's not that."

"Oh yeah?"

"I don't know what to say."

"There's lots of nonverbal ways to express what you're feeling."

Again he takes a step closer.

He *has* to be hitting on me. There is no other explanation.

Keon waits, staring down at me with the same steady gaze he had before. He wants me to do something. Should I make a move? I might as well. It's not like I see him on a daily basis around my school or something. If this doesn't work out, I can avoid him, as cowardly as that may be.

I hold my breath and close the last few inches between us by scooting a bit closer. I place my hand on his chest. He doesn't move or question the gesture. His heavy heartbeat sends shivers down my spine. I move my hand up to his neck and caress the exposed flesh. Even the muscles around his jugular could kick my ass. No part of him is neglected.

He leans down. I tilt my head back. Right before our mouths connect, he stops, and I finish the last bit, desperate once again to taste him.

My lips press against his. The heat startles me. I didn't think he would so warm or soft. The smell of his shower still lingers, and his skin tastes like savory honey. Keon licks me—lightly, testing me—and I open my mouth to continue our exchange.

His tongue runs the length of mine, and I shiver. Although my hands had been idle, I consciously force myself to graze his torso, my fingers finding the grooves of his abs and counting them while I drown in his kiss.

Six rock-hard rectus abdominis muscles.

Keon presses hard, pinning me against the counter. I suck on his lower lip, and he returns the favor with a hint of teeth. I catch my breath, and he half smiles but never breaks contact. His hot breath mingles with mine, stoking the fire building in my gut and spreading to the rest of my body.

I want this—I want him—but I stop myself and pull away.

"I, uh," I say, my thoughts an unsolved jigsaw puzzle. "You're okay with this?"

"More than okay."

"R-really? You're not joking with me?"

"Do I look like I'm joking?"

The gruff seriousness in his voice tells me everything I need to know. I stare up at him, meeting his intense gaze. Then I swallow and remember why we came here in the first place.

"We should, uh, do the things for… your shin."

Keon strokes my jawline. Up close, his dark eyes look like chocolate amber. "Yeah. You're right. Where should we do it?"

"My couch, or, uh, the bed."

He chuckles, and I know, taken out of context, my answer could be for a completely different question altogether, but I'm trying to be serious.

"Let's do this," he says as he walks back to my bedroom, never even giving the couch a second glance.

My heart rate doubles again, beating at four times the speed. I can't believe we're about to enter my room. Well, the medicine first. I should stay focused.

Still, my gaze lands on his sculpted back—I've always found muscular backs attractive—and I'm struggling to think of anything else.

Focus, Corbin. Focus.

Chapter 9
Relationship Status

Corbin Friel

I ENTER my room and Keon takes a seat on the edge of my queen-size bed. I probably shouldn't have opted for queen over twin, since the bed takes up most of the space in the room, but I've always been glad of the decision when it comes to intimate moments.

God, it seems insane that I'm with Keon, especially since my day didn't start with this as the intended ending. I should count myself lucky. I'm still in a mild stupor. I don't mind, though. No complaining on my end.

"So, what do we do?" Keon asks.

"I don't know," I say, almost a whisper. "What do you normally do?"

He lifts an eyebrow.

What does he want from me? I exhale. "I've only ever been with one other person." I talk a little too fast, so I try to slow my words. "I'm not skilled at these types of encounters."

Keon chuckles as he runs a hand over his face. "I meant for the medicine. What do we do for that?"

Heat floods my whole body. Oh, right. We were going to do that first. How have I already forgotten? I'm even holding the medical kit in my hands!

I laugh, more nervous than jovial, and walk over to him. "Lie on your stomach. I'll give you the shot in the back of your knee, and then you'll swallow this antibiotic."

Without questioning me, Keon slides up onto my bed and lies down. I rub the back of his leg. Everything about him screams *stiff*. He doesn't move. He doesn't flinch. I don't even think he's breathing. It amuses me he's so afraid of shots and medicine, but I know I shouldn't mock. I should be glad he's willing to have this done. If I hadn't insisted we do the examination, his infection would've gone undiagnosed, and then he really could have lost his leg.

I open the kit, take out some cleaning alcohol, and prep a small portion of skin, cleaning the injection area over the top of the calf muscle. Keon's tension never wanes. If anything, he's tenser—he grips the blankets of my bed like he's trying to strangle them.

Whenever I got nervous in my mother's clinic, she would explain the process. The knowledge assured me. Not knowing what was happening made it scary. My imagination would run away with all sorts of terrible scenarios.

"This is an intramuscular injection," I say. "The fluid goes straight into the muscle."

Keon growls something in response, but I can't make it out. I rub my hand along the length of his leg, and I finally hear him inhale and exhale. Is he relaxing? I can only hope so.

I stick him with the needle. To my surprise, he never moves. Most people grimace, but I guess Keon has a high amount of willpower.

"Injections straight to the veins are the hardest." I empty the contents of the syringe. "Because of the difficulties locating adequate entrance locations. This type of injection will be over quickly."

Sure enough, after a few seconds, everything is done. I withdraw the syringe, sterilize it, and then walk it back to the kitchen so I can deal with it later. When I return to the room, Keon still hasn't moved. Perhaps he thinks I need to do something else?

I sit next to him and pat his uninjured calf. "We're all done. You were a perfect patient."

He sighs heavily into my pillow. "What about the antibiotics?"

I hand him two pills. Keon takes them to the bathroom, pops them in his mouth, and drinks directly from the sink. He walks back to the bed and rolls onto his back.

With a shaky hand, he rubs the bridge of his nose. "Thank you."

"Don't mention it."

"Lie with me."

His command catches me off guard. The lustful heat had disappeared for a moment while I worked as a pretend doctor, but that brings it back full force. I scoot across the bed and rest next to Keon's warm body. He wraps an arm around me and holds me close, my head resting on the edge of his chest. The beat of his heart matches mine—accelerated, but not panicked. The memory of earlier, when our lips were locked, plays in my mind. I kiss his side, light and quick.

"Nervous?" he asks.

"What?" My mouth feels like cotton. I try to swallow but never manage it. "I'm excited you're here and… we're doing this."

He rolls onto his side so we're facing each other.

"You're very… attractive," I say, struggling to articulate my true feelings.

"Like what you see?"

"Of course."

"I'm yours for the night."

His confidence melts the last of my reservations. I want him, and he's here and willing. I can think of nothing else.

Keon Lynch

I HOLD Corbin close, pressing his body against mine. He's hard already; it's easy to tell. I run my hands across the length of his body, familiarizing myself with every inch I can reach. Then I grab his shirt and pull. He hesitates and stops me.

"My glasses," he mutters.

Corbin removes them and sets them on the tiny nightstand. I tug at his shirt again, and he doesn't offer further protest. There's a lean quality to his body. No definition to the muscles, but he's sleek and smooth. I lace my fingers through his dark brown hair, and he returns the gesture, playing with my mohawk like he's never really seen one before.

He smells fresh and clean, like he's recently showered. Something about it excites me. I nuzzle my face into his shoulder and lick at the point where his neck meets his body. When his breath catches, I know he's enjoying every second of my affection. It gets me harder and hotter. I suck his skin until it bruises, enjoying the way he pants, the taste of his raw flesh. His hands grip my shoulders, his nails digging in past my shirt.

The slight pain gets me smiling. Reminds me of some of my fight training. It quickens my pulse and brings back the thrill and excitement that comes from human contact.

I roll onto my back and drag Corbin on top of me. Everything about his presence—his weight, his hardened length, the way his breath mingles with mine—I wish this could last for hours. It's been so long since I've engaged in any sort of bedroom play.

"You don't have to leave after this," Corbin says before anything else happens. He keeps his arms posted on my chest, keeping his distance.

"You want another round in the morning?" I ask. "I'm flattered. We haven't even gotten to the best part and already you want seconds."

He becomes a shade of red like he's equipped with a light switch for the color of his face. Still, he doesn't move away or flail. He leans down closer, bringing his mouth to my collarbone and kissing the ridge.

"I mean," he says with a strained voice, "I'd like it if… you'd consider staying with me. For longer than an evening."

"I'll consider it."

"You will?"

He sounds surprised. Did he think I wouldn't want to date anyone? Then again, I really shouldn't. What if someone finds out and reports it around the fighting circles? It could be trouble… but I've already gotten into a mess of trouble already. What's a little more?

"I want to see where this goes," I say, my voice husky, betraying my lust.

Corbin gives me a nervous smile. But then he melts back down onto me and grinds his hips against mine, our dicks rubbing together, the fabric of our pants the only thing between us.

I kiss the bruise I left on the base of his neck and then lick the mark. Corbin tastes as clean as he smells. With each rocking motion, he moans, low and quiet, like he's trying to hold back any noise. The walls may be thin, but I don't care. I like it when my partner's loud.

"We should use a prophylactic," he says between heavy breaths.

What the fuck is a prophylactic? "I don't use sex toys," I say.

Corbin cocks an eyebrow. "What? I mean, we should use a condom."

"Then why didn't you say so?" I drag my teeth up his neck and nibble his earlobe. "If you want to do something that involves a condom, I like that line of thought."

He leans into my affections and continues his grinding. "A-all right."

Corbin has a nervous stutter to his voice, but his actions speak louder than words. He wants this. Maybe his mind is running through a hundred terrible scenarios, but his body has its marching orders, and he's ready to rumble.

I grab a fistful of his hair and yank back, my strength more than I counted on. I expose his neck fully, and something about the roughness must excite him, because he half moans and half whimpers. He's harder than before, an iron bar trapped by the fabric of his pants. I bite at his neck, growling with feral desire. I release him, and he locks his lips with mine, sliding his tongue into my mouth before I can take another breath.

Corbin moans while we kiss, running his hands all over my body. I undo Corbin's belt, toss it to the side, and push down his slacks. He removes his boxers and the last of his clothes, his length leaking and swollen. He yanks at my shirt, silently pleading to see me naked. I smile, break away from him, and undress in record time. For a moment, Corbin stares, never breathing, just soaking in the sight. The admiration fuels my lust. Knowing he's excited removes all doubt and hesitation.

He wants me, and I want him.

Each beat of my heart tells me there's no need to delay. I flip us both over and pin him to the bed, my hands on his shoulders, his wide eyes betraying his shock. He fans his fingers and runs them down my chest and stomach. Then he grabs my dick and strokes, half petting and half clutching. My precome gets his hand slick, and everything slides easy. I fuck his hand for a moment, but the sensations aren't enough.

"Well?" I growl. "Where's your *prophylactic*, or whatever the hell you called it?"

Corbin reaches over and opens a drawer in the nightstand. He gives me the condom, his hand unsteady, and I rip it open and apply it with the same eagerness as my very first time. I didn't realize how much I wanted this until right now. I'm so desperate for the touch, for the relief, for the companionship—to hell with the consequences or anyone hassling me for my choices.

"You like it rough?" I ask, each word wrenched from my throat. I don't want to speak. I just want to fuck him, but I have to make sure— he's small enough I worry I might hurt him in my desperation.

He nods.

His whole body trembles as I grab his hips and slide him down the bed, positioning him with his legs spread. Normally I like the guy facedown, riding him like an animal, but I want to watch Corbin's face as I enter. I want this to be personal—to make sure I do it right and he enjoys it.

The prelubed condom helps me slip into position. Already I can tell he has a tight hole, but he relaxes enough to allow me entrance without too much force. The moment I get the head in, Corbin scrunches his eyes and grabs me, but nothing looks to be contorted in pain. After a second, he opens his eyes and stares at me, ready for the rest. I tilt my head back and groan, the pleasure intense and ripping through my body as I slide in.

Corbin moans and then pleads, "Yes, please…."

God, I love it when my partner begs me to continue.

I thrust in, my self-control disappearing at a rapid rate. I continue, driving myself home, until I'm flush against his tight ass. He keeps his eyes scrunched tight, but he continues to whimper encouragements.

"Yes…. Right there…."

Corbin raises his arms and buries them under his pillows. I keep on my knees, my posture straight, and I lift his hips wherever I need to get deep. Then I pump—at first slow, but then to a punishing pace, my heart thrashing in my chest, ready for the climax.

After a few minutes, Corbin rocks against me with each thrust, yelling his moans and arching his back. His throbbing dick bounces against his stomach, twitching and leaking. I grab it and pump, adding to Corbin's feverish noises. I think he tries to say something, but it comes out as a mess of syllables and breathless pleading.

Sweat clings to everything, pooling together in droplets. It drips off me as I pound Corbin, the fire of relief building in my lower gut. Corbin swells in my hand, and he orgasms first, shooting his seed all over his chest and neck. The sight of him in ecstasy, overtaken by pleasure, is enough to send me over. I clench my teeth and groan, emptying myself inside him, straight into the condom.

Corbin sucks in his breath as I remove myself.

"Gently," he whispers.

I finish at a slow and easy pace. He breathes out and relaxes afterward, a picture of contentment.

I throw the used condom into the trash and caress Corbin's ass with my spare hand. He flinches under my touch but quickly calms. He sighs and keeps his legs spread under me. He's still semihard, and I stare down, pleased with the conquest. If it weren't so early in the damn morning—0400, to be exact—I'd do him again, but fatigue has finally caught up to me.

With a deep exhale, I roll onto the bed and pull Corbin close. He rests against my chest, his eyes closed and his breathing evening out. He must be exhausted, and I don't blame him. He's not the type of guy who has a ton of stamina.

I close my eyes.

And then my mind goes blank.

0600 AND my eyes snap open.

My body has a set rhythm. Every day I do the same damn thing. Wake up, do my morning exercises, go to work, go to the gym, come home, and then sleep. I do it with such exactness that I'm sure I could do it all without a clock, even blind.

I glance down. Corbin's arm rests across my chest, and his head is tucked into my armpit. I move him with gentle motions. The guy never wakes. He never even snorts or snores. Once free of his affectionate grasp, I scoot out of his bed and amble over to the bathroom. I take a much needed piss before dressing and then walking out into the living room and kitchen combo.

The apartment building stirs with obvious movement. The others must be up and about.

I stretch, thankful for last night. I needed it. Even the fear of my leg doesn't seem like such a big deal. I didn't even bump it during our sexual escapade, for which I'm eternally grateful. It would have sucked to be knocked out of the moment by a boatload of unexpected pain.

Should I work out in Corbin's living room? I don't see why not. I need to stay here until he wakes and administers the next round of medication. Plus, I want to talk to him about what the next step of our relationship might entail. But I can't be around all the time or even alter my schedule much. I have a few fights coming up, and I need to train and maintain my weight with a precise exactness.

The doorbell chimes throughout the apartment. I whip my attention to the door and glare. Who rings a doorbell at this hour?

I walk over, unlock the door, and open it.

Some surfer-looking guy stands in front of me, his cargo shorts and sandals the same tannish coloration. He has a tight black tank top, which shows off his wiry frame, but something about his posture rubs me the wrong way. He leans against the apartment wall like he's been waiting forever, almost annoyed, but he straightens himself the moment he gets his eyes on me.

"Who are you?" he asks.

"I was going to ask you the same damn question."

The guy glances around, trying to see past me. I step forward, and he takes a few steps back.

"I'm Corbin's boyfriend," he says. "Justin. I'm sure he's mentioned me."

Boyfriend?

Fuck.

I hate cheaters and finks—anyone who thinks a commitment isn't worth their time. I was in the military long enough to appreciate loyalty, *true* loyalty, and men who cheat on their significant others are beneath me.

And it reminds me of my father. He cheated on every woman he was ever with, even my mother. It probably bothers me more than reasonable for that fact alone.

Justin lifts an eyebrow. "So, I take it he didn't mention me?"

"He said he wasn't seeing anyone," I say, terse.

Justin runs a hand through his spiky blond hair, though the hair gel keeps it all in place. "Oh, I see. He invited you over and mentioned nothing about me. What a dog. And he acts so proper." He walks past me and into the apartment.

I grit my teeth, half tempted to throw this guy out, but that would be insane. They're a couple, obviously, or else why would Justin just walk in like this? I can't believe me and Corbin messed around last night. I hate being the participant in some sleazy sexual affair.

"You should get out of here," Justin says. He walks straight to the bedroom door and stops before going in. "I'll let Corbin know you slipped out." Then he looks me up and down. "Wow. You must have a great torso shot on Grindr. Is that how Corbin got ahold of you?"

I don't do shit like Grindr.

This whole situation leaves a terrible taste in my mouth. I exit Corbin's apartment, anger bubbling in my chest and threatening to spill over. Maybe it's best Justin deal with Corbin. I would have some choice words for the guy—strong fucking words.

Why would he lie to me? What an asshole.

Chapter 10
Training

Corbin Friel

I ROLL to my side and snuggle into the warm body next to me. But my hands find a fully clothed man—a man half the size he should be—with no substantial muscle to speak of. I snap awake and lift my head. Blurry shapes and hazy colors greet me. I need my glasses or else the world isn't right. I scrabble to retrieve them, but they aren't on the nightstand. Isn't that where I left them?

"You're so cute when you wake up flustered," Justin says, his voice laced with a casual amusement, bordering on a drawl.

"Justin," I say. "What're you doing here?"

Still, I can't find my glasses. I throw around the blankets, wondering if they fell onto the bed in the middle of the night. And to add to my frustrations, I feel... soiled. I didn't shower after my encounter with Keon, which might as well be a blasphemy, and now the sheets are tainted, and what if my glasses are rolling around this? I shudder imagining it all.

Justin rests back on my bed. "I came by to see my favorite boyfriend."

I hold back a huff. "*Favorite* implies you have more than one. And we're not dating. How many times do I have to tell you? How did you even get into my apartment?"

"That Grindr whore let me in."

"Are you talking about Keon?"

"Whatever his name was."

"Where is he now?"

Justin yawns. "I sent him on his way, obviously. I'm not the kind of guy who shares. Honestly, are you trying to make me jealous? I came by to spend time with you."

"Get out," I snap.

I can't believe he sent Keon away. We still have to do the rest of his medication, and I really want to talk to him about last night. I had fun—and it looked like *he* had fun—but I want to make sure. I don't know Keon as well as I should, I'm not very good at social interactions, and I'm not a mind reader, so straight up talking to Keon is the best course of action. Especially if I want our relationship to continue.

"Why are you so grumpy?" Justin asks. "Maybe you'll feel better once you eat. Sometimes you get hangry."

"I do nothing of the sort! Now get out. I can't find my glasses."

"Oh, these?" He twirls a blurry object around his finger. "I'll give them back. For a kiss."

"I swear sometimes I think you don't understand English."

I grab for my glasses, but he holds them above his head. Then he scoots up close and kisses my bare shoulder. I cringe away, practically growling, but Justin laughs, like he always does.

"Leave my glasses and get out," I state.

Justin sighs. "Don't be like that, Corbin. I'm not here to fight."

He has to secretly be two people because no single person can be this stupid. How many times do I have to make it clear? He shouldn't be here. I don't want to see him. He should leave. I'm more anxious and worried about Keon than anything else. I really shouldn't have allowed our sexual relationship to continue, not when he keeps trying to twist it into something more.

"I came to give you some money I owe you," Justin says.

"Fine. But give me my glasses and get out of here for a minute. I want to get dressed."

"I could help you." He leans back and stretches out on the bed. "Get you in a better mood."

Normally I'd just give in to his persistent demands—better to give Justin what to he wants so he'll go away and stop pestering me—but that has to stop. I won't do anything sexual with Justin, even if we had good times in the past.

"Not today," I say. "Not ever. We need to stop doing this. Get out of my room." I use a tone I've never used with Justin—hard-edged and forceful.

Justin must sense a change as well because he gets up. "Fine. I'll be in the living room." He tosses my glasses on the bed and exits my room.

I jump into the bathroom, turn on the shower, and force myself to enter the frigid water. I shrivel in every sense of the word. Shivering and clattering my teeth, I scrub myself from head to toe. By the time I'm done exfoliating, the water's warm but hasn't yet penetrated deep enough to soothe my muscles. I leap out of the shower and scramble to get my clothes on.

When I enter the living room, Justin's relaxing back on the narrow couch, his attention glued to the screen of his phone. I glance at the kitchen and find it empty.

"Where's Keon?" I ask.

"I told you. I sent him away."

"You really did that?"

"Yeah. Of course. I already said I'm the jealous type." He puts his phone down and scratches at his forearm. "We still see each other on a regular basis. I know you like to deny it, but we're totally dating."

I huff and stifle a tirade. What does Keon think about all this? I need to speak with him. But I don't have his number, and I don't know where he lives. How am I supposed to get ahold of him? Maybe Lala will know. Or more likely, Derek. I should give my sister a call to get his number.

"You look flustered," Justin says.

"That's what I love about you. Your legendary perception."

"So sarcastic. That's how I know you're really upset. You usually mutter all those sardonic comments under your breath."

"You said you had money for me?" I ask.

Justin kicks off my couch and ambles over. He pulls out fifty bucks. I hold out my hand, and he takes his sweet-ass time, like always, before placing it on my palm. He's sweaty, and his eyes a little more sunken in than they should be. I pocket the money and give him the once-over.

"Are you okay?" I ask.

"Concerned about me? That's cute."

He leans close, ready to kiss me, but I back away.

"What's wrong with you?"

"Ah, c'mon."

"I said no." I offer him a glare. "And you really don't look well— even if I don't want to make out with you, I am concerned."

Justin shrugs. "I feel fine. What're you even talking about?"

"You know it'll be my job to notice things about people's health, right? You look *off*. And you're scratching more than usual."

As if on cue, Justin itches at his neck. "Nah. All in your head, Bin-Bin."

Whatever. If he doesn't want to tell me what's going on, I suppose it's his business. And it's not like he's deathly ill or anything. I really should let it slide, along with everything else. The less he has reason to come over here, the better.

"Hey," I say, holding up the cash. "Thank you for this. Consider us even."

"I still owe you more."

"Forget it. I don't need it. And I'm actually seeing someone else now, so this really needs to end."

Justin doesn't say anything. I glare at him.

"Did you hear me?" I ask. "I need you to acknowledge it."

"Who is it?"

"Keon."

"Keon who?"

"Keon Lynch. The guy who was just here."

"The Grindr guy?"

"Yeah. Sure. Whatever. *The Grindr guy*. What does it matter?"

Again, he returns to silence, his expression a bit more serious than I've ever seen before.

I exhale. "We can still be friends, but this is serious. I don't want you dropping by unannounced. And we aren't going to have any more of these *hookup nights*."

"You really think you'll be in a long-term relationship?"

"Yes. I do. Now please leave."

Justin rubs his hands on his pants. He mills about for a few seconds, almost like he might protest leaving, but then gives me a lopsided smile. "Hey, I'll repay the last of the money I owe you. That's the least a friend would do for another, right?"

Something about his tone of voice gets me uneasy, but I guess he's right. "Fine. I would appreciate that."

Justin pats me on the shoulder and then opens the front door. "And if it doesn't work out, let me know. I'll be here to keep you company again." He steps out, leaving me alone in my apartment.

I glance at the time. Six thirty in the morning. Keon needs his medication in another couple of hours. And it might be too early to call my sister or Derek. I pace my kitchen and living room, my thoughts out of control and dreading every weird hypothetical. I'm more nervous about Keon than I ever imagined I would be. I haven't been with many people, so seeing him seems more important than it probably is.

I check the time. Six thirty-two.

Yeah. I need to do something to occupy my thoughts. Then I'll get ahold of my sister and Derek.

"HELLO?" DEREK asks once he answers his phone.

I sit up on my bed, breathing easy. "Hello. This is Corbin Friel."

"Oh, Bin-Bin. What's up?"

Oh God. Even Derek? I need to kill this nickname before it infests someone else's vocabulary.

"I'm looking for Keon," I say. "Do you know where I can find him?"

"Right now?"

"Yes."

Derek spends a good five seconds thinking over the question. I stare at my bedroom wall, ready to write down a phone number or leave the apartment, whatever is needed. Then Derek clears his throat.

"Uh, he's either working or he's at the gym."

"Working? I thought he was a professional fighter. Isn't that his job?"

Derek chuckles. "Yeah, I wish. Professional fighters don't get paid *that* much per fight. A couple thousand at best. And that's if you win or sell tickets. Otherwise it's a couple hundred. Not enough to live on. Not in California, am I right or am I right?"

"What does he do for work?"

"He's an exterminator. Killing bugs in stores and restaurants. Ya know."

Ah, some sort of certified blue-collar job. Not the best, but not working the register at a McDonald's either. I guess I shouldn't be too judgmental. I once worked at a Baskin Robbins to make extra cash on the side, and that was anything but respectable.

"What gym does he go to?" I ask.

85

"Some place called Harvey's Workout Zone. It's in Stockton. The northern part. Real shithole, if you ask me. A few pretty ladies go there, though."

Derek likes to share every thought on his mind, doesn't he?

"Can I get Keon's phone number?" I ask.

"Sure, sure."

I write down the number as he recites it, relief coming in with every breath. "Thank you," I say. "I appreciate this."

"No problem. Oh, uh, maybe you can do me a solid in return."

"A solid?"

"Your sister is a sweet girl. I like her."

"Okay," I say, hating the direction this conversation has gone.

"Where can I take her? For someplace special. Some place she'd like."

My sister has odd tastes. Everything she loves is something she shouldn't be doing. Since she's so fragile, all physical activity was off the table. So, obviously, she wanted to do hockey, and then MMA, and then ride horses, and then dodgeball on trampolines... the list goes on and on, escalating into whimsy with each new interest. But Derek can't do any of those things with her. She can't do them ever.

"Maybe take her to a hockey game," I say. "They have them every once in a while in San Francisco."

"Oh shit, she likes hockey? Damn. Where has this girl been all my life?"

"Hm."

"Thank you. You're all right."

Having Derek's approval isn't high on my list, but I'll take it over disdain.

"Goodbye, Derek."

"Bye, man."

He hangs up the phone, and I briefly wonder what I should do.

I'll call Keon, and if I can't get ahold of him... I'll find another way. The fact he left without even a note, even leaving his gym bag, tells me he probably left in rush. Late for work? I hope so. Better than regretting an evening with me. And better than being upset because of Justin's presence.

And I won't be able to study until I get this off my mind.

I clean my hands with a squirt of sanitizer and reach for my phone a second time.

Keon Lynch

STOCKTON DOESN'T just have shady neighborhoods. It has whole sections of city that could be described as *a seedy underbelly*. Better than Oakland, which is where I lived before, but it's not much better. Last I saw, Stockton was one of the top ten most dangerous cities to live in within the United States, and second most dangerous in California. Which is why the rent is so cheap, hence why I live here.

The biggest downside, however, is that most of the facilities open to the public are a trash heaps. I glance around my twenty-four-hour gym, taking in the myriad of graffiti tags, broken equipment, and shabby individuals, some of whom have been here sleeping for the last hour.

I do wish I had someplace to work out that was a little less of a dumpster fire. Most of the members seem to be openly in gangs—Stockton has a major problem with them—and half of the gang members have talked about their time in prison while working out.

Doesn't surprise me. The amateur fighting league is filled with thugs. They join to be "hard" and claim that they're "fighters," but most never make it to the professional level. Even people *trying* to get to the professional level never make it, really. You have to get through three amateur fights, and then you need a sponsorship to the professional level. Doesn't sound hard, but the sponsorship only happens when individuals are impressed with your skills.

That's why I moved to California. My old military CO, Harvey, owns this shitty gym and technically trains people in karate, though I don't think he's an actual sensei. He's my sponsor, and the one who got me into the professional ring to begin with. I owe him a lot, though I rarely see him. Harvey asks me to train some of his paying members in mixed martial arts, which I do for free, and that's our unspoken agreement.

Sucks not having a proper team, however. Most guys get sponsored by dojos or fight academies, so they have tons of people rooting for them, training with them, and actively helping them at every step of the process. I just have Harvey asking if I won anything and if the name of his gym got slapped on a few fight tickets or around the octagon.

Harvey actually owns a ton of places around Stockton, including a restaurant, a museum, and a movie theater. Guy likes to invest in random things and then run them with half-assed enthusiasm, hoping something will turn a huge profit. That's probably what I am to him—a minor investment he hopes works out, but he's not going to put much effort into the ordeal.

Whatever works, I guess.

I lift some weights, my mind drifting. I do this damn near every day. I have to maintain a baseline level of conditioning year-round. And I have to keep track of my progress, so the weights help me know the exact amount I'm capable of lifting. When I'm done with this, I'll do some cardio, then swim, and end it all in the steam room. Basic training, really. What I need is a competent sparring partner to hone my combat skills.

The term *sparring partner* reminds me of Corbin. Not that he would spar, but the partner bit.

I can't believe he's such a scumball. I thought he was a little more honorable than that. Who cheats on their significant other? Lowlifes and losers. It still leaves a bad taste in my mouth, and that was a few hours ago.

And here I was impressed with him. What a joke.

I grip the weight so tight I feel an unfamiliar strain in my forearm. I loosen my hold and take a deep breath. I shouldn't get too angry. I need to save any sort of rage I have for the octagon. Sometimes it helps to beat down the opponent. I prefer having the passion—passion is what really motivates me to win.

A group of guys circle close, entering my periphery at a slow rate. Four guys in total. Men I've seen hanging around outside, but they've never come to use the equipment. Do they even have memberships to this gym? Each one wears nondescript clothing. Plain black shorts, large white T-shirts. And they aren't dirty or sweaty. Haven't been working out, I see.

I glance at the check-in counter. The worker manning the front door is nowhere to be seen. Where the hell did he go?

The four get closer again, and I stop lifting my weights. I've been in enough fights to know when aggression stinks up the air. These guys are here for something, and the more I look around, the more I notice the gymgoers have vacated the main room.

"You Keon Lynch?" one guy asks, his voice betraying his lifelong smoking habit.

"Yeah," I say. "I am."

I'm not intimidated by a bunch of numbnuts in a gym. If they think they're going to do something to me, they're going to be sorely surprised.

"You need to stop making friends in this neighborhood. We don't like that you're moving in on our people."

"Is that right?" I ask.

I try to get a good look at these guys, but two of them are wearing sunglasses, one is wearing a black bandana over his mouth, and the last guy—the one speaking—has a homemade spider tattoo on the corner of his jaw. If these guys aren't from a local gang, I'd lose out on a bet.

"Don't ever come here again," tattoo guy says.

"I'm not going to do that. As a matter of fact, if you guys don't leave, I'm going to call the cops."

"Do it."

I'm tense and ready to kick their asses, but both sunglasses guys pull wrenches from the waistband of their shorts. My pulse runs hot, my whole body ready for a fight. One swings, and I back up.

The second guy swings low and grazes my injured leg.

I scream—I don't think I've ever felt something so intense ever in my life—like fire searing through my entire being.

I hit the floor on my knees, shaken and dreading the next few blows.

Chapter 11
Dirty Fighting

Keon Lynch

EVEN THROUGH my agony, my training kicks in. I roll to the side, keeping my bad leg under me, and the four guys lash out. They get two good kicks in—one to the ribs and one to the shoulder—but I take that with little damage. My thoughts dwell on the places I really shouldn't get hit—and the places I should target on my attackers. The nose. The back of the head. Throat. Kidney. Solar plexus. Any of those locations will render someone unconscious or writhing in a triple-strength dose of unforgiving pain.

I jump up to my good leg and use the toes of the other in an attempt to balance. The guy with the bandana punches me across the face, but his form is terrible and I turn with the blow to lessen the impact. I return with a strike to his side. Right in his kidney. A cheap shot if I was in the octagon—once an illegal shot—but these guys don't deserve a fair fight.

Bandana guy folds over on himself and whines. He'll be pissin' blood in the morning.

One of the sunglasses thugs swings his wrench. I catch his wrist, twist it around, and torque his arm upward. The guy stifles a yell and drops his weapon. I elbow his throat, the sharp tip of my bone jabbing right into his windpipe. He squawks and chokes as he stumbles back, both hands over the injury like he's strangling himself.

The second sunglasses thug leaps and tackles me. Panic floods my thoughts as I hit the ground on my back. I flip over to defend my weak leg, and I take my attacker with me. He's not a skilled grappler—his legs flail around without focus, and his punches are weak and ineffective. I punch him square in the middle of the chest, slamming down with my full force, right on his solar plexus. The guy loses his breath in one terrible wheeze, his eye half bulging from his head.

When I jump up, the tattoo guy slams my back with the wrench, sending a pulse of crippling pain straight to my skull. I suck in breath and fall to my knees. Again, I'm quick to shift into a defensive roll, but the tattooed thug must already know my tactics because he follows, his arm cocked for another powerful overhead swing.

I lunge at his legs, catching him off guard. He topples over, hits the floor on his back, and I move away before he can make another wild swing. I stand, and he attempts to stand, but he's slow—or at least, slower than me. I kick him in the side of the head—another illegal move if we were in the octagon. Blood splatters across his face from the ruptured ear.

But then white-hot pain blinds me for a solid second when I get a surprise strike to the shin. When my vision returns, I'm on the floor, getting hit, over and over by the sunglasses goon who recovered from his throat punch. Luckily for me, he strikes with his boot and not a wrench, but occasionally he gets my infected shin, shocking me back into submission. I'm prone, and I don't know if I can stand.

The guy kicks me in the jaw, and then the left ear. Ringing replaces all other noise. I can't even hear myself breathe, and my vision swirls.

I'm gonna get knocked out if he keeps this up.

Then he stops. Why? I take the opportunity to roll to my side and huddle into a defensive curl.

I almost gasp once I get a good look at the surroundings. Corbin is here! He says something—I can see his mouth move, but the ringing persists, preventing me from hearing—and it only seems to agitate the thug. The man rushes at him. I get to my feet, but my injured leg crumples under my weight. Fuck! What is Corbin doing here? He'll get himself killed!

Corbin takes a step back and pulls his hand out of his pocket just as the thug reaches him. The man spasms and falls to the floor, his legs twitching. Corbin stands over him, a Taser in hand, but he trembles as he staggers back, his eyes wide. Not used to the ferocity of fighting, clearly.

Corbin brandishes the Taser and yells a few things. He also holds up his cell phone, the 911 number clearly on the display.

Two of the crooks race for the front door. The last two, devoid of backup, stagger to their feet and limp after their cohorts. My hearing returns in tiny amounts. The sharp snap of the front door slamming calms me a bit. I let the thugs go—at least, that's what I tell myself, because reality says I'm in no condition to chase anyone. Corbin yells in their direction.

"The cops are on their way," he says. "You won't get away with this!"

I chortle at the cliché line. He's got a lot of balls to yell at a group of thugs, even if they are fleeing. Gang members have a habit of talking to one another. I should know. I hear them all the time in the gym, talking about how an insult to one is an insult to *all of them*. That kind of tribalistic mentality means I'll be seeing them in the future, no doubt about it.

Corbin exhales and turns to face me, a confident smile on his face. He did just save my ass. He leaped right into the thick of it and tasered a dangerous lowlife, despite the fact he would be in the midst of the chaos. It's either arrogant foolishness or a wellspring of confidence.

Corbin furrows his brow and jogs to my side.

I shake my head. "Why are you—"

"What happened?" he asks. "Getting into fights in a gym? Are you mad? That's a criminal offense."

"Is it a criminal offense to get jumped?" I snap. "Because I didn't think, *man, I need a rumble with my cardio today*, that's for fucking sure. Those guys attacked me."

My tone must have cut, because Corbin waits for half a second before straightening his glasses. "Ah. Yes. Of course. Sorry. I just walked in, and there you were in a fight, so my mind went crazy with possibilities."

I sigh, my body hurting for the effort. I can't believe a group of guys attempted to beat me senseless. My days are getting harder and harder.

"Are those goons from that bully fighting academy?" Corbin asks. "Or were they hired to harass you? What a disgusting show of cowardice."

His theory strikes a chord. I grit my teeth, imagining the exchange between some street thugs and a group of fighters. It wouldn't take much to get thugs into a fight—especially not here in Stockton, where they all try to get as many street fights under their belt as possible. They probably got a couple bucks to rough me up. And they thought I wouldn't be a problem if they rolled up in a group of four. Damn. I really need to watch my back if they're already trying to break me. I'm still two fights away from the UFC qualifier.

"They are, aren't they?" Corbin asks.

"Probably," I say.

"My goodness. Those hooligans tried to Tonya Harding you."

I force a laugh. "Yeah, it looks like it, doesn't it?" I rub at my jaw as I mull over his statements. "Wait, did you just call them *hooligans*?"

"Yes. That's what they're called."

"If you're a geriatric eighty-year-old."

Corbin brushes off his vest and huffs. "It doesn't matter who uses the word. It's an accurate descriptor."

"Uh-huh."

"I-it is! What else should I call them?"

"Gang members."

"Eh. What about *ruffian*?"

I actually laugh. "Where do you get words like that? A 1950s detective show?"

"Well… maybe…."

I can't believe it. He watches old crime shows? I love a lot of older TV shows. Even my favorite show as a kid involved a crazy cop and his talking car. Maybe Corbin and I have a lot more in common than I thought.

Before I can comment, Corbin grabs my jaw and tilts my head, staring at my bleeding ear and touching tender parts of my face. "You should lie down. Head injuries are serious."

"I'm not dizzy or anything. If anything, it's my leg…."

He kneels down in front of me and runs his hands from my thighs to my ankles. I must admit, the contact gets me a little restless. I mean, I like him there, but I'm still high on fight-mode, and his boyfriend remains at the front of my thoughts.

"Warm water," Corbin says. "You should rest in a bath or take a shower." He stands and then glances at his palms. They're crimson with my blood. He shudders. "Where are the restrooms? I need to wash. I should have used gloves."

I point to the showers, and he hustles there without another word, his pants pocket fat with his Taser. I shuffle after him, my gaze focusing on it.

"Why do you have a Taser?" I ask.

"It's nonlethal method of subduing an attacker. In most instances there are no lasting injuries. It's a safe alternative to a gun."

"Yeah, I know all that. But why do you have one?"

Corbin opens the door to the showers and holds it for me. "Lala would insist we go to all manner of questionable places when I came to visit. I think she wanted to fill a lifetime's worth of experiences into a few trips, especially since she missed out on so much. I was worried about us getting into trouble, and since I'm not a pro fighter and I don't want to carry a firearm, this seemed like the best solution."

"Fair enough."

I walk into the showers, and to my surprise, it's empty. Then again, maybe the thugs chased everyone off before they confronted me. Makes sense, to cut back on witnesses. I'm lucky Corbin came by when he did.

Then again, why is he here? How did he even know where I worked out?

Corbin stands over a sink, scrubbing his hands and muttering something like a crazy person.

"Why did you come here?" I ask as I rip off my shirt and pants. I stand on the other side of the room, near the wall of showerheads and flimsy cubical partitions, but I can still see Corbin busying himself with the soap.

Corbin glares at his hands as he continues to scrub for another thirty seconds. "I came here to speak with you. I tried your phone, but you never answered. Derek said you might be here, so I decided to check it out after my afternoon classes."

"What school do you attend?"

"The UC Davis School of Medicine."

"All the way up in Sacramento? That's an hour drive."

"Yes, well, I needed to speak with you or else I'd never be able to focus," Corbin says matter-of-factly.

I turn on the water for my shower and smirk. "Liked last night that much, huh?"

Corbin shuts off the sink and wheels around on his heel, his face pink. "That isn't what I'm here to discuss. You left my house after Justin arrived, and you forgot your gym bag. Which I brought, by the way."

"Thanks," I say. I had missed having it. The thing has most of my good workout clothes in it.

"And, well, I never got to speak with you about... us."

"*Us*? Seems to me that you just wanted a naughty little hookup behind your boyfriend's back. We don't have a relationship to speak of."

"He isn't—"

"He came in and told me," I snap. "Are you really going to deny it now?"

"He isn't!" Corbin glares. "I swear to you, he's not!" After a moment, he gets a good look at me. Then he averts his gaze and rubs the back of his neck. "S-sorry. Your showers should come equipped with doors."

I don't care if he stares. I'm a good-looking guy, I know it. And there's nothing I want to hide or feel ashamed of. Well, my mother never would've approved of my mohawk, but I like the rebel look it gives. If I'm going to be a fighter, it's important to have a recognizable image. I'm not a fan of tattoos, so I went with a mohawk and haven't looked back.

Steam mists off the water, and I step into the stream. The heat seeps into my body, right to my injuries, soothing the aches and giving me energy. Even my infected leg doesn't pulse with agony.

"Are you listening to me?" Corbin says.

I glance over my shoulder. "What? You're still here?"

"I said, Justin isn't my boyfriend. He just claims he is."

"Uh-huh. This isn't my first rodeo, *Bin-Bin*. I've heard terrible excuses before. Just leave me out of your drama."

"Wh-what? I'm being serious. Ask my sister. Lala knows all about it."

The water sweeps away my sweat and blood, creating a rose color as it swirls around the drain. I touch my face and grimace. I've got open wounds. Damn.

Corbin marches over to my stall, his gaze on the ceiling—anywhere but me. "I'm not the type of person who cheats on another. And… to be completely honest…. Justin and I were more friends with benefits than anything else. I never thought I would be in such a relationship, but life can be complicated and… well…."

I did know a few guys who never wanted relationships. They only wanted to fuck. That's fine, I don't care, but they never claimed they had *boyfriends*. Justin's actions seem a little contradictory to a fuck buddy, but Corbin seems quietly adamant about their relationship.

The infantry drills into your head the need for upstanding character and honest personal relationships. I don't want to be taken for a ride through murky drama of the lowest order. That's not my style.

"You're not lying?" I ask.

Corbin shakes his head.

"If you are, I'll kick your ass."

He snaps his attention to me, his eyes wide. "You would?"

"Hell yeah. You better not be lying."

"W-well, I'm not. But still. There's no need to threaten me."

"It's not a threat. It's a promise. I take this kind of thing seriously."

Corbin becomes quiet for a moment, and there's a piece of me that thinks he might admit he's been lying this entire time. Instead, he huffs and offers me a glare. "I suppose if I were lying, I might deserve to get my ass kicked, but that doesn't mean I approve of the barbaric nature of your promise. We live in a civilized society."

"Tell that to the four guys who jumped me," I quip.

"Those four are the pizza burn on the roof of the world's mouth. Nothing to do but ignore their presence until their time is up."

I chuckle. Perhaps he's right. But I still hope the cops get them. Where are the cops? Shouldn't they be here already? Then again, Stockton is known for its terrible response times. Last I read, there's an average of fifty deaths, one hundred and thirty-five rapes, one thousand robberies, and three thousand assaults on a yearly basis. The police have their hands full.

"Look at your injuries," Corbin says, his gaze not focused in on me. "What did they hit you with?"

"Wrenches."

"Disgusting. Truly barbaric."

"I'll live."

"You need to put some antibiotic ointment on those injuries."

"Oh yeah?" I ask. "I will once I get home."

"I have some in my car. I'll be right back."

He jogs out of the showers, leaving me alone with the warm water. I close my eyes. The soothing effect has gone, but I enjoy the heat regardless. One creak and I jump, my muscles tense for another fight. I glance around—even checking under the partitions—but I'm alone. Must have been the building settling or something. God, what the fuck am I going to do if someone actually breaks my leg? I have no idea.

I exhale.

Corbin returns with a determined look set into his narrow face. He walks up to me, straightens his glasses, and then squirts some Neosporin onto his finger.

"Turn off the water," he commands.

I comply, but once the stream stops, I get cold fast. Corbin sets to applying the ointment, even before I dry off or change. He starts with my face, gently applying a healthy coat to my cheek, busted lip, and ear. His concentration reminds me of my training. Focused. Precise. He isn't messing around.

Then he kneels again, but this time, without the running water, I can hear my own heart beat quick with excitement. The chill melts away, leaving me with a smoldering inner heat. Why must he insist on getting into such a position, especially when I'm naked? Does he know what it does to me? He must know—anyone could see it gets me hard—but he homes in on the bruises and scrapes, never glancing up, always keeping his focus.

Corbin runs his hands down my thighs again, feeling me up, looking for hidden wounds. I stare down at him, amused when he adjusts his glasses and squints at my injuries like they're personally insulting him.

I run my hand through his dark brown hair. "You're really not seeing anyone?" I ask in a low tone.

"No," he replies, not even acknowledging my touch. "Like I said, my time with Justin was more out of a need for companionship, but we aren't dating. I told him to leave me alone. He just… has a hard time listening."

He has conviction in his voice. Maybe I should talk to his sister. Then again, if I can't trust his word, why am I even considering being with him? I should extend a bit of trust if I'm going to cultivate it in return.

"Does your shin still hurt?" Corbin asks, breaking my chain of thought.

"I can't feel it right now. The warm water helped."

"That's what I thought. But you should rest and continue your antibiotic treatment. You didn't take your pills, and I haven't given you your second shot." He stands, still oblivious to my excitement. He gives me a stern look. "I insist you take the day off. Maybe two days, just to be safe. Plus, you really shouldn't be out alone when you're obviously under attack. You should know better."

Heh. He makes it sound like it's *my* fault I was attacked.

"Yes, sir," I say as I give him a sarcastic salute.

"I'm serious."

"Maybe you should watch me."

"Me?"

I run a hand up his neck and stroke his chin with my thumb. He doesn't back away or fight the gesture. If anything, he leans into it and quiets down, seemingly now aware I'm into the moment.

"I need someone to take care of me," I whisper, half smiling. "After I got all those wounds from the fight."

Corbin must have a terrible poker face because he deepens in color, shifting from a slight pink to bright red. It gets me smiling.

"I have classes," he mutters.

"Between classes, then."

"A-all right."

I pull him close and lock my lips on his. Corbin shudders. I open my mouth and let my tongue do most of the work, tasting his lower lip. Tastes like spearmint.

Corbin returns the enthusiasm, his tongue meeting mine and sliding across the rough top. He wraps a hand around my neck, keeping us together.

The door to the showers open and I break the contact, painfully aware of our situation.

"Hello?" someone asks. "This is the Stockton PD."

Corbin straightens his posture. "Oh. Hello, officers." He walks out of the shower stall. "I was just cleaning up. Please, let me tell you what happened."

I rush to grab my clothes, unwilling to explain why I was hanging out with another man in a single stall.

Once we get to my house, I'll get a new set of clothing, but until then, I guess the bloodstained ones will have to do. I'm sure the cops will love to see where those goons hit me. But I must admit, I'm more interested in getting home than making a police report. Two days of rest won't be too bad on my training, but Corbin's right.

I really shouldn't go anywhere alone.

Chapter 12
Rest and Relaxation

Keon Lynch

CORBIN AND I walk out to the gym's parking lot. The cops drive off, leaving us alone. The gym's employee claimed some people punked him into leaving, and the other gym members are nowhere to be seen. I bet those four thugs would've left me beaten and bloodied for a few hours before anyone would've found me. I'd have been lucky to survive.

Corbin points to his vehicle—the same four-door Dodge he drove when I had my last fight.

"How did you get home, by the way?" Corbin asks. "I drove you to my apartment, and you didn't have any transportation."

"It's called Uber," I say. "It cost me forty bucks I'll never get back, but it was worth it at the time." I motion with my head to the Harley-Davidson parked in the corner. "That's my ride."

"A motorcycle?" Corbin balks.

"Yeah."

"Do you know how dangerous that is?" His volume reaches levels I've never heard from him before. He gestures wildly at the bike, pointing and glaring. "Motorcycles are thirty-five times deadlier than a car! Even the slightest of collisions can lead to serious injury. And don't you dare say you're a competent driver, because the majority of accidents occur because another vehicle hit the motorcycle. It's reckless, and I can't believe you're doing it."

"Wow, you had a fucking dissertation prepared for that, didn't you?"

Corbin crosses his arms. "I've read hundreds of medical cases that involved an injured motorcyclist."

I walk over to my bike and stroke the leather seat. "You'd have a different story if you ever rode one."

"I would never be stupid enough to ride a motorcycle."

"This is a Harley-Davidson Nightster," I say, admiring the sleek black vehicle. "This bike has a vintage frame and design. And look at those black cast-aluminum wheels. Nothing compares."

"So, it's expensive?" Corbin asks, shifting his weight to his back foot and cocking an eyebrow.

I purchased the bike ten years ago, on my twentieth birthday. It was expensive then—brand-new—but I had saved up a bunch of money from my first job. Back then I didn't have any financial responsibilities, so I didn't feel bad blowing a whole chunk of change on a cool ride. But I haven't felt good about spending large sums of money since, so it's been my sole source of transportation.

"It was built in 2007," I say. "Not so expensive now."

"Did you name it?" he asks in a mocking tone, but it only gets me smiling.

"Of course I named her."

"Well? Out with it. What did you name your death machine?"

"I'll tell you. After I take you for a ride."

Corbin sneers. "Never."

"Then you'll never know her name."

"Hm. I think I'll live." He then points to his four-door car. "Guess what I named my car? *Safety First.* So I'll drive that and follow behind you and meet you at your apartment. Oh, what's your address? I'll use my phone's GPS, just in case we get split up."

I tell him and then we part ways. I don't protest, though I wish he'd let me take him for a ride. It'd be hilarious to see a guy as uptight as him ride on a motorcycle. As long as he wasn't screaming the entire way, that is. I'll convince him at some point. Nothing beats the freedom and mobility of a motorcycle.

But my headache intensifies. I really need the rest.

Corbin Friel

MY PHONE leads me to a run-down apartment building. Cracks in the paint create a spiderweb pattern that almost looks intentional. The faded red walls, bordering on the color of rust, have a washed-out look brought

100

about by long, shadeless hours in the sun. No trees for miles. Not even a single bush dots the outside of the building. The grass died ages ago.

I park my car and wait for Keon to do the same. The rumble of his motorcycle is louder than I would expect, but that doesn't upset me. Loud motorcycles are less likely to get into an accident. Motorcycles often get into other vehicles' blind spots, which is the major source of collision, but noisy motorcycles announce themselves. The chance of crashing is drastically decreased.

Keon parks, strips off his helmet, and then walks over to me. I step out of my car and give him the once-over. I guess he isn't covered in bugs or harmed from the ride, but I still don't like his bike.

Keon juts his chin toward the building. "I live in 8-B."

I glance around.

The vehicles in the parking lot have the same run-down coloration as the apartment. Five kids run across the asphalt, playing a game of tag. Their ratty clothes have oil stains from rolling under cars, but none of them seem to mind.

Keon enters the building, his duffel bag slung over his shoulder, his helmet tied to the side.

I follow him, my own backpack secure in my arms. Groups of people stand around in the hallways, chatting and smoking. I hold my breath. I've never appreciated the smell of smoke, and I end up coughing whenever lost in a cloud of tobacco. We walk up the stairs—the elevator looks like a prop in a horror movie, complete with squeaking doors, lined with rust, and a flicking interior light.

Keon leads me to his front door and opens it. I step in and freeze.

I thought *my* apartment was small…. Keon's must be half the size.

He has a black futon, a TV on top of a moving box, and a clean kitchen, though there's no table or chairs or much in the way of cooking utensils outside of a blender. Maybe he has things in the cupboards, but he doesn't have many. A single pot? Perhaps two? And he has no decorations or pictures. The naked walls give the whole apartment a hobo vibe.

Keon throws his bag on the futon and uses it as a pillow as he lies down. I walk over to him and search for a place to set my backpack. I opt for the floor, since Keon seems low on furniture.

"You don't wear it on your back?" Keon asks.

"What? My backpack? I prefer to hold it. I've had things stolen from me while wearing it before, and I haven't gotten over the trauma."

Keon chuckles but doesn't say anything else.

I open my backpack and shuffle through the contents. I have an assortment of medical supplies. Gauze, cotton balls, rags, antibiotic cream, over-the-counter drugs—anything someone might want for a minor medical emergency. I pull out some ibuprofen and a bottle of water.

"Take these," I say.

Keon does as he's told. He downs both the pills in a single swig.

"Remove your shirt and lie flat on your back."

Keon rips off his shirt, relaxes on the futon, and then exhales. I admire his gloriously sculpted muscles, and although I would never admit it, the injuries from the fight add a primal attractiveness to his already handsome physique. I don't want to stare too long, so I place both my hands on his stomach and press down with my fingers, feeling the organs within.

"What're you doing?" Keon asks.

"Checking your aorta."

"My what?"

"It's the largest blood vessel in the body. Sometimes the lining becomes thin, and then the aorta ruptures. I was just worried that, because of your fight, you might be at risk."

"And you can tell if I'm at risk by feeling me up?"

I blush but grit my teeth and soldier through it. His rock-hard abs are enjoyable, but they do make it a little harder to feel his insides, so I need to press harder and longer than with a typical individual. I don't mind. It reminds me of last night—and how wonderful that whole experience was.

"If the lining of the aorta is weakened, it balloons," I say. "It gets so big and swollen that you can feel it if you apply enough pressure. And if you know what you're looking for, of course."

"You know a lot about medicine for someone in their first year."

"Yes, well, both my parents are doctors."

"That explains a lot. And I do mean *a lot*."

I narrow my eyes and frown. "Most children take after their parents. What about your mother and father? What do they do?"

"Well, my mother hangs out in a graveyard and my father is a drunk and on the fast track to prison."

I stop my work and hold my breath. Why did I have to say anything? He must hate me for bring up such painful details.

Keon pats my shoulder, shaking me out of my thoughts. "Loosen up," he says. "You're all business. I'm not dead, and I'm not in prison, so I guess I did pretty well for myself, right?"

"Quite a macabre sense of humor you have."

"Better than no sense of humor." He lifts an eyebrow.

I straighten my posture. "Hey! I have a sense of humor, thank you very much. Give me a break. I walk into a gym and you're getting jumped by a group of guys. Sorry I'm not the jokester at the end of the day."

"Isn't laughter the best medicine?"

"No, *medicine* is the best medicine."

"I find it a little easier to deal with shit when there's a bit of levity about the subject. Otherwise things get too real. Life's already one long parade of misfortune and suffering, right? Might as well relax whenever you can."

"Hm," I say. "You are fairly relaxed."

Although he has taut muscles, it's clear he's unafraid of my touch. I enjoy the warmth of his skin, and the way he moves with each breath.

"You should relax more," Keon says. "It's good for your health."

"Is that your professional recommendation?"

"Yeah. It is. Straight from Dr. Lynch."

I chuckle. *Dr. Lynch* would be amusing. He would be the hottest doctor I've ever known, that's for sure. I wouldn't mind. I'd love to be his patient any day. Well, not really, because that would imply I'm in need of a doctor, but I wouldn't mind playing doctor.

"You okay?" Keon asks.

I take my hands off his body and wipe them off on my slacks. "Y-yes. I'm fine."

"And what about me?"

"Huh?"

"Am I okay?"

"Oh. Yes. Everything is in order. Let me tend to the rest of your injuries."

I get some bandages and gauze out of my backpack and set to cleaning all his open wounds. He watches the entire process, never glancing away or playing on his phone. Intent and curious, he narrows his eyes whenever I sneak a glance in his direction.

Then I wrap the injuries, making sure I pull the gauze tight.

"Why do you want to become a doctor?" Keon asks.

I meet his gaze, surprised by his question. Not a lot of people ask me this. Sure, they ask other medical students all the time, but with me, they all just assume it's because of my parents. *I'm being pressured to follow the family line.*

"I really love the field of medicine," I say. "It improves life and happiness, and it touches the lives of each and every person. It's a noble career that spans the ages. We wouldn't be the society we are today without doctors and nurses and specialists."

"You have a passion for it?"

There he goes with that word again. Passion.

"Yes," I say. "I would say I have a passion."

Keon leans back on his duffel bag and flinches. It takes him a second to get comfortable, no doubt because of the bruises, but he eventually settles in and stares at the ceiling, his gaze unfocused, like he's not seeing anything at all. "Being a warrior is a career that spans the ages. Maybe as long as we've had doctors."

"Maybe longer," I add.

"When I was younger… I liked doing things with my hands. I learned better when we had blocks or paints or something physical I could manipulate. Letters on pages would get mixed up for me. It was hard to sit and read something and really understand."

I never had that problem. I loved sitting and reading. The words always made sense, the stories always compelled. Test taking comes naturally, and it surprises me Keon would struggle at school. He doesn't seem unintelligent.

"But my sister was perfect with her schoolwork," Keon continues, chuckling to himself. "My mother loved her. Straight As. A little book nerd. So, when she started to excel at that, I figured, why should I compete? I would be better at something else. I would learn a sport or skill, and then I would have my own thing. Am I… making any sense?"

I reply with a curt nod. "Perfect sense." I mull over his statements for a second. "Wait. You have a sister? You never mentioned her before."

I finish wrapping his leg, and then I move to his arm. He got kicked and punched in a myriad of places, and I want to make sure the scrapes don't leave any lasting scars. Keon lets out a long sigh before answering my question.

"Her name is Alisha," he says. "She's in her fourth year of med school."

Ah, so this is the relative who had to take the USMLE. And he thought he couldn't compete with her at academics, so he focused all his time and effort on the physical—an odd sibling dynamic I can't relate to. I spent most of my childhood worried my sister might never come home from the hospital. We didn't compete, because most days I saw her, I was sitting next to her hospital bed, listening to her read me stories.

Some days, when Lala wasn't feeling well, I'd read her a story instead. I think she liked those days the most. She smiled nonstop and encouraged me when I got hung up on a word.

I wonder how Keon and his sister get along now that they're adults.

"Where does your sister go to school?" I ask.

"Someplace in North Carolina."

"When will you visit her next?"

"I…. Well, I don't know."

He doesn't know? Again, nothing like me and Lala. And the hesitation in his voice and the way he glares at the ceiling—makes me think I'm not getting the whole story. I rub his leg and trail my hand over his abdomen, caressing him in an attempt to soothe away the bad feelings. He relaxes under my touch.

"What happened between you two?" I ask.

"It's a long story."

"We have time. And I want to know."

"I got into fights with my father when I was younger," he whispers.

"Fights?"

"He beat my sister when he was drunk."

I grit my teeth, disgusted with the turn of events in his story, but I don't want him to stop. I want to know more about his life and family.

I feel like I'm only scratching the surface—that I jumped to too many conclusions and I need to right the wrongs of my assumptions.

"So you fought your father when he was drunk?" I ask, hoping he'll tell me everything.

"Yes. It happened a few times before the cops were ever called. I yelled at the officers when they arrived. They were questioning me like I was the source of the conflict, and I wasn't thinking straight... I blamed them for allowing my father to do the things he did. Why didn't they just arrest him and take him to prison? But the cops didn't like that. So we both got in trouble."

"What happened to your sister?"

"She ran away to college. Said I had anger issues. That I reminded her of our father."

He says the last sentence through clenched teeth. Every muscle in his body tenses, and he curls his hands into fists.

I don't know what to say. How can I assure him? What can you say to make deep emotional pain fade? My father is an expert at comforting his patients. He instills confidence and removes his patient's doubt. I wish I could do that here—I wish I could convince Keon he isn't anything like his abusive father.

"My sister doesn't want to associate with me," Keon intones. "She... doesn't take my calls or answer any of my emails."

"I'm sorry to hear that."

Keon doesn't reply. He closes his eyes and runs a hand down his face. I massage his chest, wishing there was something I could do. What is there to do? I can mend scrapes and bruises, but I don't know if I can do the same to relationships.

"Maybe you should talk to your mother," I say. "If you explain everything, she can talk to your sister. Things could get better."

"My mother's dead."

"Oh... I'm sorry to hear that."

My phone buzzes, and I snatch it out of my pocket. The alarm. I'll be late for my evening studying session if I delay any longer. I jump to my feet, brush myself off, and gather my backpack.

"You need to rest," I say. "I'll be back later to check on you. Try to sleep."

Keon nods. "Sure."

Then I rush out of his apartment, my thoughts nowhere near medicine. All I can imagine is Keon's family dynamic. A father he despises. A sister who won't talk to him. A late mother. I feel so lucky and privileged when I think about my own family. They love and support me no matter what.

Who does Keon have to support him?

No one.

Keon Lynch

THE AFTERNOON shifts to evening and then transforms into night. The final light of day travels down the side of my wall. I watch it while I rest, my mind preoccupied with memories of my family.

My mother died due to complications that arose from her many surgeries. Then it was just me, Alisha, and our father. That was when he became violent—almost like he was blaming us for our mother's death, no matter how preposterous that was. Especially Alisha. He yelled at her constantly, wanted her to do the housework and pick up the slack our mother left behind.

I can still hear his shouting if I close my eyes and concentrate. He had nothing good to say. All he wanted was to argue and throw his weight around.

I remember reveling in the fact I punched him. I was so proud. But Alisha hated it. She told me never to do it. Even when our father became belligerent again and again. But I had to fight back, no matter what Alisha said.

She was always kinder than me. She never wanted to hurt anything or see anyone suffer. A kind heart to match her future profession.

Alisha knew she wanted to be a doctor ever since our mother was in her accident. She wants to help and heal people—to save our mother through all the lives she would save working as a doctor. Our father wouldn't stop drinking, though, and I refused to let Alisha be his punching bag.

I hurt our father bad when we fought the third time. I didn't mean to, but I didn't know my own strength as an eighteen-year-old. I slammed him against the kitchen counter, and he crumpled to the floor in shock.

Alisha had a black eye.

The neighbor called the cops—that's when I got in trouble. I asked the cops why they never came before and why they allowed men like my father to roam the street and beat his daughter. I was frustrated at the time. Alisha didn't make matters any easier. She cried and yelled at me, said I would be just like our father—that I *was* him already.

Sometimes I wonder if it's true.

I get a rush from fighting. A primal, deep-seated rush. I like the engagement and the conflict and the brutality. Every moment facing an opponent tells me I'm alive. I'm doing something. I'm someone.

That's not why my father hurt people. He hit little girls to make himself feel better when alcohol could no longer soothe his inner demons. He didn't want a fight or a competition or to consider rules of combat. We're not alike. It's different. It has to be.

At least, that's what I like to think.

I grit my teeth and close my eyes. These thoughts haunt me. I hate imagining my life's goal is the product of my rage-filled father, and I hate the fact my sister considers me at the same level as him. But I don't want to stop. I can't.

"Fuck," I mutter.

I need something to take my mind off this. Someone to talk to. I reach for my phone, my mind going first to Corbin and then to Derek. Then again, the window is dark. I know it's closing in on 2100 hours. I doubt Corbin's coming back. He said he would, but there's no reason for him to drive an extra two hours to spend time with me. We don't know each other that well, and I'm sure he'd rather avoid me after the depressing conversation I offered him before he left. He dashed out of my apartment with lightning speed, like a second longer could cost him his life.

I dial Derek's number. It rings a couple times before clicking over to voicemail. With a short sigh, I toss my phone onto the carpeted floor.

If I'm left alone with my thoughts, they'll overwhelm me and consume my willpower to continue down this path. I've made it so far, but the goal seems twice as far away.

Why can't I think of anything else?

A knock at the door jerks me out of my wallowing. I stare at the door, an eyebrow lifted.

"Who's there?" I ask.

"It's me, Corbin. May I come in?"

Holy shit. Corbin came back? I almost can't believe it.

"Come in," I shout. "The door's unlocked."

Chapter 13
Schedule for the Future

Keon Lynch

CORBIN WALKS in with two bags of groceries, the contents bulging out the top.

I sit up on my futon, confused as Corbin walks into my kitchen and unpacks the contents. "What're you doing?"

"I purchased some food to help you recover," he replies, his focus on the food as he organizes it on the counter before putting it in the fridge or in the cupboards. "There are lots of foods that help you heal after minor injuries. Honey, coconut oil, ginseng, various types of teas… I couldn't help but notice your apartment is barren, so I took the liberty of picking these up after my study session."

Corbin puts the food away in neat positions, even going out of his way to rearrange the old contents of my fridge. He tosses things that have expired and organizes the shelves so that everything is separated by the type of food. He does the same damn thing with the cupboards. Although organization doesn't fascinate me, something about Corbin's brazen assertiveness captures my interest. I'm content to watch his compulsive need for order.

Once finished, Corbin walks over to my futon, glares down at me, and motions for me to sit up. I comply with his nonverbal command, and he kneels to look over my injuries. He never touches them directly, but he moves his fingers to edges and grazes the inflamed areas. It hurts, but not much. I can handle it.

"Have you been taking your antibiotics?" he asks.

I catch my breath and silently curse myself. "No."

"You need to take them every six hours. It only works if you're consistent. Sporadic treatment could result in the infection lingering, perhaps even becoming resistant to the medication."

"All right," I say. "I get it. I need to take my damn medication. Hand me a couple pills, will you?"

Corbin retrieves the antibiotics from the kitchen and hands them to me with a glass of water. I swear he thinks of everything. Always has a plan, always thinking ahead and—

Corbin clears his throat, pulling me from my thoughts. He takes out a small day planner from his pocket and poises a pen at the top of the paper. With his narrowed eyes and spotless glasses, he looks like a shrink from the movies, leaning over me and ready to ask questions about where the bad men touched me.

"What's your work schedule?" he asks.

I almost laugh. He really does like making schedules.

"I can make my own," I say. "I'm an exterminator, so I have a route, and I need to visit each restaurant and business once a month, so as long as I hit each one, I'm fine. I typically work from zero seven hundred to fifteen hundred, give or take."

"Hm. I see. And how often do you work out?"

"Every weekday. Seventeen hundred to twenty hundred."

"Three hours? Five days a week?"

"Surprised?"

Corbin shakes his head. "No. It makes sense. I've just… never known anyone with such an intense workout regime." He jots a few things down and clicks his pen on the paper. "Anything else you do at regular intervals?"

"That's about it."

It's not like I have many friends around here. Derek's a great guy, but he has his own workout schedule. Harvey was a great CO, and he's done a lot for me, but I haven't seen him in weeks. Who else is there?

"All right," Corbin declares. He rips out the piece of planner paper and hands it to me. "I've routed out a schedule where I'll come by in the mornings and then meet you at your gym in the evening. I've also taken the liberty of downloading the rules for Mixed Martial Arts so I can discuss strategy and techniques without being a complete know-nothing."

I take the planner paper and glance it over. Sure enough, he has times and approximate distances written off to the side. He'll be at my apartment around 0530, leave around 0630, then return and meet me at Harvey's gym around 1800, and stay until 2130. He gives himself three minutes of leeway between his lecture and driving to Stockton.

"Why?" I ask, stunned he would plan out something so elaborate.

"You shouldn't be going anywhere alone," Corbin replies with a matter-of-fact tone. "And you said you wanted me to look after your injuries. This way, I can accompany you and advise you on the best training techniques to minimize injury to yourself. Plus, I can remind you to take your antibiotics and monitor the condition of your shin."

"But this is a huge chunk of your time."

Corbin narrows his eyes, staring at me like I've said something perplexing. He runs his hands over his well-kept hair. "You said these fights meant a lot to you, right? And that you need to win two more fights?"

"I did say that."

"Well, I thought it over. I want to support your goals."

"Why? I thought you hated fighting? Didn't you say it was barbaric? And almost as bad as Roman gladiators?"

"Well, uh, I did say that. And it is a dangerous sport. Which is why I want to be there to help you. As long as you'll have me." The strained tone in his voice betrays his insecurity.

I relax back against my gym bag, touched he went to so much effort on my behalf.

My feelings about Corbin have been on a roller-coaster ride since I met the man. First I hated him, then I was intrigued, and then he helped me big-time with my leg, and I actually started liking him. Our sexual encounter was one of the best I've had in a long time, but then his *friend* came over and riled me up. I let the hate stew, but now the complications should be clear—and he's once again going above and beyond to help me.

And I would like to have someone watching my six. Corbin's tough enough to help me, even if he isn't a fighter himself. Not to mention I like his debonair demeanor. Maybe his presence will cause complications with other fighters, but I already have guys trying to break my legs, so what's one extra reason to dislike me?

They can fuck themselves. I'm not going to let any of those scumbags stop me.

"I'd like it if you stuck around," I say.

Corbin lets his breath out. Had he been holding it the whole time? He's cute when he's nervous.

I hit the back of the futon and allow it to fall into the bed position. I technically have a mattress in the other room, but it's nothing fancy, and rather unkempt. I doubt Corbin would appreciate the state it's in. Instead, I grab him by the arm and pull him onto the futon with me.

"Wh-what's going on?" he asks.

"Lie with me."

He calms down a bit and shifts around on the futon until he's comfortable. I tuck him close to my side, so we're lying next to each other, no room between us. Corbin removes his glasses and rests his hand on the crook of my shoulder. He smells of soap and sanitizer. Half of me enjoys it—makes me think of him specifically—but the other half dwells on memories in the hospitals.

Damn memories. They claw at the edge of my thoughts, threatening to devour my happiness and sanity.

"What's wrong?" Corbin asks.

"Huh? Nothing. Why?"

"You got tense, and your heart rate increased."

Nothing gets by this guy. I don't think I've ever known anyone this perceptive.

"I get depressed and anxious at times," I whisper.

Corbin wraps his arm tight over my chest. "Medical research says physical comfort can be the best when experiencing bouts of anxiety."

"Is that right?"

I turn my head, and he scoots up so we're closer. To my surprise, he locks his lips with mine, his warmth invigorating my spirit. Anything I was dwelling on disappears as I realize I have a man in my apartment— someone I might be able to call my significant other—and my evening doesn't seem quite as lonely as it did before.

Corbin plasters himself to my side, holding me close as he deepens our kiss. His tongue touches my lips, his hesitation igniting my desire to take control and show him how it should be done. But I relax and allow him to continue—slow and controlled. He sucks my lower lip and then trails kisses along the side of my jaw. His hand runs the length of my neck, brushing over the stubble I've yet to shave.

Each graze and slow touch heats my skin. I spread my legs, wishing I wasn't wearing my shorts. Corbin runs his hand across my chest and straight to my stomach, just above the waistband. He stops and plays with the grooves of my muscles, obviously enjoying the definition that took years to carve out of my body. But the fleeting touches, especially since I'm so starved for company and relief, tests my self-control.

I bite my tongue and hold back the urge.

Corbin moves back up to my ear. He licks the edge and whispers, "I have a confession."

"What is it?" I ask through gritted teeth.

"There is no medical research that states physical comfort will remove anxiety. I just wanted to kiss you."

I chuckle. He could say there was a secret cure for cancer found in popcorn and I would believe him at this point. "Then I have a confession."

He nibbles my ear. "Oh?"

"I taught you the rear naked choke as an excuse to manhandle you a bit."

Corbin stops his affections and sits up, his eyes narrowed into a squint. "You did?"

"Yeah," I say, still chuckling. "At first I was going to fuck with you, especially for all those snide comments about fighters, but then you admitted you dated men…. My mind went to the gutter, and then I just wanted to see how you would react in close quarters."

He doesn't say anything for a moment. Is he mad? I hope not. It's not like I grabbed his dick or anything while in the octagon, but maybe he's offended I had ulterior motives.

Corbin snorts. "Well, I'm flattered. I didn't think… I mean, I just figured you'd want someone…. Well, like Derek."

"Kindhearted and dumb?"

"N-no! I meant someone with a fighter's physique."

"Oh, I see. You're worried." The revelation gets me smiling. Corbin has a not-so-secret insecurity streak. The guy sure has a lot of confidence with his intelligence, so I guess it makes sense he'd find failings in his other features.

"This amuses you?"

"Yes."

Corbin stares at me with his narrow-eyed glare. But at the same time, he has a playfulness about him. What's he thinking?

Corbin Friel

SOME PEOPLE are impossible.

I can't believe he was enjoying himself while teaching me that move. I was so worried and embarrassed, I tried to push the entire event out of my mind. But here he is, laughing it up like it was a great time for everyone involved. Well, I suppose I did enjoy it. But still.

Keon offers me a casual smile. "You're not mad, are you?"

"No. I'm just wondering how I should repay you."

"Oh yeah?"

"It's only fair."

"You could always teach me some… medical thing. That requires lots of touching."

No reservations whatsoever. But I suppose men with his level of training have excess energy for stuff like this all the time. It's been proven time and time again that good workout routines improve an individual's libido.

I walk my fingers over his stomach until I reach the top of his shorts. The garment—straining with his arousal—is tight enough to expose most details. Keon's anatomy is quite impressive, and I've enjoyed the way he's gotten more excited the longer our encounter goes.

"Maybe I should have some time with you," I say, giving his shorts one last glance before returning my gaze to meet his. "To *manhandle you*, as you so eloquently put it."

"What're you thinking?" he asks, his voice low and husky.

He obviously likes this suggestion.

My blood runs hot with the idea as well. He's so handsome and masculine. I'm still in a mild amount of disbelief that I'm with someone like him. A piece of me wants to please him—to make sure it's worth it for him to stay with me. With Justin, the passion was never intense, merely exciting because it was the first time for both of us.

Keon thrills me more than anything with Justin.

I tug at the waistband of his shorts. "Remove these. I want a few uninterrupted moments to admire you."

Keon licks his lips. "Sounds good."

He shoves off his shorts and tosses them to the floor. I place my hand on his chest and guide him to the futon so that he's flat on his back in front of me. I glide my hand to his dick and stroke it with the tips of my fingers, more content to examine him than stimulate the flesh.

Keon keeps himself shaved, and he's larger than anything I've seen. His thighs, just as sculpted as the rest of his body, flex and relax as I trail my fingers farther down his body. I graze his knee and then drag my hand back up, avoiding the area he desperately wants me to play with.

"You like what you see?" he asks, a slight panting to his voice.

"You're the epitome of an old-world warrior."

"Touch me."

"Not yet."

Keon clenches his teeth. He reaches his own hand down to grab himself, but I stop him at the last second. He growls and glowers.

"This is my time, remember? I'm not done."

After a few strained moments, Keon brings his arm back to his side. His dick leaks precome, and his heavy breathing combine to make a beautiful sight. My lower gut has an intense fire building, and I swear my blood rushes to one place, and one place only. Still, I love the idea of tormenting him.

I lean down and drag my teeth along the length of his dick, allowing my hot breath to wash over his engorged skin. Keon shudders. His hands curl into fists, and he closes his eyes. I kiss around the head, enjoying every tiny noise he stifles.

Without stopping my kisses, I place a hand at the base and gently stroke up and down, slow and purposeful. He thrusts with his hips, but I hold him down and shoot him a playful glare.

"Do you want me to stop?"

"I want you to suck me off," he quips, his voice strained. "Don't stop."

I sit up and remove my hand. "You need to hold still."

"Fuck… fine."

I stop myself from laughing. He holds still and continues his shallow panting. I stare at his dick, eager to continue, my own heat threatening to burn away my self-control. "Are you negative?" I ask.

"What? Yeah. I have papers."

"You do?" Who does that? I know men sometimes do when they use quick dating sites and—

"I—" Keon takes in a deep breath and steadies himself, sweat dappling his tanned skin, "I get tested every few weeks for MMA fights. They do… physicals…. And I have my military paperwork. I'm clean."

That makes sense, and I'm put at ease. I return my mouth to his dick, but this time I lick all the way to the head, taking a line of his precome in my mouth like I'm lapping up a stray line of melting ice cream.

"Jesus Christ, Corbin," Keon says through gritted teeth.

I kiss the tip, allowing my tongue to play with the slit. He shivers and moans, his hands gripping the edge of the futon with enough force to strain the faux leather. I move between his legs, spreading him a bit, and then unbutton my shirt. I'm too heated to tolerate clothes, and I unbuckle my belt and undo my pants. Half of me wants to impale myself on Keon and reverse ride him until I reach climax, but I opt instead to continue my teasing.

I spread his legs farther, exposing him, and I drag my tongue from the base to the head in a few long and slow licks.

"Corbin," he growls. "Goddammit…."

Keon opens his eyes and meets my gaze, his expression half pleading and half frustration. I smile and lower my mouth onto his dick, taking him in one lazy movement, savoring his salty taste and the way he groans with the entirety of his breath. I relax my throat and take him all the way before traveling up with the same leisurely pace.

Keon places a hand on the back of my head and laces his fingers deep into my hair.

"Suck me off," he commands.

The gruff tone of his voice sends me over the edge. Lust takes over, and I take him in my mouth all the way, enjoying the way he bucks and thrusts, hitting the back of my throat like he needs to bruise it. I moan through each pump and please myself the entire time, already at the edge of my orgasm. Then I struggle for air and half gag on his length, but he grabs my chin and lifts me away for a moment, allowing me to breathe.

He brushes a thumb over my lip. "You're real good at this," he whispers in a deep tone. "It's going to be difficult not fucking you every night."

His enthusiasm infects me, and I return my mouth to his dick, excited to please him. He mutters encouragements under his breath as he bucks up into me. I stroke myself at an ever-increasing rate, enthralled by the sensations and moment. I love looking up his sculpted body to catch him staring down at me. It's blurry—wish I had my glasses—but there's enough for me to know he's watching.

Then his thrusts get desperate, and he says my name through gritted teeth.

The hot sensation of his climax fills my mouth. I swallow, sucking the last bit off of him before pulling away, and the action gets me close. I hate the thought of coming on furniture... but I'm too far gone to calculate where. I finish myself into my hand and keep it there, unwilling to allow it to spill, even though my body convulses and twitches with the deep tremors of satisfaction.

Keon sits up. I'm surprised when he grabs my shoulder and pulls me close, pressing me against his chest like a hug, but he doesn't let go. I take a few deep breaths as I listen to the pounding of his heart. It slows with each beat, calming down after the excitement.

"That was great," he says.

"Just *great*? Was it that underwhelming?"

He laughs. I love his laugh. Deep and with a low rumble, showing off his perfect teeth. How do his teeth stay that way as a fighter? I know they wear mouth guards, but I figured something terrible would happen eventually. Or perhaps Keon is lucky.

"What words should I use to describe it?" he asks.

"Superb."

Another chuckle. "You think pretty highly of yourself, don't you?"

"Am I wrong?"

"No. You're right. It was superb." He kisses me, but I hesitate, and he stops.

"I need to wash my hands," I say, still holding the jellified remains of my climax in the palm of my hand. It leaves a soiled feeling I can't shake.

Keon lets me go. "Sorry."

I stand, my legs shake a bit, and then I wander into the kitchen. The moment the water in the sink is running, I wash the bodily fluids from my hand, content to have saved the furniture from the mess.

"You enjoy it?" Keon asks.

"Yes," I say, the taste of him still lingering on the edge of lips. "You're quite captivating."

"Huh. Superb and now captivating. Never heard those compliments before."

"I have a robust vocabulary."

He laughs. "Well, Dr. Thesaurus, why don't you come over here? I want you close."

I shut off the water and walk back to the futon—it's not a long trek. He grabs my arm and pulls me back into his embrace.

"Are you okay?" I ask.

"I want you to stay with me for the night."

His request catches me off guard, but I like it. "All right."

Though I wish I had brought my toothbrush and comb. Some things I can't live without. But Keon seems like he needs company, and I don't want to abandon him.

So I rub his shoulder and nuzzle the base of his neck, enjoying the rugged scent of his after-sex sweat. And besides, it's better I'm here. What if someone else comes to attack him? Four guys attempted to break his legs. He needs all the help he can get.

Chapter 14
Better Workout

Keon Lynch

I LIFT my weights, counting the reps in my head. A light burn courses through my shoulder and biceps—I've become accustomed to the sensation and even revel in it. If I push myself, I'll reach new heights. I stop after eight reps and switch arms. The key to fast muscle growth is to avoid static routine. Today I'll do eight reps before switching, but tomorrow I'll do eleven, and the next day I'll do seven. If I did the same number each time, my body would fall into a slump, building only enough stamina and muscle to do the exact number I always lift.

Corbin sits next to my machine, reading on his tablet. He pokes the screen, scrolling at a decent clip, silent and sitting with a straight posture. People give him odd looks. While they wear grungy sweats and tank tops, Corbin felt it necessary to come dressed in slacks, a button-up shirt, tie, and vest. His shiny black shoes are the cleanest thing here.

"Interesting," he says, never taking his eyes off the tablet screen. "In MMA fighting matches, it is no longer a foul to grab the opponent by the clavicle."

"What's the clavicle?" I ask.

"The collarbone."

Hm. That is interesting. I always thought that move was illegal. It's a nice little handhold on the body, should I grapple a guy in the right position.

"It's a foul to claw or pinch, however," Corbin continues. "Which is odd, considering they allow *punching people*. I mean, would you rather be pinched or punched? I think the answer is obvious."

"They don't allow the use of pinpoint pain," I say as I finish my eight reps with my left arm. I switch back to my right and continue. "You can't twist skin either."

My sweat pools together and runs down my body in rivulets. I don't care. I'll take a shower after this and clear it away later. But I do hate when it gets down to my wrists and palms. A slick grip could result in me dropping the weight. I've had one fall on my toe before—worse than anything in the octagon.

I grab my towel to wipe some of the sweat away, but Corbin jumps up and startles me.

"Wait," he says. "Use this."

He rummages through his backpack and pulls out a clean towel—white and pristine, compared to my ratty red towel. I take his and wipe off. Once done, I toss it on the workout machine next to me. Corbin grabs the towel and then folds it into a small square. He places it near my feet.

"This is a shared space," he says. "You should have more respect for your fellow gym members."

I cock half a smile and then motion to a guy on the treadmill. Corbin glances over just as he snorts and spits a wad of phlegm onto the floor. The resulting splat had more volume than any I heard before. Must've been extra soggy.

Corbin shudders. "Dreadful."

"I thought I was being halfway decent," I say.

A large guy lumbers over to my weight-lifting station, and I stop my reps to get a good look at him. He's solid muscle, but not in a good way. I doubt the guy could turn his head, and his arms are so bulging with muscle he couldn't put them down to his side, even if he wanted to. His tight T-shirt would scream in agony if it had a voice. The damn shirt might bust apart at the seams at any moment.

"Get off the station," the guy says, his tone more a grunt than anything else.

"I'm still using it," I say.

"I don't care. I wanna lift some weights. Get off."

"I'll leave in a couple of minutes. I still have a few reps to finish."

"You two faggots will leave when I say you leave."

Before I can handle this escalating situation, Corbin stands and straightens his glasses. "Excuse me, but do you own this gym?"

I leap to my feet and put an arm in front of Corbin. "Never mind him."

"No," Corbin barks. "You don't deserve any more bullying. This man should wait his turn and watch what he says. Like an adult."

The meathead gives Corbin a sneer. He pats his arms and then kisses his left bicep. "I need the equipment to keep these pretty. The girls like 'em."

Corbin forces a single laugh. "Only because there is no workout routine for a face."

I jump between Corbin and the man, tense and ready if the man swings. He steps forward, growling, but I slam my hand on his chest and glare. He matches my gaze and flinches, no doubt sensing my conviction should he push this fight. The guy might be muscled, but I'm sure I can choke him out just as well as any other.

"Prissy bitches don't belong here," the meathead says. He shoves me away from the weights and takes a seat. "Control your girlfriend, or else I'll do it for you."

"Classy," Corbin says under his breath.

I take Corbin by the upper arm and guide him away from our beefy friend. "Listen, I really appreciate you're here, but I don't want to get into any more fights before I have to, do you understand?"

"But did you hear him?" Corbin motions to the muscle-bound man, glowering. "Demanding the equipment? Insulting your sexuali—"

I tighten my grip on Corbin's arm, and he gasps. I loosen my hold, forgetting my strength, but I can't believe he was just going to announce our sexuality to the entire gym. Obviously these men aren't the type that'll respect other people's decisions. It's best to hope they get hit by a car or go back to jail rather than getting into a fistfight with each and every one.

"Not here," I whisper through gritted teeth. "Don't mention *us*."

Corbin jerks his arm out of my grasp. He cleans his glasses with the sleeve of his shirt. "They must already know. Didn't you hear him? Name-calling us all sorts of colorful words."

"He doesn't know—he was just trying to casually insult us with the stupidest and easiest things his tiny mind can come up with."

But everyone might know now. The other gym members give us quick glances over their shoulders. They saw I gave up my machine when the meathead came demanding it, which isn't the reputation you want with a group of street thugs who view violence as a tool, but I won't let them jump Corbin either. We just need to keep our heads down and ignore these fools.

"This doesn't seem like a reputable place to train," Corbin says, panning his narrowed gaze across the room. "You should switch your membership. I'm sure Stockton has several other gyms with far better equipment. And patrons."

"Look, that's not an option."

Our argument draws everyone's undivided attention. With a quick sigh, I take Corbin into the locker room and close the door, separating us from the others. Chlorine, soap, and mold mix together to make an odd scent that hangs in the air, thick as fog.

"If you're going to watch me train, you need to play nice with everyone else. The owner sponsors me for my fights, and even if I *could* leave, everything else is too expensive. I don't have the money for them."

Corbin stares at me for a long moment, his slight frown telling me he's unconvinced.

A couple guys walk out of the showers, not even bothering to use their towels. They have tattoos from their neck to their toes, each so amateurish and terrible they might as well be magic eye illusions. Corbin gives them a quick glance before snapping his attention to the ceiling, his face flushed and his posture stiff. I don't mind if they're naked—I've seen enough people naked in the military that nothing could faze me now—but I am worried they'll take offense to staring.

I avert my gaze and keep it centered on Corbin.

"Did you get anything I was saying?" I ask.

The door to the locker room opens. Corbin and I jump back, but the moment I see Harvey, I relax.

Harvey is an odd combination. Beer belly. Thick, reddish mustache. Pronounced sideburns. Muscular arms. A tree-trunk neck. The guy could be a 1930s lumberjack if he wore flannel and jeans. Today he's dressed in a pair of military-green cargo pants and a black T-shirt. He gives me the once-over before turning his attention to Corbin.

"What's going on?" Harvey asks, his voice gruff and laced with a strange accent. Almost Southern, but not quite.

"What's wrong?" I ask.

"I got people out there saying you were starting a fight." Harvey jabs a finger into my chest. "Well? Were you?"

"He most certainly was not," Corbin interjects.

I shove Corbin behind me. "I wasn't in a fight. Some jackass didn't want to wait his turn for the equipment, so we had some words."

"Which one? The drunk on the StairMaster, or the guy who eats steroids for breakfast?"

"Steroids."

"Oh, well that asshole ain't gonna have a membership here anymore, I guarantee."

Harvey slams back out of the locker room, the stomping of his boots echoing around us until the door shuts. Corbin wrests himself from my grasp and crosses his arms.

"You weren't this bold when we first met," I say, remembering how he trembled like a lamb in front of a wolf. "What's gotten into you?"

"People would try to pick on my sister," he says, his whole body tensing. "Because she was sick. I hate bullies. I have no reservations when standing up to them whenever I see they're harassing another."

"You just don't stand up to them on your own behalf?"

Corbin opens his mouth and then closes it without speaking. I nailed it. He's concerned about protecting people but shrinks away when he's the sole target. It's cute, but I don't need protection from Harvey.

Harvey bursts back into the locker room, slamming the door with enough force that the two naked guys jump. I like Harvey. He has the personality and energy of a bulldozer.

He turns his glare to Corbin. "And who're you?"

"He's my manager," I say, fast enough to cut Corbin off. "For my fighting."

"Manager, eh? You're getting real serious about this, aren'tcha?"

"Yes. Only two fights left before the qualifier."

"Oh?" Harvey strokes his mustache. "When's the next one? I want to attend."

"Two weeks from now," I say.

Corbin perks up, his eyes wide. "Two weeks? You never told me that. Everything I read about fighting says you need at least four weeks of recovery before you take another."

"That's the recommended time frame, not the required amount. I don't have the luxury of waiting."

I can only attend so many fights due to location and weight class. If there aren't any fighters in my weight range who want to fight, I'll be screwed. Fortunately for me, I have two lined up, in locations I can get to. But only two.

Harvey motions me to the side, and I step over to speak with him.

"He's your manager?" Harvey asks. "And he doesn't know when your next fight is?"

"He's... new."

Harvey grunts. "Whatever. Don't let him screw you up, kid."

"I'm sure I can handle it."

"Well," he says as he lifts his gut and straightens the belt of his pants, "if anyone else gives ya a hard time, just let me know. I want to see you on the TV. That's when you mention my gym, right?"

"That's the plan," I say.

And I mean it. Harvey has done a lot for me. If he wants me to give his gym a shout-out in the octagon, I will. We walk back to Corbin, who gives us a hard stare. Did he hear everything? Probably. Harvey isn't a quiet individual.

Harvey pats Corbin on the shoulder. "Make him a champion."

Corbin replies with a smile. "As his manager, that's what I intend to do."

Heh. He's really embracing that lie, isn't he? I've never had a manager before. I've done all my scheduling and promoting myself. It's not hard, but it does get tedious.

Maybe Corbin will really help with his organizational skills.

"THERE ARE a lot of techniques in mixed martial arts," Corbin says.

I finish my squats, my mind half on Corbin and half on the remaining time I have before the fight. One week to go. I need to watch my weight, I need to keep my training up, but I have to stop all workout routines that might injure me. It would be a goddamn laugh if I disqualified myself from the fight because I strained something overpreparing.

Corbin lifts an eyebrow. "This rear naked choke is popular."

"It's a beginner's move," I say. "Most people learn it quick."

"Hm. What's a difficult move to perform?"

"Anything with the word *flying* in the title," I say with laugh. "Flying armbar, flying knee…. Any of those moves require you to be at the top of your game."

"Why is the word *flying* even in any of those moves? Surely it doesn't mean they're performed in the air."

I drop down to the mat and start my series of push-ups. I should do eighty today to keep it light. "Flying means both your feet leave the mat to perform the move. Normally, with a standard armbar, you take your opponent to the ground and then forcibly extend their arm to the breaking point. With a flying armbar, you grab your opponent's arm while you're both standing and you jump onto his body, basically, forcing him to support your weight, while you're also torquing his shoulder. If you do it right, you take your opponent to the ground, already straining his arm, so he taps in seconds."

"That does sound difficult."

"Trust me. It is."

"Is there any advantage to flying maneuvers?"

"They're sudden and unexpected. You can catch a cocky opponent off guard if you do them correctly."

I finish a set of twenty push-ups and break for a few seconds, my arms posted. I need the strain of a slow workout, not the burn of something fast and intense.

"You need a training partner," Corbin says. "I don't think I can practice a flying armbar with you under the best conditions."

I glance over at him, some of my sweat-drenched hair in my face. "Yeah. I do need one."

"What about Derek?"

"He trains with his own guys. He doesn't have time to come train with me."

"He has time to spend with Lala," Corbin intones. "So maybe he has time to spend with you. I'll look at his schedule and coordinate. I think it's in your best interest if Derek helps."

"Don't pester him or anything."

"I'll be polite."

Derek will likely fold. He's too good a guy to deny someone's request. That's why I never asked. I felt guilty, especially after all he's done for me. But maybe Corbin can actually figure out a time schedule that will work and won't impede Derek's own routine.

I can only hope.

WE STAND in the lobby of the California State Athletic Commission. The high ceilings and ornate pictures add a bit of sophistication to our surroundings and remind me of my time in the military. Not the time in barracks or overseas. Hell no. But there were moments we had to wear our crisp dress uniforms and present ourselves to generals, sometimes in or around fancy buildings, like the one here in Sacramento.

Our line moves as if a corpse is the sole person helping people. Corbin glances at his phone every couple seconds. He puts it back in his pocket, waits, and then yanks it out, like he felt a buzz, but nothing's there.

"Expecting a call?" I ask.

"My sister typically asks to do something with me every Friday before class. She hasn't called today. Maybe she's ill. Or depressed. I'll give her a call once our business is done."

He puts away his phone with a huff of finality, as though the matter has been decided. Then he rummages around in his other pocket and pulls out a piece of paper. He flashes it my way and I take it. It's a list— food supplements with the best yield for muscle building, right along with calorie counts.

"Is this for me?" I ask.

Corbin nods. "I know you use protein powder, but a powder with whey would be more beneficial."

I've never tried whey powder before. And according to his list, it's lower in calories and higher on the muscle potential. He must have done some comparative research on my behalf. He's... really going out of his way. He must be giving up time on everything else.

We're here to register Corbin as my official manager. We don't need to do it, but if he is, he can come backstage with me to all the events and never has to pay for anything in a place where I'm fighting. It's more a convenience move, but I still appreciate his wiliness.

"Thanks," I say. "For everything you've done for me over these last few weeks."

Only four days until my fight.

Corbin lifts an eyebrow. "I live in Sacramento. This isn't so far from my apartment. And it's better than hanging in your gym."

"I meant, thank you for altering your whole schedule to help me. At the gym, in the apartment, the antibiotics…. Everything."

"Don't mention it."

Don't mention it, he says. Like it's no big deal. Nobody was jumping to help me this much before, not even Derek. Yet here Corbin is, sacrificing his free time and skills to ensure I have the best chances possible.

"Why all of this?" I ask.

"It was your speech in my mother's clinic," Corbin replies, once again glancing at his phone like a guilty addict.

I wait for a moment, hoping he'll elaborate, but he never does.

"Don't stop talking," I say. "What speech?"

"The one about having nothing else but this dream. Your passion to be an MMA fighter. It obviously means the world to you. I doubt our relationship would last ten minutes unless I was willing to support you at some level, and I don't like to do things flippantly, so here we are."

So here we are, huh? I smile. I guess this has been a crazy ride.

I must admit, thinking about his dedication to me twists my chest into knots with enough guilt to choke on. What have I done for him? I know he enjoys my company, especially physically, but that can't be enough. I should do something for him—something specific and tailored to his wants and dreams. But what? Who could I ask that would have insight on the matter?

My thoughts grind to a halt the moment I spot two familiar members of the Alpha MMA Academy. Clark and Anderson. They mill around the front door, chatting it up like they're here for casual business.

"Wait here," I tell Corbin.

He narrows his eyes but otherwise doesn't protest.

I stomp over to Clark and Anderson, my blood hot and my mind focusing on the things in the room that could be used as an impromptu weapon. A potted plant or a pen. Who knows what these guys will do?

I slam Clark in the shoulder before he even knows I'm here, knocking him back into the wall. He's a good thirty pounds heavier than I am, and pure muscle—I could feel it, even through the shirt.

Clark tightens his jaw.

"You have two seconds to explain," he says, his teeth clenched.

Anderson jumps behind me, taking up the flanking position without a second's hesitation.

"You're sick," I say to Clark. Anderson doesn't scare me. I beat him quick in the octagon. I can do it again.

"What're you talking about?"

"Hiring thugs to come after me in the gym? Don't try to deny it. They were after *me* specifically."

Anderson grabs my arm and torques it behind my back. He twists my wrist at the same time, and pain shoots up my arm and into my shoulder. Clark grabs the collar of my T-shirt and shoves me back against Anderson's chest. He digs his fingers into the fabric of my clothes.

"Are you high?" Clark asks. "We wouldn't send thugs to beat your ass. *We'd do it ourselves*."

"Hey!"

Corbin jogs over, his phone in his hand. Clark and Anderson both let me go and step away, though they reek of aggression. I can tell they want a fight.

"I'll call the cops," Corbin shouts.

A couple security guards—who had been flirting with a few girls standing in line—finally see what's happening and hustle over. I had been expecting a brawl, even if I didn't want it, but this outcome is better. Clark had genuine conviction in his voice. The Alpha MMA Academy didn't hire the thugs.

"We better not meet like this again," Anderson says as he shoves past me. He and Clark exit the Athletic Commission before any questions are asked.

But if they didn't hire thugs to cripple me… who did?

Chapter 15
Date Night

Corbin Friel

HALFWAY UP the stairs to my apartment, my phone buzzes. I'd answer, but my hands are filled with books and a single bag of groceries. It stops after a few rings, but it starts back up again a few seconds later.

Has to be Lala. She's the only person I know who calls with the persistency of an attention-starved child. Then again, she hasn't been calling or texting me for the past two weeks. Well, she called a couple times, but she normally calls twice a day, not twice a week.

Maybe I shouldn't ignore her call. I wouldn't want her to think I'm ignoring her.

I place my books and bag on the stairs and answer my phone.

"Hello?"

"Ah!" my sister gasps. "Bin-Bin! I'm so glad you answered. I just had the most wonderful date."

"Date?"

"Derek took me to a hockey game. Can you believe it? He likes hockey! I told you it was a great sport."

"It's almost as violent as MMA," I say. "And more people are involved. People with knives strapped to the bottom of their shoes. I don't see how anyone could enjoy that sport."

"Oh, pishposh. It's wonderful. And Derek was wonderful. It was a Sharks game, so you know it has to be good. He bought me a jacket with the Sharks logo on the back, and it was so warm."

"Wonderful."

Lala pauses for a minute. "It's the first time I've seen a hockey game in the arena."

I mull over the statement. I've never taken her to a game, and I guess neither have my parents. I know she's loved hockey since she was younger—again, any sport she wasn't allowed to participate in suddenly became her favorite sport ever—but I'm surprised to hear she's never attended a game in person.

Lala gasps again.

"What is it?" I ask. "Are you okay? Do you need me to come over?"

"No. I need you to explain yourself."

"Wh-what?"

"I got so swept up in my date with Derek that I almost forgot I was angry with you!"

"Why?"

"You're dating Keon? And you didn't tell me? I thought we told each other everything!"

She's shouting loud enough I swear the whole apartment building can hear her over my phone. I hold it a few inches away from my ear and frown.

"We've only been seeing each other for a few weeks," I say.

"Are you serious? That much time has gone by and you didn't say *anything*? Now I'm really offended."

I exhale, unsure of what to say. I've been so busy helping Keon with his training—and just watching to make sure no one harasses him—that I haven't had time to revel in our relationship. I'm glad Lala is having lovely dates. Keon and I typically spend the evening cuddling on his futon. He's so tired after his training, and I enjoy the warm embrace of his powerful arms….

It's been quite nice. Pleasant and calm. Not the excitement I think Lala wants to hear.

"Wait," I say. "How did you find out we were dating?" Do Derek and Keon talk? Did Derek tell her all about us?

To my surprise, Lala offers me a nervous chuckle. "Oh, you know. Uh, Derek said a thing, and I put it all together."

"Really?"

"Yup. Cross my heart and hope to die."

Now I know she's lying. Lala only says that when she's trying to hide something. So how did she figure it out?

"Look at the time," she says. "It's almost ten. So late. I have to go to bed."

"But—"

"I'll talk to you later, Bin-Bin! And I'm still mad at you. You should have told me. But you can make it up to me later. Have a good night!"

"Lala, I—"

She ends the call before I get another word in. I sigh.

Like Lala is one to talk. She's apparently been spending all her time with Derek and hasn't said a thing to me about their relationship. Apparently, it's all sunshine and unicorns, but it's only a matter of time before Derek does something to ruin it. I don't have facts or logic to back up my thoughts, it's just a gut feeling I have—or maybe a secret wish. I don't know which. I'm still not a fan of them being together, even though he seems to make her happy. But I won't say anything. I'll just wait for the inevitable.

I pick up my books and bag when my phone buzzes a second time. With a groan, I set my stuff back on the stairs and answer.

"Lala, I'll tell you whenever something exciting happens," I say into the receiver.

"When something exciting happens with what?" Keon asks.

"Oh, Keon." My mouth goes dry. His deep voice melts through the phone and into my ear. I haven't spoken with him on the phone lately, and I enjoy every second way too much. "Sorry. My sister just wanted to know whenever we did anything exciting. She likes to talk about everything in my life."

"We haven't done anything exciting?"

"Er, well, of course we've done things that are exciting," I say. "I meant something that can be discussed in polite conversation."

"Heh. I have something Malala can talk about."

"You do?"

"I was calling to ask if you wanted to go out tomorrow, just the two of us."

"Is this a date?" I ask.

"Yeah. Before I stress over my fight."

"I would like that."

"Good," Keon says, stiffer than normal. "I'll pick you up from your apartment around six tomorrow."

"I'll be ready."

"Perfect. I'll see you then."

I hang up the phone, more energized than I was before. Funny how a simple relationship can change someone's perspective on life. Already I feel much happier than a few weeks ago. I know Keon and I might not work out—that's just the reality—but right now I can't quell the urge to smile. I wonder where we'll be going on this date.

Once I reach my apartment door, I set my bag down and stick my key in the doorknob. When I turn, I discover it isn't locked. Odd. I don't think I've ever forgotten to lock my apartment. I'm not worried, because this place rarely gets visitors, and I've never heard of it getting burglarized, but I don't want to make it a habit.

I enter and the first thing I notice is a peculiar smell. Like… cleaning products. Something similar to Windex. I keep my apartment clean, I know, though I never stink up the place with an overload of chemicals. It isn't good for the respiratory system or the brain.

While contemplating the source of the odor, I place my books and bag on the kitchen counter. After spending time with Keon in his terrible gym and walking up four flights of stairs with a heavy stack of my books, my body has a fine layer of grime and sweat I can't wait to wash off. I shuffle to my bedroom, but right before I switch on the light, someone grabs me.

"What the—" I shout.

"Shh, shh," someone replies in a familiar tone.

I jerk to get away, but the person wraps their arms around me and keeps me close. The smell of cleaning products—specifically ammonia—is strong now.

"Who are you?" I demand, yelling loud enough that I hope it wakes the neighbors.

"It's me, Corbin. Calm down."

Justin. Of course. He got into my apartment. I should've known.

"Why are you in my room?" I ask. "What're you doing here?"

I squirm again and get halfway out of his grasp, but Justin keeps a tight grip on my clothes and keeps me close.

"I don't feel good," he whispers.

I stop struggling and squint through the darkness. I can't make anything out. I reach over and flip the light switch.

Justin draws me back into a tight embrace. In the few seconds I get to look at his face, I can tell he hasn't slept much. Black bags under his eyes, pale skin, red sclera—even a child could see the ill effects of something ravaging his body.

And he's the source of the smell. His damp clothes, sticky with his sweat, reek of chemicals. I take in a few deep sniffs. Perspiration carries trace amounts of toxins the body wishes to excrete. Specific chemical odors only occur when the kidneys and liver are overworked and unable to process dangerous substances out of the body.

What the hell has Justin been ingesting that would result in this kind of odor?

He hugs me and squeezes tight. "I knew you could help me."

"What have you been eating?" I ask as I pat his back.

"I'm not hungry."

"You must have done something to your body. Perhaps you've been eating expired fish, or—"

"I need to lie down."

He drags me over to my bed and throws us both to the mattress. I worry about his foul odor infecting my furniture, but it's clear he's been here awhile. My bed will never be the same.

When I attempt to get up, Justin jerks me back down by the front of my shirt.

"Watch it," I snap.

"Stay with me. I need you."

"You need a doctor."

"You're a doctor."

"Not yet." I break his grip on my clothes, but he wraps his arms around me again, latching on with the force of a barnacle. "Justin. Stop this."

"*Please*. No one else understands. I'm scared, Corbin."

Scared? What's he talking about?

I relax and rest back on the bed, Justin clinging to me and nuzzling into my neck. I try to keep calm, considering he's ill, but his bizarre mannerisms continue to build. And his clothes have a few stains along one side, like he fell or got skidded through the dirt. Even his hair, which he normally keeps spiky and gelled, hasn't been touched in some time.

Justin kisses my neck. I bunch my shoulder up and block his affections.

"I'm seeing someone," I say. "I'll sit here and comfort you, but you can't do this. We're not together."

"You're not still seeing the same guy."

"Yes, I am."

"Bullshit."

"It's true."

"A few friends of mine said—" He takes a deep breath and shakes his head. "—well, I guess they didn't. So it doesn't matter. All I want is to be with you, Corbin. We've known each other for years. You're the only person I trust."

I sigh and stare up at the ceiling. Justin glues himself to my side, his body warmer than mine. Much warmer. He must be sick, but it seems self-inflicted, rather than a virus or disease. I hate to see him like this. Even if I don't want him as a significant other, I don't want him to suffer.

I wrap an arm around him and stroke his back. "You'll be okay, Justin. I'm sure you have friends and family you can trust."

"They all hate me," he says. "I never do what anyone wants. I'm always a disappointment."

"That's not true."

"My father wanted me to be straight; my mother wanted me to go to college; my friends all want me to be into all the things they are. I'm just a disappointment to all of them. Even you ditched me because I'm not a muscled gym rat, apparently."

"That's not why," I say, holding back a tirade. Now isn't the time to go into his shortcomings. This "illness" could be messing with his perceptions.

"I saw the guy you hooked up with," Justin whispers. "I know what you're doing, but I want one thing to go right for me. I want to have one thing all my own."

"Are you referring to me? You want *me* to be the one thing that's all your own?"

Justin doesn't answer. He runs his hand up and down my chest and stomach, grazing his fingers along the buttons of my shirt. His hand gets lower and lower with each cycle, until he reaches the top of my slacks.

The mere physical stimulation affects me, but I've got enough perception to understand where this is going—and I want none of it.

"Stop," I say.

"What? We're not doing anything wrong."

How many times do I need to tell him? Why is he always like this? I'm on the verge of yelling, but again, he doesn't look like he's in the right state of mind to even fully understand.

"I want professional help," he says.

"Okay. I support that decision."

"Can I borrow some money?" he asks. Before I can respond, he adds, "Just a little. Just enough to get help."

"I thought you had a job?"

"I do. I do. But it's not enough."

"Justin…." I sigh. What's with him?

"I paid you back some, right? I'm trying. Just help me out, Corbin. Please. You're the only one I can turn to."

Against my better judgment, I say, "Fine. I'll give you some money. But you better get the help you need, okay? You don't look right. You don't smell right."

"I know."

"I am worried about you."

"I know," Justin says, stroking my jawline. "You're a good guy—I knew you'd help."

I STAND at the edge of the parking lot next to my apartment, pacing the white line next to my car. Each time I glance at my phone, I'm reminded that a watched pot never boils. It's 6:56 p.m., then 6:57 p.m. Each minute slower than the last. Why am I so anxious? Keon and I have been together for a few weeks. It shouldn't be different than when we hang in his apartment.

But we've never been on a proper date before.

"We're handling this all backward," I mutter to myself.

I chuckle as I stare at my shoes. I don't want our relationship to turn into what I have with Justin. I want this to work, so I have to make it work.

The rumble of a motorcycle heralds Keon's arrival. I straighten my posture as he steers the sleek vehicle into the parking spot next to mine. Strapped to the back of the bike is a second helmet.

Oh no.

I cross my arms as he steps off the Harley-Davidson, ready to give him yet another explanation about why I hate motorcycles, but the words catch in my throat when I see what he's wearing.

He takes off his helmet, straightens out the hair of his mohawk, and brushes off his fitted leather jacket. Even his jeans can't contain his muscles—or the bulge of a well-endowed man—and it takes me a moment to remember that staring is rather impolite. I gaze slightly off to the side, avoiding eye contact and taking shallow breaths.

"Corbin," he says. "That's a new look for you. I like it."

"Thank you."

I wanted to be more "casual" than what I normally wear, so I opted for my only pair of jeans, a black tank top, and a loose button-up shirt over it. Not fully buttoned, of course. I spent some time in front of the mirror calculating the best ratio of buttoned to unbuttoned buttons. Three seemed to be the best to achieve a mellow appearance while still retaining a bit of class.

"I brought a second helmet," Keon says. "I really want you to experience a motorcycle ride at least once in your life. That way you know what you're missing out on."

"It's dangerous," I snap. "Unnecessarily dangerous."

"It's a thrill. Trust me. I've driven motorcycles for years. You're in safe hands."

I step back toward my car and stare at it for a few seconds. Cars have temperature control and music and *seat belts*.

"Where are we going?" I ask. "If it's somewhere close, maybe I'll consider it. Maybe."

"That's a surprise."

"Is it, now?"

"That's right. No spoilers."

I keep my arms crossed, my mind flipping back and forth. A part of me doesn't want to disappoint Keon. He's obviously excited to ride the damn death machine. But the other part of me doesn't want to die on our first date.

Keon shrugs. "Look, I'm not going to force you, but I'd appreciate it if you give me a chance. If you're too uncomfortable, we can always take your car."

"Hm."

Car or motorcycle? Maybe one time won't be too risky....

What have I gotten myself into?

Chapter 16
First True Date

Keon Lynch

CORBIN TAKES my second helmet, and I can't help but smile. I knew he'd give it a try.

"What?" he asks. "Dying on the first ride is statistically improbable."

"I'm a bad influence on you."

"Definitely."

His quick snark gets me laughing. He joins in, but his is a little more nervous than I want to hear. He spins the helmet around in his hands and gives my bike a few quick glances out of the corner of his eye, like it might attack him at any moment if he lets his guard down.

I pat the seat. "I promise I'll take good care of you."

Corbin replies with a sneer, like he's regretting his decision. Before he can protest, I pull my helmet on and swing my leg over the seat. Corbin fidgets with his glasses, measuring them with his fingers and comparing it to the base of the helmet. I've worn sunglasses under my helmet before, so I'm confident he can wear his. Sure enough, he figures out a way and shoves on the helmet.

I start up the bike. Corbin takes his time getting on the back, like he can't decide the best angle to approach. Finally, he hops on, but he keeps a few inches away from me.

"Get close," I say.

"I don't want to crowd you," he replies, his voice muffled through the helmet.

"Can't be avoided. Just scoot over."

Corbin slides up against me. He wraps his arms around, but again, he keeps his distance. It's cute, though I doubt he'll stay this way once we're moving. I rev the bike, pull forward a few feet, and Corbin grips me so tight I swear he's trying to squeeze me in half. Even his legs seize up on my sides, threatening to cut off circulation.

I get to the edge of the parking lot, and the moment my front tire touches the street, Corbin finds a way to tighten his grip. His fingers twist into my leather jacket, and his whole body hardens to steel. I chuckle to myself, hoping this isn't a deal breaker for our relationship.

Once we're out onto the roads, I keep under forty miles per hour. I could go faster—a *lot* faster—but if I even tap another vehicle, Corbin will leave me, disavow all motorized transportation, and likely become Amish.

The sun sets in the foothills, blanketing California in a fleeting moment of reds and oranges. Even under the tinted visor of my full-cover helmet, the blaze of colors could impress any world-weary soul. I nudge Corbin. He should see this, and I suspect he's had his eyes closed since we left his apartment.

The roads between Sacramento and Stockton aren't so bad. Straight highways and a few turns. Corbin loosens up after a couple minutes on the frontage road. The lack of traffic and the constant casual speed make for a pleasant ride. He glances around, though not too much. He keeps his head buried in my back.

I take one hand off the handlebar and scratch his knee. Corbin presses himself against me, loosens the grip on one hand, and strokes my shoulder. It doesn't last, however, and he goes back to securing himself to my body with the strength of a barnacle.

The cool breeze, easy maneuvering, and engine between my legs combine to create a fantasy of freedom in my mind. I could go anywhere and do anything. A car is too bulky to travel everywhere, but my motorcycle weaves between vehicles and obstacles with little trouble. While other people have to slow for traffic or wait behind terrible drivers, I can swerve around them and continue on without a care in the world.

We enter Stockton after the sun has set. The evening isn't as wondrous as the crimson sunset, but I enjoy the bright lights of the city contrasting with the darkness of night regardless.

I pull my motorcycle up to a series of buildings near the edge of town. From the outside, it's hard to tell what they are, and after I park my bike, Corbin takes his helmet off and glances around, one eyebrow lifted.

"Enjoy the ride?" I ask after I remove my own helmet.

"I'm sure my blood pressure went to dangerous places a few times," he says. "But it wasn't terrible."

"Wasn't terrible, huh? I'll take it. Anything's better than immediately recoiling away in fear."

"It's still a needless risk. If you want adrenaline in your blood, you can go to an amusement park."

"People die in amusement parks, ya know."

Corbin huffs. "A lot less than on motorcycles."

"Admit it," I say as I pat his back. "You enjoyed the ride."

He looks away and glares at our surroundings. "Where are we?"

Dodging the statement. I see how he is.

A short breeze washes over the near-empty parking lot. No lights illuminate the windows. A pack of abandoned dogs trot by, sniffing at the overflowing garbage cans. I can totally understand why Corbin dislikes this place.

"Wait here," I say. "I'll be right back."

"You're leaving me here?" He crosses his arms and glares at the surrounding darkness. "I mean... what if you get attacked by thugs again?"

"Scared? Don't worry. I'll protect you."

I wrap an arm around his back and drag my knuckles along his spine. Corbin leans against my chest and huffs a second time. He's funny when he's disgruntled.

"Why would you bring me here?"

"I'm hoping you'll enjoy it. Just wait here. I'll be back in just a minute, I swear."

I let him go and jog toward the buildings. I slip between two and make my way to the back parking lot meant for the employees. True to his word, Harvey is waiting next to the back door, leaning heavy on the wall and staring at his phone.

"Hey," I say. "Is it all set?"

Harvey rams his phone into his jean's pocket and sneers. "Yeah, yeah. It's ready." He tosses me a set of keys. "Make sure not to break anything. And don't do anything you wouldn't want on camera. This place records everything."

"Thank you for this."

"I'm serious about not breaking anything. This was one of my worse property purchases. I have to pay three times as much insurance, and it barely turns a profit. Lady I purchased this place from said it was a turnkey operation, but that's jack shit right there. I need to sell it as soon as possible, and I can't do that if everything's busted."

"I'll take care," I say. "And Corbin isn't the kind of guy to mess anything up."

"All right. I'm gonna take off. Lock the place up when you're done. And don't worry, the security guard knows you'll be here."

"Again, thank you."

Harvey hits my shoulder with a fist and walks off to the lone truck parked by the dumpster. I'm not sure if Corbin will like this date, but his sister seemed to think it was the greatest idea anyone has ever had, so I'm hopeful.

Then again, he might hate every second and I'll blow this relationship one painful step at a time.

Corbin Friel

MY STOMACH grumbles.

I didn't eat all day in anticipation for tonight. Hunger is the best sauce with any meal, but I'm bordering on ravenous. Justin always accuses me of becoming hangry, so we better eat soon or else I'll start consuming my patience.

Why did Keon bring me to what appears to be an abandoned business district? Not the classiest locations for a meal and certainly not the safest. Where is he? The longer we're separated the more my imagination plays tricks on me. Every disturbance of the wind is a thug lying in wait. The crunch of my shoes sounds like someone sneaking up behind me.

My blood pressure rises all over again.

Keon jogs out of the alley between buildings and rejoins me. I consider hugging him the moment he returns, but I restrain myself. Best not to appear needy and weak on our first date, especially if I'm frightening myself with my own delusions.

"Ready?" Keon asks.

I nod. What could we possibly be doing?

He juts his chin toward the largest building in the row, one nestled between a closed coffee shop and an old school supply depot. The building looks like a warehouse—two stories, no windows, and a dull brown paint job. The large double doors are the only thing throwing me off. What is this place? It's like Willie Wonka's chocolate factory, but instead of a gold ticket and whimsy, a homeless man just pops out and gropes you.

Keon unlocks the front door. I lean in close to see what's inside, but he blocks my view. He lifts an eyebrow and offers me a playful smile.

"Close your eyes," he says.

"What? Why? Are you intentionally hiding the purpose of this building?"

"I want you to be surprised, but this place is all business up front. The party's in the back."

"So this is the mullet of date locations?"

"Heh. Something like that."

"Well…."

I'm still dubious about the building, but Keon can handle anyone who jumps us. I hope.

"Okay," I say.

Keon takes my glasses, leaving me blind to the surroundings. The blobs and shapes share the same general color palette, blending together into a mass of browns, grays, and shadows. I grab Keon's arm and hold on tight. I grit my teeth the moment he opens the door. It screeches in protest, like a wail warning us away.

God, I need to toughen up. It's a rickety old building. What could happen?

We step inside, and Keon jerks me close.

"What's wrong?" I ask.

"Nothing. I just don't want you to run into anything while you're blind."

"What's in here?"

"It's fine. But don't touch anything. Seriously."

What a way to calm my nerves. What's in here? Fine china? Bombs? Of course it's not bombs, but my imagination won't stop going for the deep end.

"Let's go," Keon says.

He guides me deeper and deeper into the building. He flips a few switches, and lights flood the area in full force. Some things sparkle and glitter, but I really can't make out what they are besides something made of glass.

Then we reach a large rectangular room with an open center. Objects cluster against the walls. Are things on stages and podiums? Keon hands me back my glasses. I affix them to my face and gawk at our surroundings.

I had no idea.

Keon Lynch

"HERE IT is," I say. "What do you think?"

Corbin stares, his expression unreadable.

I glance around. Museums aren't my thing. I went to a few while in elementary school, so I associate them with something a child would be interested in. Malala said Corbin would appreciate history, however, and when I told her this museum had a medical history section, she almost swallowed the phone whole when she gasped. She said Corbin would be ecstatic.

He doesn't look thrilled, though.

"This is a bunch of medical history stuff," I say, trying to fill the silence with conversation. "And I figured we could eat here."

I motion to a table set up in the back. The circular table has a white cloth draped over it, a couple of chairs, and a picnic basket. There's also a lit candle—the tall type, like in cheesy romance movies—and I roll my eyes hard enough to strain them. I can't believe Harvey did that. What a cheeseball.

"We're allowed to be here?" Corbin asks.

"Yeah. Harvey owns the place. He said we could be here as long as we wanted."

Corbin walks up to the first exhibit. I join him, uncertain of what I'm looking at. It's a chair—old-school, probably hand carved—made of oak and polished smooth. But the seat is missing the middle portion, like some sort of early-age toilet. The armrests have grips at the ends, however, and grooves for the fingers to wrap around.

"Wow," Corbin says. "This is an eighteenth-century birthing chair."

"Wait, what? People gave birth on this?"

I guess that explains the handgrips. Fuck.

He straightens his glasses. "Pregnant women would sit here, and the midwife would stand behind the chair and massage or coach her."

"I see."

"Oh! And look at these."

Corbin hustles to the next thing under a display case. It's a stack of white marbles. Misshapen marbles, but still as large.

"These are bladder stones," he says.

I hold back a laugh. "They just have some dude's bladder stones out for display?"

"These are unusually large and prominent. And so many of them. It really makes you wonder what the diet was of the people who produced these. Bladder stones are concentrated minerals formed in your urinary tract. They must have been eating things with bits of rock in them to product bladder stones this large."

Damn. He knows a lot. And Malala was right—now he does seem genuinely excited to be looking at this stuff. I'm glad. I don't have the spare funds to take him someplace fancy, but I still wanted to show him I care about his interests as well.

"Oh, and look at this! An old book on medical procedures. Look at these pictures! How antiquated. Did you know that during the Renaissance they thought the brain was made up of only seven paired brain nerves? We've discovered so much since then. Fascinating."

The way he talks about the book reminds me of my sister. Alisha said the same thing about studying medicine. *Fascinating.* That was the word. She couldn't put those books down.

Corbin turns to face me. "Thank you. This is amazing."

"I'm glad you like it."

"You probably aren't as interested in this as I am."

I chuckle. "Hey, if you can learn jiujitsu moves and the rules of MMA fights, I can learn a little about… birthing chairs… and bladder stones."

He laces his arms around my elbow. "You're adorable when you talk about esoteric medical things."

For the first time since I've been with the man, I get flustered and red in the face. But I like this. Maybe, if I ever talk to my sister again, I'll at least have some interesting things to discuss with her.

"Why don't we eat?" Corbin asks. "I'm famished."

I walk him over to our table and take a seat. I made Corbin a few ham sandwiches and myself a single plain chicken breast. I also brought along some fruit—grapes and bananas—and a couple celery sticks, just in case I need something to chew on to stave off the hunger.

Making weight is a bitch sometimes. I have to make sure I lose a few pounds between now and weigh-in. Which is less than twenty-four hours from now.

"I've been thinking," Corbin says as he prepares his meal in a tidy fashion. "Have you considered attending college under an athletic scholarship? You're skilled enough. Many colleges have wrestling programs. I know you said you weren't good at schoolwork, but the staff at these schools help individuals with dyslexia. I think you could earn a degree and continue fighting, if you wanted."

"Nah," I say as I poke around the piece of my grilled chicken breast. "I need to make money. I can't stop. Not yet."

"To pay for your apartment? You could get a dorm or—"

"Not for that."

"Do you have debt? Because—"

"It's not that either," I say, glaring at the plate in front of me.

"Should I stop asking?"

"It's fine…. I use almost all my money to pay for my sister's medical schooling."

Corbin's eyebrows shoot up, practically disappearing into this hairline. "You do? But I thought your sister didn't speak to you? I thought you didn't even know what school she goes to?"

"I don't," I say with a sigh. "And she doesn't know I pay for it."

Corbin cuts his ham sandwich in half. "Your family has more drama and relationship twists than a midafternoon soap opera."

"You're telling me. All I need is a bout of amnesia and it would be complete."

"How do you pay your sister's debts without her knowing? I'm extremely curious."

"Well, before our mother died, she had a trust fund set up. She told Alisha the money was for her college, but my dad had access to it as well, and he used it all before Alisha even got to school. I… spoke with the attorney after me and my sister had a falling out. Alisha never knew the fund was empty, so I asked the guy to pretend like there was still money in it. I send him a check every month, and he uses the money to write my sister out a new check—from this fake fund."

"Why?" Corbin asks. "Why not just tell her?"

"I tried offering her money. She refused it. She said she didn't want to have a reason to be in my debt—like she thought I would hold it over her or something. I figured this was for the best."

Alisha wanted a new life, far from the trash can of her childhood. I don't blame her. I hate remembering my early life as well. And I want her to succeed. I couldn't help my mother, but I can do something for Alisha.

Which is why the UFC is really my last chance to achieve anything for myself. All my other options are gone, even something like a college scholarship because I have to work.

Corbin moves his chair around the table until he's sitting next to me. He places a hand on my knee and eats his sandwich with a deep look of contemplation etched into his face.

"Your fight is tomorrow?" he asks.

"Yeah," I say.

"Are you ready for it?"

"I think so."

"You think so? Or you know so?"

I give Corbin a sidelong glance. "What's that supposed to mean?"

"You can't start doubting yourself. There are several studies about the *self-fulfilling prophecy*. People who believe something often see it come true, whether it be positive or negative. They subconsciously fulfill their own desires. So, as your medical advisor, I suggest you continue with brimming confidence."

I pull him close. Corbin tenses for a second and then leans against me.

Normally, the night before a fight, I would be in my apartment, watching a movie. Alone. Sometimes doubting my capabilities. Sometimes convinced I could make it. I prefer this kind of night.

I tighten my grip on Corbin. I prefer this kind of support and camaraderie.

"Thank you," I say. "I'll try to keep your advice in mind."

Corbin nuzzles up against my neck and kisses me at the base of my jaw. "You've got this."

Chapter 17
Two-Hit Combo

Keon Lynch

I STEP onto the scale. The judges weigh me in at two hundred and five pounds. The exact right weight for a light heavyweight fighter. Technically the range of weight is one hundred and eighty-five to two hundred and five, but every pound I have over the opponent is only a benefit in my favor, which is why everyone wants to be at the max limit for their weight category.

I step down and allow the photographers to snap a few pictures for the after-fight results. I do a few poses, but before I can leave, one of the photographers points me over to another fighter.

"We need a few shots with your opponent," the lady says.

My opponent. Zane Kennick. He's thinner than me, but his arms and chest teem with coiled muscle and bulge in places mine don't.

I watched a few of his fight videos the moment I heard he would my opposition. Zane has a mean jab-and-uppercut combo. He starts by punching a fighter dead-on in the nose, smashing it to the point of breaking. The gushing blood and broken cartilage get in the way of breathing. The moment the injured fighter opens his mouth to take in air, Zane hits them with an uppercut, right under the bottom of their chin. Uppercuts damn near shatter jaws normally, but if your mouth is open, the strike adds a whole new level of pain from the teeth smashing together, even with a mouth guard.

It's a terrible combination—one I need to avoid at all costs.

When I step up close, Zane holds out a hand to shake. I take it and smile while the shutters of a million cameras snap all around us. He gives me a bro-style hug. I allow it, and he pats me on the back, his breath on my shoulder.

"I'm going to fucking destroy you," he whispers.

Ice runs through my veins—I'm ready to fight him right here, if that's what he wants.

But Zane steps away from me, all smiles, like nothing happened.

Corbin is right. Fighting, in part, is psychological. A blow to the confidence can wreck a guy as much as a blow to the kidney. Zane wants to get a few cheap shots in before our fight. I can't let him get under my skin.

I walk away without a reaction. Best to play deaf. Zane might rattle other guys, but I have a fight to win.

Derek jogs over to me and motions to the door. "Hey. Corbin and Malala are out in the car. You ready to get your eat on?"

"Sure."

"You okay? You look a little tense."

I guess I didn't hide it as well as I should have. "I'm fine," I say. "I just need to concentrate."

Corbin Friel

ALTHOUGH I'VE done this before—watching Keon weigh in, eating with him, spending time before the fights—it's like I'm seeing the event in a whole new light. A terrible, nerve-racking light. I disliked watching two men beat each other senseless before, but watching someone I care about get into the octagon? I dread every moment Keon will risk his well-being for his life's goal.

And I don't know why, but Keon doesn't seem like himself. Even as we sit in the fighter's waiting room, he's quiet, pensive.

The back room for this fight event is different than the last. Each fighter gets their own closet-sized room with a tiny table and a couple chairs. We have the ventilation of a tomb, and the heat of a breezeless day in the desert, but the staff of the event has graciously provided us with as much warm water as we can drink.

Derek holds Lala in his lap, and they whisper their conversations to each other. We're close enough that I can still hear everything, though I doubt they care. Lala curls herself up in Derek's grasp and stares up at him with a permanent smile.

Somehow, despite the sweat-inducing environment, those two remain cheery.

"What're you thinking about?" she asks.

"I'm thinking about the first round," Derek says. "What're you thinking about?"

"Do people ever gamble on MMA fights?"

"Uh, I think they do online."

"Do you ever do it?"

Derek forces a single laugh. "Who, me? Nah. That's illegal here."

"Oh, okay."

She pecks him with a kiss, and he runs his hand through her long black hair.

How are they still in the honeymoon phase of their relationship? I figured Derek would've made a fool of himself by now. Yet here they are, so attached at the hip they might as well be conjoined twins.

Maybe I should introduce Lala to some of my med school friends. I doubt Derek compares to any of them. Then again, it would be a douchebag move to sabotage the relationship.

My phone buzzes, and I glance at the screen. I stop breathing for a moment when I read the caller ID: Justin Riddle. He doesn't usually call me. It takes me a moment to run through the myriad of possibilities. What does he want right now?

Keon lifts an eyebrow. "Who is it?"

I tuck my phone into my slacks pocket. "Justin. It can wait."

Keon straightens his posture, his expression shifting from neutral to hardened. "You're still seeing him?" The words come out with a sharp edge.

"It's… complicated," I say.

"Bullshit. Just tell me you aren't seeing him, Corbin."

I open my mouth to explain, but I swallow the words before I get anything out. Keon's terse tone and tense posture betray his anxiety. Discussing Justin's problems shouldn't even be a topic for conversation at a time like this. Keon needs to focus.

"I don't see Justin anymore," I say.

"Good. If you two are over, you're over. I don't want to see him around."

"You have nothing to worry about."

I'll explain the money-borrowing situation after the fights. It's not like Justin and I are doing anything wrong. Keon will understand—but not right now. It would be a distraction to bring up all the details.

Keon wrings his hands and glares at the floor. The heat might be getting to him, along with the stress of an impending fight, of course. What would my father say here? He would have something comforting and inspiring.

"Is there anything I can do for you?" I ask as I place my hand on his knee.

"No."

My chest tightens. The inability to affect the outcome of today's fight weighs heavy. If I had the power, I'd make it so Keon already had everything he ever wanted. I feel helpless being forced to sit on the sidelines and watch.

Only a couple hours before the fights begin. At least, as his manager, I'll be able to stay with Keon here in the back and watch him fight from the corner with Derek. Lala will be alone in the audience, but she'll be sitting in the front row, so she'll be close.

What if Keon loses? How will he react? What will he do?

I wish the night were over. I don't want to contemplate the possibilities.

Keon Lynch

MUSIC FILLS the arena, loud enough to quicken my pulse and get me restless.

But I can't seem to focus like I have in the past. I'm worried about my infected shin and about my opponent and about how close I am to victory. I can't seem to get out of my own head. And the more I think about it, the worse it becomes.

I wait behind the door for my name to be called. The announcer yells to the audience, getting them pumped for our match. Normally I wouldn't pay attention, but I listen now in an attempt to distract my thoughts.

"Next up, we have our light heavyweight match," the announcer blares.

The cheering of the crowd shakes the building.

The announcer continues, "In the red corner, fighting out of San Jose, California, with a professional win-loss record of five to two, we have Zane 'the Two-Hit Wonder' Kennick! Zane's wins have all been with a devastating knockout. Will we get more of those tonight?"

The applause churns my stomach.

"You're up," one of the bouncers says as he opens the door.

I step out to make the short walk to the octagon. To my surprise, I'm met with more cheers than boos. The audience claps, and a few give me encouraging thumbs up.

The announcer, a gaunt man in a fitted suit, motions me into the octagon. I step through the cage, and he smiles wide.

"And in the blue corner, fighting out of Stockton, California, with a professional win-loss record of five to zero, we have Keon 'the Watchman' Lynch! He's never lost, ladies and gentlemen. Will he keep his record clean tonight?"

Now the boos hit. Not as much as in the past, when I was a complete nobody, though I can still hear them.

Zane hops around on the other side of the ring, his fists up and his piercing gaze locked on mine. I can't lose to him. I can't lose to anyone.

The announcer leaves the octagon. "Let's begin!"

The bell rings.

Zane and I both lunge for the middle of the cage. He throws a jab, but I step away, an inch from the blow. He's fast. Just like his videos. And his beefy arms pack a mean punch—I could feel the force of his blow as his fist flew by my head.

I kick his inner thigh, right below his black shorts. He jumps back, still dancing around on the balls of his feet. I get up close and kick him again in the same spot, my strike leaving a slight red mark and echoing throughout the ring. One or two hits won't hurt him too much, but if I land a targeted assault on the same spot over and over again, it'll add up. Once his leg is sore, he'll slow down, and I'll have a better chance of winning this match.

Zane leaps at me with a heavy overhand punch. I jump away and slam into the edge of the octagon, my back against the chain-link fence.

The familiar heat of battle courses through my veins, filling me with a burning desire to win. Each movement of my muscles brings with it a pleasant burn. I'm tense. Coiled. Ready to strike.

I kick Zane again, this time hard enough to stagger him. Zane switches stances, so that his injured leg is more behind him—protecting it. And his expression changes too. Something hate-filled and menacing. He wants to win as much as I do.

We circle around the octagon, facing each other the entire time. I'm too focused to hear the crowds or the announcer or even the time for our match. All I can hear is the steady beat of my heart.

I step forward, and Zane does the same. I feint a kick, and instead I hit Zane with a left hook, my fist connecting with his cheek.

Zane throws his powerful jab at the same moment—right as I'm recovering from my close counterpunch. He hits me in the nose, even while I'm stepping back. There's a slight crunch and click inside my ears, and hot blood splatters across my chin and shoulder.

I jump back, and so does Zane.

Fuck!

I can't breathe through my nose. All I get is the terrible scent of copper and the clogged sensation of being congested. I open my mouth to get a few gulps of air and then close it tight, opting to hold my breath rather than risk Zane's infamous fight-ending uppercut.

But I can't fight the whole match without breathing.

We dance around in circles, never getting too close. I throw a few kicks, but they don't connect. I paint the mat of the octagon crimson.

The bell rings, signifying the end of this round. I have two more rounds to end this before it goes to decision and a group of judges decides who won. If I don't submit or knock Zane out, I'll be subject to their opinion—the fight could go either way.

A waterfall of blood pours from my nose, coating most of my front. There's not much pain, probably due to the fact I'm soaked in adrenaline, but I know there'll be a fuckton of pain in the morning. For now, I hold my gloved hand to my nose, blocking the flood of fresh blood.

While Zane's coaches rush to give him water bottles before round two, Derek and Corbin join me in my corner of the octagon. Derek sets down a stool and I take a seat.

Corbin places a towel under my busted nose. "Does it hurt?"

Corbin Friel

KEON SHAKES his head.

My hands tremble as I examine his face. His nose isn't out of place or crooked, which is a good sign. I doubt the ridge bone in his nose is broken.

"Can I touch it?" I ask.

Keon nods.

I run my fingers along the sides and middle of his nose. He doesn't flinch or protest, which is also good, because I feel the dented portions of his flesh much easier without the movement. He breathes through his mouth the entire time, the mouth guard in the way and preventing him from getting good airflow.

"It's not bad," I say. "It's probably your septum—the part that separates the nostrils. I don't think you've dislodged the cartilage."

Derek rubs Keon's right shoulder. "What's wrong, man? You're not yourself out there. You never get hit."

Keon doesn't answer.

"Wrap it up," the sideline referee says. "Round two begins in sixty seconds."

Derek gives Keon a water bottle and does his best to wipe away the copious amounts of blood.

What's wrong with Keon? He really hasn't been himself the entire day. I kneel next to him, wishing I could just comfort him, but I know I shouldn't do anything overtly affectionate in the middle of the fight, especially not when we're center stage.

"Keon," I say, my voice low. "You make an art of fighting. I've seen it before in the way you move, the way you train, the way you talk about this. I don't know what's wrong, but I know you can win."

My whole body shakes. What else can I say?

Keon pats me on the shoulder and I snap my gaze to his. He has a calm look about him that wasn't there before. Then he strokes the side of my neck with his thumb. A small gesture, one probably unseen by the crowd outside of the octagon, but it reassures me and quells my trembling.

How is it he's comforting *me* at a time like this? I should be the one assuring him.

"Time's up," the referee barks.

I step away from Keon, my whole being yearning to stay.

"I'll be here when you're done," I say. "No matter what happens in your match."

And then I exit the cage, almost afraid to watch the rest of the match.

Chapter 18
Ringside

Keon Lynch

I MUST admit, having a team to support me makes a big difference. Even if it's smaller than most, it helps.

Derek takes my water and stool and I hop out to the center of the cage. Zane meets me there, a tight smile on his face. His enthusiasm infects me. I smile back, no doubt a disturbing sight given my messed-up face, but I don't give a shit.

The bell rings.

Zane shoots in with his signature uppercut. I lean away but stay close enough to punch him in the gut. I have to gulp down air as I move around him afterward. Zane folds and then attempts to backhand me as he turns. Again, I dodge his blow.

Zane doesn't let up. He throws another punch, and then another. I'm on the defensive, taking steps backward until I hit the fence. I have to block the strikes with my forearms. Zane pummels away, opening his own mouth to drag more air into his body as he unleashes another series of unrelenting blows.

I drag my back along the fence in an attempt to get away from him, but nothing helps. Then, when he slows, I return with a heavy punch of my own. Zane leans away to avoid it, and I punch again, giving myself more room to escape him. Sure enough, once Zane takes a step back, I run from the edge of the octagon and return to the center.

Zane takes his time chasing after me.

"He's tired," Derek shouts from my corner. "Get him! He's tired!"

I can't allow Zane to punch me. So I lunge at him. Zane blocks his face with his arms, but I grab his legs and slam him to the mat. I jump on top of him, straddling his stomach. Zane wraps his legs and arms around my body, keeping me close, preventing me from slamming him with a series of ground-and-pound punches.

"I'm not tired, bitch," he hisses into my ear.

I try to break free of Zane's hold, but he's stronger than me. Gritting my teeth, I grab one of his arms and attempt to twist—if I can get an armbar, I can force him to submit. But again, he overpowers me through sheer muscle alone.

Fuck.

And then Zane does the same thing to me—he grabs my arm and twists, moving it into a position so he can overextend my elbow. With enough speed and surprise, I roll over Zane and rip my arm from his grasp. I jump to my feet and stagger back.

I need a new plan.

Zane stands, sweat rolling off him, but he's not breathing heavy. And unlike me, he doesn't have a bloody nose getting in the way. My blood is smeared across most of his chest, but he doesn't have any open wounds to speak of.

He strides toward me, confidence spurring him forward. If he hits me with an uppercut, I'll lose. If I take him down to the mat, I'll lose. If I wait until the time runs out, I'll lose. I have to take a gamble.

When he's a foot away, my body tenses, ready to give me 100 percent. I leap at him, legs first, both feet off the ground, and hook his legs. The momentum throws him backfirst on the mat. In that moment of confusion, I grab his ankle—his legs are nowhere near as muscled as his arms—and then I torque that son of bitch as hard as I can. I overextend the foot, bending it backward, practically feeling the muscles and tendons ripping under my grasp.

Zane screams and taps on the mat.

I let him go and take a deep breath of blood and air.

He submitted.

I win.

Corbin Friel

"UNBELIEVABLE," THE announcer says. "If you blinked, you would've missed it. Keon Lynch wins with a flying scissor heel hook, ladies and gentlemen! Perfectly executed. Zane had no idea what hit him!"

I allow myself to breathe. For a moment, I thought Keon would lose. I almost looked away—anything to avoid watching him struggle. But he won. And it was an impressive win. The whole arena audience is up on their feet, cheering and clapping with the force of a hurricane. Even Zane's buddies seem impressed enough to offer up a few moments of golf claps.

Derek grabs my shoulder and shakes me. He says some things, but without a microphone, I can't discern a single word through the chaos. I try to calm him, but he doesn't listen. He shakes me again, hugs me, and points to the cage.

Lala unfurls a banner with Keon's name on it. She waves it around the front row, shouting alongside the best of them.

The announcer grabs Keon's arm and holds it over his head. Afterward, Zane gives Keon a hug, and the two share a quick handshake.

Zane seems like a nice sportsman. Maybe Keon will make a friend of him.

Keon and Zane are led off by the medics to allow for the heavyweight fight, but I don't care about any of that. I keep close to Derek, and we go to the back room to wait until Keon is done with his postfight procedures.

"Do you think they'll find out about his shin?" Derek asks the moment we're alone in the back room.

"I doubt it," I say. "Not unless they take blood tests."

"Sometimes they do."

I snap my attention to him. "They do?"

"Yeah. Sometimes. If they suspect really bad drug use."

"Do a lot of fighters use drugs?"

Derek shrugs. "I dunno. The pressure can get intense. Some guys take stimulants or steroids to get that edge, ya know? Sometimes people take so many supplements they accidentally test positive for Turinabol."

"Turinabol?"

"It's a type of steroid. For sick muscle definition."

Ah. Yes. For *sick* muscle definition. That's the best definition by far.

I hold back a powerful eye roll.

Well, so long as they don't take blood tests, I doubt they'll figure out Keon's marrow infection. A urine test would reveal the antibiotics, but those can be taken for a wide variety of reasons, and sometimes people preemptively take them in preparation for surgery or other medical procedures.

And I doubt they would ding Keon for that kind of drug use.

The door opens. Derek and I tense, but Keon steps into the room, and we both relax, like we were synchronized through empathic means.

Before Derek says anything, I rush to Keon's side. "Are you okay?"

Keon, already dressed in a clean T-shirt and shorts, wraps an arm around my back and holds me close. "Just one more fight," he says, ignoring my question. "Then I'll have enough wins to participate in the UFC qualifier."

"Yeah. That's good. You'll do it. But are you okay? How do you feel?"

"Pain is fleeting. Glory lasts forever."

He says each word with unbridled conviction. He smiles, despite the busted nose and forming black eye. His happiness eases the tension in my gut, but I still want to tend to his face.

When I attempt to step away, Keon tightens his grip. I glance up at him and lift an eyebrow. He leans down and kisses me, his lips rough and laced with a hint of soap and copper. Something about the way he slowly runs his tongue across mine stirs all sorts of urges I didn't have a few seconds ago. I shiver under his touch and return the favor by nibbling on his lower lip. Already the heat between us causes me to melt into him. He really must be ecstatic for his victory.

"Aww," Derek says.

I end the kiss and shoot Derek a glare. He's still here?

Derek hits a fist into the palm of his opposite hand. "If you two are done celebrating, we should get going! And Malala sent me a text saying she's ready for food."

Lala didn't send me anything of the sort.

"I don't know," I say. "What if Keon needs to rest?"

"We should go eat," Keon says. "I want to celebrate. With you. And Derek and Malala."

"I-if that's what you want."

"It is. Let's go."

To my surprise, Derek opts to take us to BJ's Brewhouse, a middle-to-fancy restaurant open until the wee hours of the morning. I would never normally go to a place with a name like *BJ's*—my first guess would be it's a gay strip club specializing in glory holes—but I'm pleasantly surprised with our surroundings.

It's huge. Full bar and restaurant, complete with tables, booths, and conference room. The high ceilings and modern décor give the place an aura of sophistication IHOP won't ever achieve. The menus even come with a beer selection guide, to help us navigate the myriad of beverages brewed on-site. Quite nice, actually.

Keon scoots into my side of the booth and keeps close the entire time. At all points, his leg touches mine, or his hand rests on my knee, or he slings an arm across my shoulders. Whenever he can, he nuzzles my neck and runs his teeth along the edge of my ear.

I'm hungry, both for food and his touch, and I revel in Keon's affection. I close my eyes and lean into him, a small piece of me wondering if I'm too desperate for contact. Who needs food? We could go back to my apartment and eat there.

"You two are so cute together," Lala says, breaking me from my pleasant trance.

I straighten my posture. "Shouldn't you finish your salad?"

Lala pokes at lettuce, a coy smile creeping across her face. "You were so adorable and tender when you were in the ring with Keon. I took pictures to show Mom and Dad."

Blood rushes to my face at the thought of my sister photographing intimate moments between me and my significant other. And then showing them to our parents? I swear she makes me feel like a child.

Keon doesn't even acknowledge the conversation. He trails kisses along my neck.

His manhandling treatment the entire evening has been strange—Justin never did such a thing—but it's welcomed. I admire confidence, since I sometimes overdoubt myself into nervousness. Keon knows what he wants, and it's obvious he wants *me*. That kind of recognition dispels my fears.

Derek holds Lala just as close, which lowers my mood a bit. At least he isn't as amorous as Keon. That's my only solace.

Before I can say anything, a group of men enter the restaurant, each wearing a similar blue T-shirt with the name Hideki Dojo written across the back. They cheer and make a ruckus all the way to their table. I count ten in total, and they pat one man on the shoulder several times, some even lifting a glass of water in his honor.

Keon's hot breath reminds me of his proximity.

"Do you want to keep doing this?" I whisper. "I thought you didn't want to do this in front of… fighter people."

"Fuck 'em," he says. "If I can kick Zane's ass, I can kick most of theirs if they try to make a fit. I'm tired of having doubts. They only destroy me."

I must admit, his brazen conviction kills my desire to remain dignified. I run my hand along his inner thigh, ready to celebrate with him in any way he sees fit.

But Keon and Derek both tense at the same time, and I'm put on edge myself. Four guys from the Hideki Dojo walk over to our booth, each one just as ripped and intimidating as the next. Will they do something here? In an upscale restaurant? I thought we were safe among the trappings of wealth, but I guess goons don't have any decency.

"Are you Keon Lynch?" the leader of the small group asks.

Despite the man's athletic physique and numerous bulging muscle groups, his face looks like something I drew with my left hand. Too many blows to the head, no doubt.

Keon turns to the guy. "That's right. What of it?" he asks, curt.

"Whoa, whoa," the man says, both hands open and up. "We came over to congratulate you. That was a sweet bout, my man. You have talent."

Another guy nods. "Really amazing. We thought you had lost, but you pulled it out of the bag. I hope they recorded that, because it's replay material."

The tension in the room fades, and I find myself breathing easy. These guys aren't here to mess with Keon—they're here to bro out and talk about fighting.

The messed-up-face guy smiles. It doesn't do him any favors.

"I've seen you fight a few times," he says. "I thought your winning streak might've been a fluke, but it's clear you got the goods to back up all that attitude. And balls. Who attempts a flying scissor heel hook in the middle of a match? That's impressive. I've got mad respect for you."

"Thanks," Keon says. He gets up out of the booth and offers a hand. One by one he gives them all bro-style half hugs, with a few quick pats. "I've seen you guys around as well. Congrats on winning the welterweight fight."

One of the Hideki Dojo guys rubs at the back of his neck. He, too—like Keon—has a black eye and red nose. They've both cleaned up, but it's clear they've been in an intense fight.

"It was hard fought," the other fighter says. "But worth it."

The man with the gnarly face points to their table. "Why don't you join us? We'd love to hear your thoughts about the fight. And I don't think I've ever heard of your sponsor before. Harvey's Workout Zone? Is that new?"

Lala claps her hands together. "We'd love to!"

Funny how she was silent the entire conversation, but now she's happy to accept their offer on Keon's behalf without a moment's hesitation.

"Sure," Keon says.

He takes my arm and guides me out of the booth seat and straight to his side. Without any subtlety or attempt to hide his actions, Keon kisses me in front of the Hideki Dojo guys. It's not a quick peck. It's a few-second show of affection that ends leaving me dazed. Keon immediately returns his attention to the others, like this was all a test—daring them to react or comment.

For a moment, no one says anything.

"We should probably get a bigger table," the man with the messed-up face says, breaking the silence between us. "Fourteen won't fit without a few more chairs."

The others nod and rearrange the place before the waiters even get here.

And that's it. No snide remarks about Keon's sexuality. No looks of disgust or retraction of their invitation. Even Keon relaxes a bit, satisfied with their response.

I like this Hideki Dojo place.

KEON AND I return to my apartment by three in morning. Stuffed full of food and drunk on the merriment of the evening, I unlock my apartment door and hold it open for Keon.

His injuries still bother me when I get a good look at his face in the light, but I know they're superficial. Black eyes will fade, and a broken nasal septum will heal. There's no reason for me to get fussy. I just like to be fussy sometimes.

Keon doesn't even give me a minute to get settled. He grabs me by the shoulder and pushes me back against the wall, obviously restraining some of his strength as he does so. I meet his serious gaze, and my legs nearly buckle. He reeks of testosterone and lust, and his wounds give him the aura of a battle-hardened warrior.

I never realized how much I was turned on by something like that.

He runs his hands the length of my body, undoing the buttons and pushing things aside until my skin is exposed to the cool air of my apartment. I get goose bumps, both from the chill and the pleasure of his touch.

"Keon—"

"You have thirty seconds to decide where we do this," Keon says, gruff and terse. "After that, you're losing the decision."

It's hard to think when all the blood in my system is centralized on one throbbing location. I gulp down air as Keon presses himself against me, equally as hard and excited. The question takes a few moments to register as I stifle the urge to beg him to take me.

Keon grabs my jaw and forces me to stare at him.

"You're running out of time."

Chapter 19
Sister Troubles

Corbin Friel

I MOTION toward the bedroom. Keon shoves me toward it, never taking his eyes off me. We enter my room, and while I mostly focus on Keon's husky breathing and tanned skin, a small part detects the odd chemical smell I've come to associate with Justin.

My heart stops, and my lust wilts into dread.

Is Justin here?

With an unsteady hand, I flip the light switch and glance around. Keon latches onto my neck, sucking at my skin and sliding his tongue along the furrows of my jugular.

"What is it?" he growls.

"N-nothing."

No one's here. Had Justin come and gone? What's his problem? Why would he do that?

I take a deep breath, the odd cleaning-chemical taint on the edge of my perception. Keon pushes me toward the bed as he rips off his shirt and tosses it to the floor.

"I've changed my mind," I say, hating the idea Justin rolled around on my sheets with his terrible odor. "We should go somewhere else."

"This isn't the time for teasing," Keon says.

He grabs me by the collar and removes my vest and shirt the rest of the way. Then he yanks off my belt with one forceful motion and I swear I'm fully hard afterward. But I can't let go of the doubt and disgust.

Keon goes to shove me onto the mattress, but I grab his biceps—rock hard, always pleasant, and distracting. "Please," I say. "We should do it elsewhere."

"Why?"

"I… haven't cleaned it in a while."

I figure Keon will be disgruntled or irritated. Instead, he cracks half a smile. "I should've known." He guides me toward my bathroom and shoves me in.

"What're we—"

"You want it clean?" he asks with chuckle. "We'll keep it clean."

He turns on the shower and shuts the door. He has a predator aura—if he wasn't into men, I'd think he was going to kill me. All other thoughts disappear as he removes his shorts and kicks them off to the side. I only have a moment to admire how swollen he is before Keon takes my glasses and sets them in the sink.

With the world blurry, I squint to gather the details. Keon must know I have limited vision, because he takes over completely. He removes my slacks and boxers, his hands never touching my aching dick, even though I want nothing else. I'm on the verge of begging for it when he guides me into the shower. A part of me fears slipping and falling, but Keon keeps his strong arm around me the entire time.

The hot water and steam mix with my heated blood, intensifying my need for relief. I don't know what Keon wants, so I wait as he shuts the shower door, confining us to the narrow space, our bodies practically touching at all points. The stream of water across my bare skin—my hypersensitive dick enjoys even the slightest stimulation—almost causes me to moan.

Keon leans down and picks me up by the thighs like we were the stars of an athletic porno. He presses my back against the shower stall and spreads me so I'm exposed to him completely. I wrap my arms around his neck, my whole body trembling.

"Relax," he growls into my ear.

My heart rams against my rib cage, and my dick rubs along his solid abs, both excitement and hesitation colliding in equal amounts through my thoughts.

"I want to do this bareback," he says between heavy breaths.

He waits a second for my acknowledgment. I nod, still in shock that he can hold me up.

"You won't get tired?" I ask. What if he drops me?

Keon laughs and never actually answers.

He releases one of my legs, allowing me to half stand on tiptoes as he licks two of his fingers. He watches me the entire time, his saliva coating his digits like he's blowing them. I can't find my breath. Despite the water's attempt to wash away the impromptu lubricant, Keon reaches his fingers up under me and coats the entrance to my ass with gentle strokes.

Even the soft graze of his fingers has me shivering and close to release.

Keon lifts me up again, both legs well off the ground, and effortlessly lowers me down until the crown of his dick is positioned right where it needs to be. I hold him tight, the water unable to get between us.

Then he allows gravity to do the work for him. The initial entrance hurts—the stretching slightly burns—and I let out a strangled grunt. Keon turns his head and kisses my ear.

"You okay?" he asks.

"Y-yeah," I mutter into the base of his neck. "Just… give me a second…."

With each second I go a little lower, my body adjusting to the presence of Keon. Once he's fully in, I shudder, overwhelmed by the intense sensation of being fully impaled. I don't think Justin's ever taken me as deep. My toes curl, and I dig my fingers into Keon's skin.

"Please," I murmur into his flesh. "Continue."

Through sheer strength alone, he lifts me up and allows me to slide back down. After a few motions of this, I'm gasping for breath, riding the edge of orgasm. He picks up the speed, his teeth clenched and grinding.

I stroke myself, needing the extra sensation, enjoying how the water now spills down the front of me—loving the way my knuckles graze Keon's rock-hard stomach. He groans with each lift and thrust, and I can't stop myself from adding to the lustful chorus.

Right at the peak of my enjoyment, Keon picks up his pace, ramming home as though he can't control himself any longer. That's all it takes—I come with such potency my legs try to straighten themselves, but Keon keeps me pinned. I spasm in his grip, my guttural moan echoing off the bathroom walls. The shower washes away the semen, leaving me clean and prolonging ecstasy with each droplet of water that teases my sensitive body.

Keon slams up into me, rocking me from the tranquility of orgasm. He reaches his climax and empties himself inside of me—an experience I've only had a few times in my life—but I enjoy every second of it.

He grunts and slumps forward for a moment, though he never drops me.

I kiss his neck and shiver.

"Are you okay?" I ask.

"You're tight as fuck in this position," he says through shallow breaths. "We need to do this more often."

Keon exhales and sets me down. Unfortunately, my legs buckle, and I grab hold of his shoulders to keep myself up.

"S-sorry," I say.

"It's fine. I like it when you're weak-kneed."

"I think this has more to do with blood flow."

"Whatever the reason."

He grabs my shampoo bottle and squeezes some into his hand. I rest my forehead against his chest and allow my breathing to return to normal. Keon is so fit and accustomed to physical activity that he's already recovered. His godlike stamina will be hard to keep up with.

Keon runs the shampoo through my hair and lathers me up. I snap my gaze to his and lift an eyebrow.

"What're you doing?"

"Washing your hair," he says. "Pretty obvious, really."

I enjoy the way he massages my scalp, but my indignation won't rest. "Why?"

"You don't have your glasses, right? I figured I'd help you out."

"I'm not blind without my glasses, thank you very much. I shower every morning without someone else's assistance."

"Maybe we should change that."

His flirtatious comment causes my mouth to go dry. The thought of Keon in the shower with me every morning is rather pleasant. Not the washing-my-hair bit, however.

"Don't you think this is foolish?" I ask as I attempt to move away. There's nowhere to go, however, and I end up in the corner, soap all around my head and shoulders.

Keon drags me back into his embrace and continues with his task. "Do you like it?"

I want to deny it, because I feel like a child, but I do enjoy the closeness of it all.

I don't reply, and Keon chuckles.

"I like doing it," he says. "So why try to hide? You don't need to pretend when you're around me."

"You… like this?"

"Yeah. I like touching you. I like the indignant look you give me sometimes. I like it when you get flustered." He grazes his knuckles along the base of my jaw. "I like that you were there for me. And that you said you'd be there no matter the outcome."

I slide my hands up and down his chest, my vision clear enough to see the water run in rivulets down the natural lines of his muscles. I can't find the words to express myself, so I wrap a hand around the back of his neck and pull him close. I slick my hair back, wiping away the soap, and then lock our lips. I respond by melting into him, losing myself in the way his tongue plays across mine.

We break apart, but Keon stays close, his lips grazing mine as he speaks. "Thank you for being there."

I stroke his skin, unsure of what to say. I didn't do it for a favor or recognition. I was there for him because I wanted him to succeed—because I wanted to be there if he was injured. But his tone is so serious and his body tense. What should I say to reassure him that I need no thanks?

I smile, my thoughts dwelling on a single key point I hadn't thought of until now.

"You do still owe me something," I say.

"Anything."

"You never told me the name of your motorcycle."

Keon is quiet for a moment. Then he laughs. He presses his forehead against mine and squeezes me close.

"Really? You want to know my *death machine's* name?"

"That's right. You said if I went for a ride, you would tell me. You never did."

"Ever see the TV show *Knight Rider*?"

I mull over the question. "I heard of it, but I never watched it."

"There's a super intelligent AI car that rolls around with a police officer. Together they bust criminals. My sister and I loved the show as kids. So when I went to the Harley dealership and they showed me a Nightster, I immediately thought of the car from that show."

"What's the car's name?" I ask.

"KITT."

I stifle a laugh. "You named your sleek, manly, killer vehicle *KITT*?"

"You better believe it. KITT was a badass. Any vehicle should be lucky to be named after him."

I wipe water off my face in an attempt to conceal my smile. "Whatever makes you happy, I suppose."

Keon lifts my chin and kisses me again, slow and careful, more tender than he ever has before. I tremble for a second, confused by the emotions that run through my mind. When he ends the kiss, I want to tell him this moment is perfect, but I stay silent. Best not to ruin the mood by being overly sappy.

Keon shuts off the shower. "Come on," he says. "I'm tired. We should hit the sack."

My bed comes back to the forefront of my thoughts. Should I mention Justin? No. Not now. Not in this perfect moment.

"Don't worry," Keon says as he guides me out of the shower. "I sleep on a futon at home. I don't give a shit if your bedding isn't up to snuff. We'll rip off the sheets and sleep on the mattress."

I guess that'll do for tonight. I'm spent, and I need my rest before I can think straight.

And I can't wait to sleep with Keon in my arms. I don't want to think about anything else.

MY PHONE buzzes.

And then it buzzes again. And again. And again.

I open my eyes and stare at the wall of my bedroom. It's a reasonable hour—10:00 a.m. on a Sunday—but I'm pleasantly sore from the waist down and running on far too little sleep. I roll over and snuggle next to Keon's warm body. He breathes evenly, undisturbed by my phone twirling around on the nightstand.

170

Again, it buzzes, demanding to be heard like a newborn with colic.

With a powerful exhale, I roll back over and snatch up the phone to answer it.

"Lala?" I ask. "I'm tired. What is it?"

"Corbin?"

The voice hits me with the shock of a bucket of ice water to the face.

"Mom?"

"Yes," she replies, her voice strained. "I'm sorry to bother you. It's about Lala. Everything is fine, but there was an accident. She's being transferred from the hospital to my clinic as we speak to finish with recovery."

"What happened?" I sit straight up, all grogginess dispelled.

"Apparently she went out jogging with a friend and tripped. She fractured two of her bones."

"Which ones? What type of fractures?"

"Her femur and ulna. Both impacted fractures. She'll be fine."

I take a deep breath and leap off my bed. "I'll be there within the hour."

"I'll speak with you then."

My mother hangs up and so do I. In a mad dash to get out the door, I grab the nearest clothing, even if it's dirty, and throw it on. I don't care. Anything to get technically covered. I grab my glasses last and slap Keon on the back.

He jerks his head to the side and glares. "What's going on?"

He's on his feet before I can say anything, tense and flexing like he might need to beat someone's ass at any given moment.

"I need to go to my mother's clinic," I say. "It's Lala. You can stay here, or you can come with me, but I'm leaving in sixty seconds no matter what you decide."

Keon nods and grabs for clothing as well.

Out jogging with a friend? I bet I know exactly who she was jogging with. She's been Derek's shadow ever since they started dating. I bet he even put her up to the jogging as well. Completely reckless and endangering her for no good reason. I knew Derek would be a bad match for her, but I never suspected he would cause her harm, even if it was indirect.

I'll tell Lala what I think of him now. She can't be with Derek, not if he's going to push her to unsafe activities.

I won't allow it.

Chapter 20
Painful Tidings

Keon Lynch

THERE'S AN anxious energy about Corbin as he drives us to his mother's clinic. He's obviously flustered—he accidentally put my T-shirt on in his haste to get out the door, and the fitted workout shirt looks odd contrasted with the slacks—I just wish I knew what to do in order to calm him down.

He parks and leaps out of the car. He says nothing to me and keeps his gaze down the entire walk. It fuckin' sucks seeing him like this, but I'm not capable of changing reality. All I can do is be there for him like he was for me.

Corbin and I enter his mother's clinic. Unlike before, the lights illuminate the area, revealing vibrant pictures of transfixing landscapes and potted plants with gorgeous flowers. I'm still not comfortable, but I'm no longer on edge walking through the place.

A few staff members nod and wave to Corbin, and through virtue of being with him, I'm allowed in the back area without any fuss. Corbin runs straight to an older woman the moment he lays eyes on her. She has his same jawline and lips—there can be no denying their blood relation.

It must be his mother.

"Where is she?" Corbin asks.

"In the last room on the left," she says.

Corbin doesn't say anything else. He turns and jogs straight back to the room, not even offering me a glance or explanation. I hesitate for a moment, debating on whether I should see Malala at the same time. Perhaps Corbin should have some alone time with her.

My nervous shifting catches Corbin's mother's eye.

"And who are you?" she asks.

I rub at my neck. "Keon Lynch."

Her eyes widen, and a smile sprouts across her face. "Oh. The pro fighter. Lala has told me all about you."

"She has?"

"That's right. But where are my manners? My name is Dr. Susan Friel. A pleasure to meet you."

"Same."

Dr. Friel walks over and looks at me from head to toe. She's shorter than me, almost by a foot, but she holds herself tall and confident. Her once-brunette hair has silvered, but not entirely. The laugh lines on her face give her a pleasant expression, even when she's not trying.

Her smile widens. "So handsome. No wonder Corbin adores you."

Adores, huh? I can't restrain a slight smile of my own.

"I'm sorry we had to meet under such upsetting news," she says. "But I'm grateful I was able to meet you before too long. Corbin is busy, I understand, but we don't talk as much as I'd like."

She reminds me of my mother. I haven't visited her grave in years. Maybe I should do that in the future—after the UFC qualifier.

Dr. Friel points to the hall. "I believe you're friends with Derek, correct? He's waiting in the room down there. The last on the right."

"Not with Malala?"

"He goes back and forth. He's a little agitated, if you ask me. Perhaps you can calm him down?"

"Sure. And it was lovely meeting you. I'll tell Corbin to call more in the future."

"Don't worry. I was dating in med school once myself. If I wasn't studying, I was spending all my time on dates and flirting. I can wait until he's done before I pester him to call."

She reminds me of my mother. So understanding. Or maybe my memories are rose-tinted. It feels like forever since I last saw my mother.

I shake away the thoughts and head for the room Derek is in. It's not like Derek to forsake being supportive and helpful. What does he have to be agitated about? I'm sure Malala would prefer his company while she recovers over being alone. At least I know I would.

Once I enter, Derek turns to me. With his eyebrows knit together, he ambles over, his hands jammed into the pockets of his running shorts. He doesn't look me in the eye.

"What happened?" I ask.

"Nothing."

"The girl has two broken bones. Try again."

"No, I mean it. We were out jogging, perfectly normal, and then we're on this road with a ditch by the side, one out of town, ya know? Maybe a couple miles from her house. She trips and falls, and then she can't get up, and she's in a ton of pain."

"That's it? She tripped?"

"Yeah. I swear it. She told me she has brittle bones, but I didn't think it would be that bad."

"What happened after that?" I ask.

"Whaddaya mean *what happened after that*? I picked her up and ran her back to her house, of course. Neither of us brought a cell phone, and I wasn't going to leave her there."

Derek paces the room, his gaze glued to his feet. I walk over and grab his shoulder.

"Something else is wrong."

He shakes his head. "I didn't realize she was so... fragile."

"I thought you already knew that."

"I did, but... I didn't know the extent. What if I hurt her? It could happen so easily. I don't think I could forgive myself if I did. God, I hated seeing her cry. She's always happy. It killed me."

I can't even begin to imagine how worried I'd be if I were with someone who could break at any minute. And Derek isn't a weak guy. He can snap the bones of normal guys with little effort. Could he go an entire relationship without hurting Malala by accident? That's a pretty big gamble.

"Whose idea was it to go jogging?" I ask.

Derek forces a short exhale. "I go jogging every morning. Last night I stayed at her place, so when I got up, I went to head out. She wanted to go with. She said she normally hits the treadmill at the gym, but maybe there's something safe about a static environment. No rocks to trip on. Anyway, I tried to tell her I would be back shortly, but she's stubborn. I should've insisted we go to the gym, but at the time I didn't think it was worth arguing about."

Damn. Corbin's gonna be pissed when he hears it was Derek's fault they went out jogging. It's not really Derek's fault, though. He didn't give Malala brittle bones—and he was there to carry her back.

I let go of Derek's shoulder and take a step back. "Did the doctors say she'll be okay?"

"Yeah. But that doesn't change the fact I could still accidentally hurt her at every turn. It's been eating at my thoughts, man. All I can think about. I remember hating the kids in school for grabbing her crutches and making her fall. What if I'm that guy?"

"I think it's a little different when it's an accident."

"Outcome is the same, though. She's still hurt and crying."

I don't know what to say. I guess he's right. There will always be a chance he could hurt her. No getting around it. But what will he do about it? What *can* he do about it?

Derek resumes his pacing. I keep my mouth shut. Maybe it's best if he and Malala handle this.

Corbin Friel

I RUB Lala's uninjured arm as I sit next to her bed. Her long black hair is free of her standard ponytail, though tucked behind her ears, keeping her face clear and revealing her bright smile. Sometimes I wonder if it's a front. She always smiles in hospitals. Even when we were younger— even when she was severely injured—always a smile on her face.

"The fractures aren't bad," she says in a singsong voice. "All I need is a splint for the leg and a cast for the arm. I should be back to normal in a few months." She holds up her casted arm and gives it a gentle pat.

"That's good," I mutter.

"It was a deep irrigation ditch. Good thing Derek was with me."

"Did he help you out?"

"Oh yes. He carried me all the way back to my house. He ran too. I hated crying in front of him, and every time I thought about it, I got frustrated and cried more. Do you know how that goes? It's a terrible, infinite circle that just results in more crying." She laughs. "But having him close really made it better."

"I'm glad you're all right."

"Mom said I could leave later tonight."

"I'll be by every day to help you out."

Lala waves away my comment. "I'm sure I can get by. Mom also offered me the spare bedroom in her house. And Derek can always help me."

Feh. Derek. What was his role in this, anyway? I should speak to him. I'm *going* to speak to him. While my sister adjusts the pillows on her bed, I stand.

"I'll be right back."

"Okay."

I exit her room, march straight across the hall, and enter Derek's makeshift waiting room. Keon perks up at the sight of me, but he doesn't say anything. I stop in front of Derek, and he crosses his arms, a picture of uncomfortable.

"Did you encourage her to go jogging out by a bunch of irrigation ditches?" I ask.

Derek shrugs. "She went out because of me, yeah."

"What's your problem? She can't do things other people can. You have to keep that in mind when you're with her. Do you understand? Or should I say it slower? She has a bone condition that requires special care."

"Yeah. Yeah, you're right. She told me, and I should've listened."

"And yet you still went out?"

"Yeah."

"Unbelievable. You have all the common sense of a potato. My sister will have a cast and splint for months because of you!"

Derek only nods.

"So what're you going to do about this?" I ask.

"I'm gonna tell her it's over."

His response takes me by surprise. Even Keon lifts an eyebrow, but again, he says nothing.

My chest tightens, and my first thoughts are to yell at him. Derek wants to break up with Lala? What an asshole. Lala is ten times better than he is. He should feel lucky to be in her presence! Then again, this is exactly what I wanted. I even came here to encourage him to leave her— funny how I flipped a one-eighty the moment he suggests doing it.

But I shake my head. This is for the best.

"Good," I say. "I think she should date someone a little more her speed as well."

"I never want to be the one that causes her any pain."

"There's no chance of it now."

"I'm, uh… gonna go talk to her, then. Sorry about everything. I didn't think it would turn out like this."

Without another word, Derek leaves the room.

Keon stares at me, an unreadable expression etched across his face. I turn away, bothered by my own response to Derek's suggestion. He wants to leave? He didn't even fight to stay with her? He didn't make an excuse for his behavior, or say it was a fluke? Anything? Lala isn't *that* fragile. She can have a normal life and can do lots of physical activity thanks to modern medicine. Derek doesn't need to be afraid of hurting her.

Here I am again, trying to argue for them to stay together. Which is silly, because I hate Derek.

So why do I need to keep reminding myself of that fact?

"Do you think they should be together?" I ask.

Keon walks over to me and rubs my shoulders. "I don't know. I want to stay out of this as much as possible. It doesn't seem like my place to tell anyone what they should be doing."

"Lala isn't a porcelain doll."

"Seems like she is."

"W-well, not really! She's delicate. There's nothing wrong with that."

"Why didn't you say that to Derek?"

"Because…."

I don't know. I keep saying he's not worthy of my sister, but they were always happy together. Even now, when his jogging is what caused her fall, she's content and exuberant about life. Maybe I should've told him to stay.

"I'm going to speak to my sister, and then we can leave," I say.

Keon nods. "All right."

I scratch the odd T-shirt I'm wearing as I fall into an abyss of doubt.

But it'll be all right. Lala is always happy. She'll get over this soon enough.

The whole clinic seems to hold its breath as I enter the hall. Derek exits my sister's room and then heads for the front door, never offering me a goodbye. He must have succeeded in delivering his terrible news. I hope Lala took it all right.

When I walk in, I see she's no longer smiling. She stares at her lap, her fingers curled into the thin blanket, her hair taken out of her ponytail and obscuring her face.

"Lala?" I ask as I reach her side. "How are you feeling?"

"Corbin.... Derek left me."

I take a seat on the edge of her bed. She turns away from me. I rub her shoulder. Nothing. Her still silence is unnerving. When is she ever like this? It's not like Derek was her one true soulmate or something. She'll get over him.

"Forget about him," I say. "You have to admit he was slow on the uptake. People like him are the reason we have directions on shampoo bottles, for goodness' sake."

She turns back to me, silent tears streaming down her cheeks, marring her appearance with a sadness I've never seen from her before. I scoot close, until my shoulder is against hers, and I wrap an arm around her back.

"Lala, it'll be okay. He's not worth crying over."

"You don't understand," she whispers, her voice strained. "This always happens."

"What does? Losing a boyfriend? You've barely dated anyone, and you're still young. You'll find somebody."

"No."

"What do you mean *no*?"

"I've been on hundreds of dates, Corbin." She wipes at her face, her lower lip trembling. "I... I never told you about them because... because they never lasted more than a few days. Every time I tell the guy I've... I've got this brittle bone disease, they get disgusted or s-scared, and then they leave."

I hold my breath, my chest tightening into a terrible knot.

Her tears continue to flow, no matter how many times she wipes them away.

"I thought Derek would be different," Lala says. "He already knew. He saw me in elementary school. And now he's gone too. I… I'll never find anyone, Corbin. Why would anyone be with me when they could have a perfectly normal girl, huh? I bet Derek wants… wants an athletic girl who can keep up with him and… and I'm not that. I'll never be that. I'm just… pathetic."

Lala buries her face in her free hand and strangles back her sobs, but it doesn't work. When I rub her back again, she jerks away from me.

"Leave me alone," she snaps.

She shakes as she hunches over and drowns her face in the blankets. Her hair spills onto the bed like inky waterfalls, covering everything and blocking my view. She doesn't get up or attempt to speak, not even when I slide off the bed and head for the door.

With each step I hear her sobbing become more intense, and the pain in my chest intensifies.

Keon Lynch

CORBIN ISN'T the same.

Sure, he meets me at the gym, spends time with me in the morning and evening, and we bunk up on most weekends, either at my place or his. But he's not the same. He rarely speaks, and he doesn't laugh.

I stroke his hair as I wonder what I should be doing. It's almost dawn, but I can't sleep, so I hold him close and enjoy the way he takes in breath. Sometimes he talks during his sleep. I like listening because it's always entertaining. One night he tried to order a sandwich. He must have been half awake, because when I told him I wasn't a Subway, he got upset and demanded his sandwich or else he'd call the sandwich police.

Dreams can be insane sometimes.

Thinking about that gets me smiling. Life really is different with someone to cuddle. Derek and Lala don't have that anymore. They must be hurting. Everyone can feel it from here to the moon.

Derek has been the worst of all. He doesn't answer my calls and hasn't been around his gym lately. I got a text from him that read: *sorry, I can't make your next fight.* That was weeks ago. My last fight before the qualifier is steadily approaching, and my only corner man can't be there. I'll need to find someone else.

And while Corbin is great emotional support—and medical support—he doesn't know enough about fighting to really help me in the cage.

I grab my phone off Corbin's nightstand and scroll through the texts. A couple days ago, I got a message from the Hideki Dojo guys. They wanted to know if I would switch sponsorships. They want me in their program, and they're willing to waive the monthly price to be a member. It's a sweet deal, but I worry. I can't abandon Harvey, not after he's given me so much. If I can continue to advertise his gym, I'll join the Hideki guys, but if I can't….

At least with the Hideki Dojo I would have several people in my corner. And I would have a sparring partner. And a crew.

Again, I tighten my grip on Corbin.

I enjoyed having Corbin, Derek, and Malala as my fight-night crew. Their presence at the last fight made the difference, I'm sure of it. But now Malala and Derek won't be attending, and Corbin needs the emotional support more than I do.

But I don't have time to wait around for everyone to get their shit together. The MMA fights won't wait.

Maybe I should join the Hideki Dojo, no matter if I can continue to promote Harvey's gym or not. I'll call them in the morning.

Chapter 21
Unpaid Debts

Corbin Friel

THE HIDEKI Dojo has the casual atmosphere of a close-knit group. Keon and I stand at the edge of the room, observing the members go through their routines. They have a karate class, weight lifting, jiujitsu training, judo instruction, and a whole wall dedicated to belts, trophies, and ribbons. I'd be impressed if most of them weren't from children's divisions.

The abundance of kids leads me to believe this is more of a family establishment rather than a dojo strictly to train up MMA fighters.

The man with the beefcake body and messed-up face—whose name is Elei—points to one of the training mats. Four men roll around, caught up in their sparring.

"We don't have many guys interested in MMA right now," Elei says. "But the guys we do have are really serious about the sport. They train six out of seven days, and we're hoping to make a name for ourselves."

Keon nods along with the words, his eyes glued to the people sparring.

I shift my weight from one foot to the other. This place seems wholesome. Much better than Harvey's Workout Zone. I doubt Keon will have any problems here. If someone walked in looking for trouble, they'd likely be sent to the hospital in an ambulance for their efforts.

"I like this place," I say.

Keon nods. "Yeah."

Elei clasps his hands together. "I'm glad to hear it. If we have more fighters like you in our team, I'm sure we'll become one of the best dojos in the Sacramento area. We're always looking to grow."

So Keon gets a free ride in exchange for publicity. They can claim he's one of their fighters, implying he got his skills through their dojo, when in reality they just scooped him up before everyone else came to their senses and realized Keon is talented. And if Keon really does make it to the UFC level, this place will become moderately famous, no doubt.

"Why don't you train here until your next fight?" Elei asks. "We want to make sure you're happy with our little fighting family before you make any permanent decisions."

"I appreciate that," Keon says.

He throws down his bag and heads for the people sparring. I hang back a moment, taking note of the karate session—wondering whether or not I should join something similar—before heading in Keon's direction. Elei grabs my shoulder and stops me in my tracks.

"Hey," he says. "It's great you're super supportive of Keon's career."

"Oh. Yes." He keeps his hand on my shoulder, and I lift an eyebrow.

"You don't look like the type of guy who works out. Or trains for fighting."

"That's because I don't."

"Maybe it'd be best if you wait for Keon in the lobby or came back when he's done."

I grit my teeth, ready to argue, but Elei holds up his other hand.

"Hey, hey," he says. "We ask the girlfriends of all the other fighters to do the same thing. It's just a… significant-other policy. So they don't get distracted."

"But I'm his manager."

"And his significant other?"

"Well, of course."

"Still a distraction."

That's preposterous. Keon never gets distracted when he's training. He's focused and determined, and it's not like I'm going to grope him between sit-ups or something. But when I pan my gaze around the room a second time, I realize Elei's right—everyone here is either an instructor or actively training. The parents, and other random people, wait in the lobby.

Damn.

"All right," I say. "Tell Keon to text me if he needs a ride." I suppose he could always take the bus or an Uber or something.

"Sounds good. On Friday nights we like to end our training with a little BBQ in the back. You're more than welcome to join us."

"Thank you."

I hope Keon doesn't mind that I'm going to leave. I'm sure Elei will tell him why.

THE LONG walk up the stairs to my apartment seems lonelier than usual.

I shouldn't be upset by this turn of events. It's easier to study for my tests in my apartment rather than at Harvey's Workout Zone. I'll have all my books, and I can listen to online lectures, which aren't practical options when I'm sitting on some workout equipment.

But I still enjoyed doing it. Even if Keon and I were engaged in separate activities, the proximity made the entire thing infinitely better. And we could occasionally talk, or I could ask him questions about MMA. I can't really do that now.

And every moment I spent with Keon helped me avoid thinking about my sister. I can't think of a good solution for her problems. It frustrates me beyond reason.

I reach my apartment door, lost in my thoughts. That changes the moment I insert my key and find the handle unlocked. A chill settles over my body.

Justin.

All feeling is quickly replaced with righteous anger. Why is he still entering my apartment without my permission? Doesn't he know I have a ton going on in my life? School, my sister, Keon, a jam-packed schedule—I don't have time to waste on unnecessary drama.

This is the final straw. I open the door, intent on yelling at him and sending him packing, when I'm greeted by an unusual sight.

Justin waves to me from my couch. Another man sits next to him—a weaselly guy with jet-black hair and eyes so far apart I swear they're trying to escape his face. Tattoos mark him in a few distinct spots. His neck, in front of the ear, his forearm. Each faded and hard to decipher. His ratty jeans, scuffed-up tank top, and heavy jacket aren't adding to his sophistication either.

I'm about to ask about him, when a third guy shuts my apartment door behind me.

My mouth goes dry the moment I get a good look at him.

He's like Keon—muscled and tall—but he has the same kind of faded tattoos of the man on the couch, along with a myriad of faded scars across his skin. And he's so close. I jump away, shaken. He locks my door. The click of the deadbolt ices my veins. All anger I had before evaporates into dread. What's going on?

"Hey, Bin-Bin," Justin says. "I was wondering when you'd get back home."

His casual tone does nothing to ease the tension.

I turn to face him. "Justin. I… didn't think you'd be here. And with company."

"Oh yikes. Where are my manners? This here,"—he motions to the weasel on the couch—"is Frankie. And you should know my other friend. He's a pro fighter."

I don't even bother looking at the goon hovering around behind me, his breath practically washing over my hair. "I don't know all the pro fighters, Justin."

"His name is Alfonz Moreno. He's got a long record. How many wins does Alfonz have, Frankie?"

"Are we counting prison?" Frankie asks, his voice just as oily as his pockmarked face.

"Sure. A win is a win, right?"

"That's a good sixty-three wins, then. Alfonz knows how to hurt a guy."

I straighten my glasses with an unsteady hand, unnerved by each new fact that settles into my thoughts. "Justin… can I speak to you in private?"

"Of course."

He slides off the couch and motions to my bedroom door. We walk in together—the eyes of the other two following us the entire way—and he shuts the door the moment he's in.

Up close, Justin doesn't look right. His wan complexion has a slight sheen of sweat, and the bags under his eyes have deepened since last we spoke. His clothes are nothing like his usual easygoing wardrobe. He has cargo pants and a dark hoodie, each garment reeking of chemicals more than the last.

"What're you doing here?" I demand.

"Shh," Justin says as he steps up close to me.

I move away until my heels hit the wall. Justin posts an arm on the wall by my shoulder and hovers a few inches in front of me. His breath has a foul taint, and his pupils are dilated more than they should be.

"Justin," I whisper. "I'm really worried about you. Who are those guys? What're you doing here? You're freaking me out."

"You don't give a shit about me, Bin-Bin. Don't even pretend."

Justin brushes my hair with the knuckles of his spare hand. I don't move or react to his touch.

"I do care about you. Tell me, are you... on drugs?" That's the only explanation for half of these symptoms.

Justin strokes my hair again. "If you care about me, why'd you leave me?"

"We weren't right for each other."

"But some asshole fighter is right for you?"

"You don't know him," I say. *He's everything you're not.*

"If you really cared about me, you'd be with me."

Justin leans forward for a kiss, but I turn away, holding back a gag. Should I fight him? My skin crawls, and my chest tightens with anxiety. If we fight, the other two will get involved. I should try to convince Justin to see reason.

With a sigh, Justin steps away, like he can hear my inner disgust.

"Look," he says. "I came by because I have a way to pay you back all that money I owe you. We got a nice deal that'll make everyone involved some extra Benjamins."

"K-keep it. I don't want any part of this."

"You haven't even heard the plan. It's brilliant."

"I don't care. You broke into my place, and you brought... people here... and I want you out. Please. If you need to talk, I'm willing to talk. But I don't want to be a part of some money-making scheme."

Justin hooks his thumbs in the belt loops of his jeans. "Of course you don't want any money. You're some spoiled rich kid with parents who take care of you. But us *trash people* need some dough every now and again. I owe a lot of people money, Corbin. Not just you."

"Aren't you working?"

"Yeah. I'm working. Every day."

The way he says it—slow and laced with deception—tells me it's not the job I thought.

"What're you doing, Justin?"

"It's none of your business, really."

Oh Jesus Christ. If he's on drugs, and he's seeing guys like *Frankie* and *Alfonz*, there's a good chance he's not doing anything reputable. But why? Justin was never like this. Sure, he had no drive or ambition, but he never wanted to hurt anyone.

No wonder I never saw his uniform or even heard of his schedule. I can't believe how blind I've been. Only heinous drugs like meth would cause someone to sweat Windex from every pore.

"You need help," I say. "Real help. Professionals. Maybe the police."

"Fuck off, Corbin. I have this under control." He steps up close to me, more aggressive than I've ever seen him. "You're gonna help me with my money problem, not give me a bunch of Saturday-morning cartoon advice, got it? I have a bookie who's taking bets on the next fight in San Diego. And guess who I see on the fight card? It's your Grindr whore and my good buddy Alfonz."

Oh no. I can't even breathe. I already know where this is going.

"Guess who's favored to win?" Justin asks. His lip curls up into a smirk. "Grindr Whore has a better professional record, and he's been on a winning streak. Completely favored to win. That means, if he loses, everyone who bet against him will make fat stacks of cash. I'm talkin' a good thirty grand, maybe a little more, if we can get a few more people in on it."

Again, I say nothing.

Justin snaps his fingers. "All you need to do is make sure Keon loses. Pretty simple, right? It only takes one measly fight."

"Don't be insane," I whisper. "I can't stop Keon from winning."

"Sure you can. I've seen all your little notes about health and fitness scattered around the apartment. You made that douchebag a whole list of foods he should be taking. I'm sure you could slip something into his diet the day of the fight, couldn't you? Something that'll interfere with his concentration. You're a smart guy in med school—you know all the right chems to throw into someone's food to get them doubling over in pain."

"I'm never going to do that, Justin." I put my hand in my pocket and curl my fingers around my cell phone. "You're sick."

Justin posts his arm back on the wall and his face in close to mine. "I think you'll do it."

I don't like cursing, so I hold back a *fuck you*, but my expression only gets Justin smiling wider.

"Think about it," he whispers. "Because if you don't help me out, you might find three or four guys waiting for you after class. Or by your apartment. Or in the gym. And they're gonna take thirty grand out of your skin."

Three or four guys? At the gym? I grind my teeth together, holding back my urge to yell.

It was Justin who sent the thugs after Keon—the four guys who jumped him in the gym. Why? Did he hate Keon for taking me away? It had nothing to do with Keon, but I guess meth messes with a person's brain too. Justin isn't thinking straight. He's not himself at all—he's a stranger I've never met wearing the skin of Justin and parading around like a wannabe gangster.

"I'm not going to do it," I state. "Ever. I don't care what you—"

"Shh," Justin hisses.

He places two fingers over my lips. I jerk my head away, never wanting to taste any part of him ever again.

"It's not just you they'll visit," he says. "Lala is a frail girl. You need to really think about her safety… especially now that she doesn't have her own personal bodyguard hanging around her at every hour of the day."

I snap my gaze to his, my heart stopping in the middle of a beat. "You wouldn't."

"No, no, no. I like Lala. I'd never lay a finger on her. My friends, on the other hand…. They'll be mad if they don't get their money. And since I told them you and your sister were gonna help me, they're going to blame you if this doesn't work out."

My vision darkens for a second as my thoughts wrap around the terrible reality of the situation. A group of lowlifes will harm me and my sister if Keon wins his fight. What can do I do about this? Who should I go to?

Justin must read my expression like a book because he replies with a laugh. "You're so cute when you're flustered. What're you thinking about? How you're gonna stop me? You don't even know who my friends are, Bin-Bin. If you try to get me arrested, you'll still find my buddies waiting for you in dark corner one day. And I saw Lala's cast photos on her Facebook. If that's what happened to her falling into a ditch, I can only imagine what getting roughed up would look like."

"Who are you?" I ask, breathless. "The Justin I know would never do this. Never."

He meets my gaze with a glare. "What the fuck do you know? Like I said, you don't give a fuck about me, so don't try to act like you know what I would, or wouldn't, do. I have my own goddamn problems now. Besides, don't we have more of a history than you and the Grindr whore? This should be an easy decision. Losing once isn't the end of the world. And Keon doesn't even need to know. Slip him something in secret, and everyone wins."

God, I hate every second Justin's so close to me. Each word he utters is like oil in my ears, oozing through my thoughts and sending shivers down my spine. He's disgusting—but he's right. I don't know how I would prevent me or my sister from getting hurt. I wouldn't even know where to begin.

So am I trapped? I *have* to harm Keon?

No. There must be another way. Keon wants this with all his being. If I sabotage his goal now, I could never forgive myself, even if Keon never found out. Then again, I'd also never forgive myself if Lala got hurt because I was too stupid to see the warning signs about Justin.

"You get it, right?" Justin asks. "You don't have a choice."

I bite my tongue.

He continues, "I figured you and Keon would've been over by now, but I guess you can't get enough of his dick. Does he plow your scrawny ass every night? Oh, better yet, tell me which one of us gives better head?"

I sneer. "Classy."

"What? I'm just curious." He kisses my clenched jaw with a slow and deliberate motion. "Hey, I'll give you a couple thousand once this is all over. You know. For old time's sake." He kisses me again, but I can't lean any farther away than I already am. "And I'll throw in a few more thousand if you get on your knees right now and remind me why I loved staying over so much."

I shove him away, my body shaking. Each breath I take fuels a fire that's been building since we entered this room.

"What the hell is your problem?" I growl.

Justin brushes off his hoodie and walks back over to me. "I'm trying to be nice." He grabs my shirt collar and yanks me forward. I stumble, and then he trips me. I hit the floor between my mattress and the wall. Before I can stand, Justin slams his knee into my lower back, pinning me to the floor.

I stifle a grunt and grip the carpet, shocked by the pinpoint of pain.

"Don't make this difficult," he says as he runs a hand down my side.

"Please," I mutter into the carpet. "Not like this."

For a moment, Justin doesn't move. Then he stands, releasing me from the floor. I get up to my feet, rubbing my lower back, thankful he has a shred of decency still remaining in his drugged-up body. But he returns to my side and fingers my vest buttons.

"I hate that you're with him," Justin says. "I really do. And the more I think about it, the more I think we should have fun like we used to."

Well, one thing's still the same—he's persistent. I doubt he'll let this go now that he has it in his mind.

"If we do this quick," I say, "will you leave afterward?"

"What? No cuddling?" He chuckles at his own joke. "Of course I'll leave, Bin-Bin. Whatever you want."

"Then… let's get this over with."

Justin smiles. He takes a seat on the edge of my bed, and I walk around to the other side. He rips off his hoodie and throws it to the floor, leaving on his simple white T-shirt. But the moment I get directly behind him, I lunge and get an arm around his neck. Before he can break free, I place my other arm on the back of his neck and lock them together— trapping Justin in a rear naked choke.

Although I'm not the strongest man alive, the choke cuts off blood flow with even a simple amount of force. I focus all my efforts into keeping my hold, even when Justin digs his dirty nails into the skin of my arms and claws at the flesh. But he isn't that strong either. He can't break free.

After a few seconds, his efforts wane. Right before he passes out, Justin kicks the wall with all his might, the bang of his heel echoing throughout my apartment. Half a second later and the bedroom door flies open. Alfonz rips me off of Justin and slams me into the wall, his strength undeniable.

I block my face and glasses with my arms, but he grabs the collar of my shirt and jerks me close.

"Stop," Justin says between ragged coughs. "It's fine. I'm fine. Everything's under control."

Frankie ambles in and frowns. "Did you get what we needed? The kid's on board?"

Alfonz shakes me hard enough to rattle my teeth. "You're gonna go along with the deal, right?"

He has the same pungent Windex odor as Justin. And his breath could cause the dead to retch.

"I understand what you want," I say, my voice strained. "Now get out of my apartment."

Both Frankie and Alfonz turn to Justin.

"Let's go," Justin says. "Corbin knows what he needs to do, and he's gonna do it if he knows what's best for him."

Alfonz releases my shirt, and I stumble away, my breathing shallow. He gives me a sidelong glare before heading out of the room with Frankie and Justin in tow, leaving me alone with my predicament. I wait until I hear the front door to my apartment close before I lean against the wall and fall down into a sitting position.

How did this happen? It's my fault for getting involved with Justin like this—I should've moved on fully or seen the warning signs earlier or anything else than go along with his downward spiral. And now look what I've done. He's threatening me, my sister, and Keon. And he's right. Even if I go to the police, it won't stop anything. It'll only guarantee someone gets hurt.

What am I going to do?

Chapter 22
Plans

Keon Lynch

A SOFT knock on the front door wakes me. I've always been a light sleeper, ever since my first tour of Afghanistan. The thought I could be shot at any moment never left me.

I glance at the clock. 0200. Who would be knocking on my door at a time like this? It better be a good fucking reason because I'm not in the mood to dick around with randos when I have to get to work in a few hours.

I pull on a pair of boxers and walk to the door, unconcerned with modesty since my guest is unconcerned with manners. The moment I open it up, I catch my breath.

"Corbin?"

He stands in the dark hallway, his head hung. He rubs at his arms and shifts his weight from one foot to the other. "May I come in?"

I stand aside and motion to the apartment. "Yeah. Help yourself to anything you need."

Corbin shuffles in and takes a seat on my futon.

"What's wrong?" I ask as I shut the door and lock it.

He doesn't answer.

I sit next to him. The long sleeves of his shirt are dotted with the black spots of dried blood.

"What happened?" I ask.

"I've had a rough night."

"Let me see."

Corbin holds out his arm. I pull back the shirt and recognize the injury straight away. Nail gouges. Those sting like a bitch, but they heal fast. Unfortunately they leave scars more than any other small wound. Not sure why.

But why does he have nail gouges in his arm?

"Who did this?" I ask, anger poisoning my blood.

"It was m-me," Corbin mutters. "It was an accident. I, uh, fell down the stairs at my apartment and accidentally scratched myself."

"How?"

"I wasn't paying attention. Grabbed my arm instead of the railing."

The knowledge calms me a bit, but it's too late to save me from going into fight-mode. I sigh, and it takes some of the anger with it.

What does Corbin always insist I do when I have minor scrapes?

"You need some antibiotic ointment," I say.

Corbin glances over to me, his glasses low on his nose. He has a hopeful look, better than the melancholy mask he wore a second before.

I stand, grab some Neosporin and bandages, and return to Corbin's side. He watches me smear the ointment across the injuries, his face flushed. Once the wounds are slathered, I cover everything with the bandages.

"Not very often the doctor gets to be the patient, right?" I ask.

"You have a surprisingly gentle touch."

"I can be rough, if you'd rather."

Corbin cracks a smile. But it's gone in the next moment, like happy emotions are as difficult to hold as water.

"Something's wrong," I say. "Why keep it from me? It's not like you to play cryptic."

"Keon, may I stay here with you for a few weeks? I... don't want to stay at my apartment anymore."

"Why? Do you have PTSD from that stair fall?"

He doesn't answer. He doesn't even respond to my joke. Obviously something has gotten to him, but I can't do anything about it if he never tells me. And I hate the way he keeps his gaze downcast. I don't like it when he doesn't look at me. It's like he's hiding from me by staring at the floor.

"Of course you can stay here," I say.

"Thank you." Corbin exhales, but none of his tension leaves him.

Maybe I should try to put him at ease with some simple conversation.

"You missed out on the BBQ," I say. "The Hideki guys really know how to cook. If I don't watch myself, I'll never make weight."

"What did they make?"

"Teriyaki chicken. Beef kabobs. Some corn on the cob. Salad. Good shit."

"Hm."

Then he returns to his state of silence.

Tsk. Corbin's really testing my patience. Why won't he just tell me? We've been through a lot together already. I thought he wouldn't hesitate to unload his problems, but here he is, soaking in them like his own personal marinade. I get it—sometimes people want to wallow—but this is taking it to a whole new level.

"Is this about Malala?" I ask.

"Y-yes," Corbin says. "It is. That's exactly what this is."

"What about it?"

"I'm worried about her."

"Worrying doesn't change the outcome. It just makes you feel bad in the meantime," I say. "That's what my mother used to say. You can't sit here and tell me you don't have any ideas on how to make your situation better."

"I feel like I'm trapped," Corbin mutters. "Like there are no good solutions."

Trapped? Sure, Corbin can't fix his sister's illness, but saying he's *trapped* is a little dramatic for the situation. But Corbin has always been a little melodramatic. The way he reacted to my motorcycle told me that much.

"Why don't you sleep on it?" I ask. "We can talk about it tomorrow once your classes are over."

He nods along to my suggestion and stands. To my surprise, it doesn't look like he brought anything with him. No bag of clothes or a toothbrush or comb. He's going to regret that. I don't have anything spare except for clothes, but they aren't the kind Corbin gravitates toward.

I lead Corbin to my tiny bedroom and open the door.

Corbin's never actually seen my room. We've slept on my futon a number of times, or I've gone to his place, but he's never entered my room. And for good reason. I have a box spring on the floor, no bed frame, with a mattress on top. Piled in the corners are my clothes. One corner for clean, the other for dirty. My good clothes are in the closet, but otherwise I'm quite casual about how I keep my space.

Corbin glances around, his gaze homing in on the disheveled bed and waterfall of wrinkled socks pouring off my dirty pile.

"Sorry about this," I say as I gather up the clothes and shove them into a basket. "I'll keep it cleaner if you're gonna stick around."

"It's fine."

"You say that, but I know you're cringing internally."

Again, Corbin cracks half a smile. "You know me too well."

"Anyone with two functioning eyes can see you like things crisp and clean." I tap his vest with the back of my hand in an attempt to emphasize my point, but my attention is drawn to the straggly nature of his clothes.

He fell down the stairs? The more I think about it, the more I think it's bullshit, but what else could've happened? Most of his neighbors are old folks who keep to themselves, not an angry mugger looking to take Corbin's wallet. And Corbin isn't the kind of guy to get into a random fight.

But he's determined not to tell me, apparently.

"The sheets are clean," I say, motioning to the bed. "And I purchased the mattress when I moved here, so it isn't bad."

"Uh-huh."

I strip off my boxers and crawl onto my bed. Corbin takes his time undressing, making sure to fold his clothes before setting them on the floor. He takes his glasses off last and leaves his boxers on before shutting off the light and getting onto the bed next to me. He never sleeps in his boxers.

"Too disgusted with my bed to sleep naked?" I ask, half sardonic, half apologetic.

"No, it's not that. I just… want to sleep like this."

A strained silence comes between us.

I pull him close, his tense muscles hard to miss. I graze his arm with the pads of my fingers, curious about his thoughts. Corbin rests his head in the crook of my armpit, his breathing shallow.

Is he planning on leaving me? His cold mannerisms and unwillingness to speak make me think that's the case. But then why would he ask to stay for a few weeks? I don't want to lose him, but maybe he's done with this and would rather focus on his career and schooling. Maybe I should talk about my hopeful plans for the future—the plans I fantasize about if everything goes the way I want.

Maybe then he'll see I'm serious about making a life and a living beyond these few fights.

"Do you know how much money guys make in the UFC?" I ask.

Corbin shakes his head.

"The lowest-ranked guys make a good forty to fifty thousand per fight. And if they win that fight, they get a bonus, sometimes five or ten thousand extra. Not only that, but they can win the *fight of the night* bonus, which can be another fifty grand on top of that."

"I had no idea," Corbin says.

"I'm not even done. The fighters get major commercial sponsors. Have you seen the shorts of those UFC fighters? They have all sorts of advertisements on the sides. Each of those ads pays the fighter per fight. And since the UFC works on a pay-per-view model, most fighters also get a percentage of the revenue on the sales."

Corbin says nothing.

"The highest-paid fighters get millions a year," I say. "And the big-name people can demand half a million per fight just to show up. With that kind of money, all sorts of possibilities are open."

"What do you mean?"

"Well, I can't fight forever. Maybe a few years in the UFC, if I'm lucky. If that happens, I'll be able to make enough to pay for Alisha's school, and then open up a small business of my own. I was thinking a gym or a fight academy. Maybe even a motorcycle dealership."

"Eh," Corbin says with a grunt.

"The point is—my plan is to make it enough so I don't have to struggle. After that I can train other fighters and be a coach."

"Why haven't you told me this before?"

I snuggle close to him and stare into the darkness. "It wasn't as close as it is now. I have one more fight, and then I'll be in the qualifier."

"Isn't that another fight before you have a UFC contract?"

"Yeah, but I can't even imagine losing that. In my mind, it's just this one last fight before I make it so close to my dream I'll be able to grab on and never let go."

Corbin has a set future as a doctor. Everyone knows it's just a matter of time before he has his own clinic, making a steady living, living out his telos. I hope he understands my goals aren't shortsighted or small. And I can have a fight academy anywhere he has a clinic—we don't need to separate because of our goals. They can work together. Hell, maybe I can even pay for two people to go to med school.

I'd like that.

And if Corbin helps even one person who has gone through a car accident—someone with a shredded liver who needs a transplant—it'll be like I somehow helped a family avoid the tragedy mine went through.

But Corbin doesn't respond. If anything, he's tenser than before and shifts around in my arms like he's agitated. What's wrong? I thought he'd enjoy hearing this.

Maybe I should speak to his sister. She knows him better than I do.

I ENTER my apartment a few minutes after noon. Today I got through all my clients in record time. I laid down a few cockroach traps, checked a hotel for bedbugs, and assessed a restaurant's problem with pigeons. Not bad—and now I'll have a little extra time to work out and train.

I throw off my uniform cap and unfasten the buttons of my shirt when a knock at the door interrupts my routine. A light, almost hesitant knock. I open the door and lift an eyebrow.

"Hello, Keon," Malala says with music in her voice.

She waves with her good arm and smiles wide enough to brighten any dark corner.

I glance around. Corbin is nowhere to be seen.

"What're you doing here?" I ask.

Malala strokes the sling that holds her casted arm. "Oh, well, Derek gave me your address a while back. I hope you don't mind me visiting?"

"I don't mind," I say as I step aside to allow her in. "But I don't understand why."

"I need to talk to you."

Ironic. While a piece of me wanted to talk to Malala, I figured it could wait until the weekend, not a random Thursday afternoon.

She walks in with a limp, and while I know she's wearing a splint on a leg, I can't see it under her flowing dress-like pants. She stops in the middle of my kitchen-living-room combo and gives my home a quick once-over.

"Wow," Malala says. "So… cozy."

"You don't have to lie," I quip.

"Oh. Good. Because it's totally a bachelor pad. And not in the good way. More in a sad, depressing way, really."

"I'm aware."

"Bin-Bin must hate it."

"He's been polite enough not to comment."

Malala covers her mouth with two fingers, but it doesn't hide her smile. "Sorry about that. I couldn't resist."

"How did you know I would get off work at this time?"

"I didn't. I've come by three times already. I figured you would eventually be home, and here you are! With enough persistence, any plan will work."

That's a unique way to look at things.

Malala takes a seat on my futon, and I know she's going to be here awhile. I fiddle with my uniform shirt and opt to button it back up. I guess I'm going to be here for a while longer.

"So," Malala begins, her word drawn out. Then she stops.

I wait.

She looks away from me and stares at the cold television. "Uh, I want to talk to Derek."

"Okay."

"But I want to talk to him in person. I didn't really say anything the last time we spoke. In my mom's clinic. I wasn't myself, and I didn't get to tell him how I felt."

A piece of me wonders why Malala is telling me this. Wouldn't Corbin be a better option? Not that I'm going to tell her to leave.

"I wrote out a few prepared speeches," she says as she rummages through her pockets and withdraws at least ten sheets of paper. She straightens them out on her lap and stares down at them. "I want to say just the right thing, and I was hoping you'd read these before I see Derek."

"Me?" I balk. "Why me?" This isn't up my alley.

"You're Derek's friend, right? I want to know if you think these will help or if I should say something else."

"What're you trying to do? Get him back?"

Malala exhales, straightens her posture, and turns to me with steadfast resolve. "I'm not going to let my medical problems take anything more away from me. Maybe I can't play all the crazy sports or be super athletic, but I can still have a life and friends and a family all my own. Derek said he didn't want to hurt me, so he left, but leaving me hurt more than any of this stupid falling business. I want him to know that I'm the one that'll make decisions about what I feel safe enough to do, and that he doesn't hold any responsibility for my injuries if I sometimes make a mistake."

She stops for a second, but I don't say anything.

Malala continues, "He doesn't have to be with me... I don't want to force him. But he shouldn't pretend I don't exist! He won't even return my phone calls. Is he that afraid? I have to set us straight." She returns her gaze to the television and mutters, "And if I change his mind about us being a couple, that's okay too."

"You're not mad at him for leaving you?"

"Of course I'm mad! But I can understand too. He was really upset, and I should've explained things better."

"Why not talk about this with Corbin? He's been upset ever since that incident."

"Corbin has helped me a lot. I want to prove to him I can handle my problems. On my own."

Malala glances over at me, and I lift an eyebrow.

She offers a nervous chuckle. "Well, and with a little bit of your help."

"Speaking of Corbin," I say. "He's been weirder than normal lately."

"Yeah?"

"How should I deal with that?"

"Has he told you what's wrong?"

"No. He's been as cold as a corpse and twice as silent."

Malala rolls her eyes. "Yeah, Bin-Bin can get that way. You just need to keep asking. He has a bad habit of giving in if he's pestered too much. I think he doesn't like confrontation. Or maybe he wants to be like his dad. His dad is super nice to everybody. But Bin-Bin is a little… uh… too sarcastic to be totally like his dad."

I don't want to break the man to get him to talk to me. I want to help him deal with whatever problems he has. He's been there for me in more ways than one—I'd love to show him that I can be there for him too. But he has to give me that chance.

Malala pushes her papers over on the futon and smiles up at me. "So, you'll help me, right?"

"As long as you realize I'm not very good at this."

"That's okay. I just want you to say things like *looks good, Lala*, and *I'm totally moved and awestruck by your fantastic writing, Lala.* Boosts my confidence, so then I won't worry."

I laugh. Whatever floats her boat.

"Oh," she says. "And don't tell Corbin, okay? I'll tell him after I've spoken to Derek."

"When are you going to speak with Derek?"

"Probably after your next fight. That's in a month, right?"

"Yeah."

"Good! It's a plan."

I sit down on the futon and scoop up the papers.

Yeah, I guess we have a plan.

Chapter 23
Trust

Keon Lynch

I'M SO fucking sore. Not even a warm bath took the ache of the exercise. But I can't slouch. I've only got a few weeks before the fight.

Corbin rests back on my chest while we watch *Die Hard*. The futon has limited space, so we're so close we might as well be one person. I like the smell of him, and each breath he takes is a soothing reminder I'm not alone. He takes my hand and laces his fingers through mine, a simple gesture my thoughts linger on, content to feel the warmth of his touch.

"*Die Hard* is based on a novel," I say between high-powered action scenes. "It's called *Nothing Lasts Forever*."

"Did you read it?"

"No. I just know it."

"Hm."

"I also know that Bruce Willis wore rubber feet shoes during the scenes where he runs across glass. You can see how freakishly huge his feet are if you pause the movie."

Corbin tilts his head back to look at me. "Why do you know so much about *Die Hard*?"

"I had a crush on Bruce Willis when I was younger," I say, almost embarrassed to admit it. Then again, he's hot as fuck in that movie. Who didn't have a crush on him?

"He is very capable."

"And confident. I love confidence." More than the muscles or the action. I probably would've loved the villain just as much if he hadn't been so evil. The villains always reminded me of my father, and then I never could look at them the same way.

"That's probably why I joined the military," I say aloud, more to myself than to Corbin, lost in my own musings. "I had fantasies of kicking bad-guy ass and walking away like a badass. It was never quite like Bruce Willis, but I guess I had a few moments in Afghanistan."

"Tell me about one."

"I was on patrol when a car bomb went off in a nearby vehicle. There was a kid inside. Age four or three. He was still alive and crying for help. I managed to pry open a door with the barrel of my rifle and pull the kid out before the heat got too bad."

I technically still have some burn scars on my elbow, but no one ever seems to notice. The kid got rushed to the hospital, and afterward the family came to see me. The relief and happiness that their child was okay has stuck with me to this day.

Die Hard continues on my tiny screen, but I'm not even paying attention anymore.

"Doctors save people," Corbin whispers. "It's not as dramatic or badass, but the intellectual pursuit of defeating an enemy like cancer has always intrigued me. But I never had a crush on any movie doctor. I always had my mother and father as role models."

I mute the TV.

"You must have had a celebrity crush," I say. I nibble his ear and he shudders. "Who was it? Were you one of those guys secretly in love with boy bands?"

"N-not any of that!" His face burns up, even the edge of his nibbled ear. "It was Will Smith. Happy? When I was younger, I saw him in *Independence Day* and I've followed his movies ever since."

"Any movie he's ever naked in?" I ask in a playful tone.

Corbin huffs. "That's just—I mean, I wouldn't keep track of that. No one would."

"Bruce Willis is full-frontal nude in *Color of Night*."

Corbin sits up and rubs the bridge of his nose under his glasses. "How can you shamelessly admit you watched a movie for the sole purpose of seeing an actor naked? It doesn't seem sleazy to you?"

"Hey. He filmed it and put it out there. I happily watched. I don't see where the crime is."

"S-still."

"C'mon. I know you've done the same thing."

Corbin stands and mutters something under his breath all the way to the kitchen. After a few more huffs, he says, "Will Smith has a gay scene in *Six Degrees of Separation*. But I didn't watch the movie for that sole reason, thank you very much. It just… happened. And I must admit, I hadn't come to terms with my sexuality at the time, and it made me feel flustered, and… well, it's a short scene. But I watched it a few times."

"What's *a few*?"

"More than I care to admit."

I chuckle. His reluctance to admit his secret crush is adorable. And I might have to watch *Six Degrees of Separation*. I've never even heard of it, but imagining a younger Corbin awaken to his sexual urges while watching it puts the movie at the top of my list.

Corbin fiddles with something in the kitchen, but I'm too sore to crane my head back and see. "What're you doing?" I ask.

"Making something to eat. Would you like anything?"

"Can you make me a protein shake?"

"Yes."

"That's all I need."

Corbin stops. With the TV muted, the whole apartment is eerily silent. Is he not moving? I wait for a moment, wondering what he's up to, but I don't ask. He's been off—even now, even when he was in my arms.

"Keon," he says.

"Yeah?"

"What if I told you that I have medicine to keep your leg from getting infected in the future?"

"I'd say that sounds awesome."

I run my hand down my calf. No matter how hard I squeeze, there's no pain. There hasn't been any pain for weeks, actually. I'm still taking antibiotics, but only for a few last days. Corbin really helped me out. I don't think I would've caught the problem without him—and maybe I would have done irreparable harm to body.

"If I brought you some pills… would you take them as I instructed?"

"Yeah," I say as I stretch out on the futon.

"You wouldn't demand to know the contents of the pills? Or do any research about the side effects?"

"If you say I need them, and they aren't banned by the fight commission, I'll take whatever you want me to take."

What an odd series of questions. I've trusted him this far, and he's never let me down. He even helped with my food and fight schedule. At this point I might swallow nails if Corbin said they would make the difference in my fighting performance.

I have no reason to doubt, and he's such a smart guy—whatever he thinks is best, is best.

Corbin Friel

I RUN a shaky hand through my hair and stare down at the protein powder and pills.

Justin was right. This would be easy. Keon doesn't even bother getting off the futon to see what I'm doing. He says he'll take anything I give him, without investigation or suspicion. That kind of faith in my abilities rocks me to my core. He trusts me. And here I am, contemplating his downfall.

I turn the pills over on the counter. They contain acetaminophen—an oral medication used to treat pain and fevers. A small dose, like the stuff found in Tylenol, isn't bad. But the amount I have….

It'll cause nausea, vomiting, and abdominal pain. And it won't hit all at once. It takes time. Seven hours. Twenty-four hours. The liver processes it at a slow rate. Acetaminophen also destroys the liver if taken too frequently, which can lead to its own host of problems.

I could crush up this pill and pour it into Keon's protein shake. The symptoms would cause him to lose any fight he's in. There's no doubt in my mind.

My chest twists into knots. Each beat of my heart sends waves of agony through my system. The thought of hurting him—especially when he relies on me—burns my lungs and makes it hard to breathe.

I push the pills into the trash and press my forehead against the wall.

Doctors don't hurt people. They don't betray their patient's trust. And Keon….

Keon is different. Special. I… care for him more than I think is healthy for this point in the relationship. He makes me feel safe. It's why I ran to him after I picked myself off the floor of my bedroom. I never should have left his side. This wouldn't have happened if I had been with him.

"You okay?" Keon asks.

I step away from the wall and wipe my sweaty palms off on my slacks. "Y-yes."

"You're quieter than usual."

"Sorry. I'll strive to make more noise."

Keon chuckles and says, "Just strive to make us some food, all right?"

"Right."

What am I going to do? No matter how many times I ask myself, I don't know. We're so close to Keon's fight, and I'm running out of time. Maybe I should tell Lala to get out of town. Maybe we should just both move out of California.

Is that a reasonable response? No. Of course not. And my mother would never condone Lala getting too far away from home without a good reason. And what will I tell her? That my ex became a drug addict lunatic that's threatening my life over some money? They'll all end up getting hurt, and it's my fault.

So what else is there to do?

Keon Lynch

TWO DAYS until my fight.

I've tried looking up information about my opponent, Alfonz Moreno, but I can't find a damn thing. That's not true. I found some criminal records, nothing that would prevent him fighting, though, and his official MMA profile has him marked as a "jiujitsu artist," but that doesn't help me. Most guys record their fights and keep them on the internet—even I do it. You can watch your old fights and see where you need improvement, and sponsors typically want to see a clean record of fights before backing a fighter.

So why wouldn't Alfonz have any of his available? His record says he has six wins and five losses. Eleven fights. Not even his opponents uploaded them?

I lace up my shoes while Corbin packs my gym bag and his school bag. All morning he's been lost in a melancholy daze. I'm losing him, somehow. Each day he keeps his secret from me is another day he grows distant.

"Hey," I say. "How about we take my bike to the gym?"

"Sure," Corbin says.

No fuss. No protest. He doesn't even balk.

Something is terribly wrong.

I grab my bag, and he grabs his. Tonight he didn't have lecture, so we have a few hours extra. I'm not going to do any hard training, not with the fight looming around the corner. I can't risk getting injured. If a doctor says I'm unable to fight, that'll be the end of it.

Corbin and I leave my apartment and head for the parking lot. No conversation. I saddle up my motorcycle, and we both strap on helmets. Corbin sits behind me and grabs on for dear life before I even start the engine. At least he's not so depressed he's forgotten this part.

I take off onto the road, and the evening winds wrap their cold embrace around my entire body. Corbin shivers with all the force of a washing machine the moment we hit thirty miles an hour. We probably should've worn thicker clothes. Corbin has his normal attire, and I have a T-shirt and sweatshirt. Not the best combo, but it'll be fine.

A few miles from the apartment and Corbin's teeth chatter enough that I swear I can hear them over the sound of the engine. I pull over and park on the side of the road. When I remove my helmet, Corbin does the same.

"Wh-what's g-going on?" he asks between ragged breaths. "We sh-should get there as s-soon as possible."

Corbin Friel

KEON REMOVES his sweatshirt. Confused and uncertain of what's going on, I rub my arms and wait. He steps close, throws his sweatshirt over my head, and then tugs it into place. I slide my arms through the sleeves and straighten my glasses.

"W-won't you get cold?" I ask.

Keon runs his hand along the edge of my jaw and tilts my head up. He kisses me, his lips warm and his breath hot. The experience dispels the cold more than the sweatshirt.

For a moment, all my worries fall away. Why does Keon do this to me?

"I'll be fine," Keon says. "Put your helmet back on."

I comply with his demand, my insides raging between guilt and adoration, and wait until he's situated back on the motorcycle before latching on to him. His sweatshirt smells like him. I enjoy the scent—probably a little too much—as he pulls back onto the road and heads off toward our destination.

His skin sprouts goose bumps from the chill, but Keon never devolves into shivering like I did. Although I hate removing my arms from his waist, I wrap my arms around his shoulders and shield his biceps from the wind as much as possible.

It doesn't take long for us to reach our destination. To my surprise, it's Harvey's Workout Zone and not the Hideki Dojo.

"What're we doing here?" I ask as I rip off my helmet.

Keon runs a hand through his disheveled mohawk. "I've decided I want to stay here." He gets off the bike and stretches.

"I thought you liked the Hideki guys?"

"I do. But Harvey was by my side the entire time. I can't stand leaving him at the end. Besides, I hate their rule about you sitting in the lobby. I'd rather work out here and have you available between sessions than chat with the Hideki Dojo guys."

"But...."

Me? I swear he's killing me with kindness.

I haven't even been good company lately. I know it. A small part of me hoped Keon would get disgusted with my lack of communication and demand I leave. The guilt of being with him—of not telling him about Justin—gnaws at my soul. Every second I stay with him is tantamount to me taking advantage of his kindness. He should leave me, and I should turn myself in to Justin and his thugs in the hope they're satisfied with just breaking my bones and not Lala's.

It's taken me a while to come to this conclusion, but that's what I should do.

"Tell me what you're thinking," Keon commands.

I straighten my posture and stare up at him from the motorcycle seat. He rarely takes such an aggressive tone, and it unnerves me for a second.

"What?" I ask, half lost in the moment.

"I see the look on your face. And the way you hold yourself. What's going on? Tell me. Right here, right now."

"I...."

"Corbin, I've been nice. I've had patience. But no more bullshit."

Should I tell him? The moment I mention Justin, I'm sure he'll want to end this anyway. But he has the hard-set expression of someone who'll die before they leave without answers.

"It's about Justin," I say, my mouth dry. "I've made a terrible mistake."

Chapter 24
Second Meeting

Keon Lynch

I GRIT my teeth and hold my breath as I wait for Corbin to elaborate.

"I loaned him money," Corbin quickly adds. "And he kept coming by my house to talk about it. His behavior continued to worsen. He would be cheery, then distant, then confrontational, and he smelled of chemicals. I should've seen the warning signs, but I never thought to consider Justin would use harmful drugs like methamphetamines."

I cross my arms, attempting to rein in my growing rage. I close my eyes and take in slow inhales.

Corbin continues, "The last time I saw him, he brought a few of his *friends* along. They... they threatened to hurt me and my sister unless...."

Unless? *Unless*? I open my eyes and glare at the man, but Corbin stares at the ground, his voice distant.

"Unless I made you lose your next fight. Justin wants to bet on your opponent, Alfonz Moreno. Alfonz was at my apartment as well. Justin says he'll make thousands of dollars if you lose."

He takes in a ragged breath.

My body has all the warmth of a glacier—anger has numbed the last of my feeling.

Corbin removes his glasses. "I... gave serious thought to it, Keon. I'm so sorry. I d-didn't do it, though. But the fact I even played out the scenario in my head haunts me. But if I don't do it, he's going to have his friends hurt my family. Justin says they're all betting against you, and they want the money."

Corbin covers half his face with his hand. "I don't know what to do."

I step closer to him, and he flinches back, trembling. His shoulders bunch around his neck and he looks away from me, shielding his face.

Reminds me of my sister. After I beat my father, she did the same thing. She was afraid. Afraid I would hurt her.

But she's one of the few people in this world I'd never consider hurting. Just like Corbin.

"Don't," I say. "I'd never hurt you."

Corbin crosses his arms tight over his chest and still refuses to meet my gaze. "I thought, and rightly so, you'd be upset. I might deserve a punch or two, to be honest."

Never. I said I'd kick his ass if he cheated on me, but this is a completely different situation. I'm more upset that he didn't come to me straight away—he should've said something the moment a fuckstick like Justin threatened his well-being. And what kind of low-level thug would threaten Malala? She's not even involved and just a low blow to hurt Corbin further.

"Where is Justin?" I ask.

"I... don't know."

"Call him."

Corbin snaps his attention to me, his eyes wide. "What? Why? He has ruffian allies, and associates with the worst of the worst. What if I call him and he mistakes this as an invitation to see me again? I've been trying to avoid him this entire time. That's why I've stayed at your apartment."

"Good. Call him, and find out where he is."

"Wh-what're you planning? You can't go see him. Even if the police arrest him, his friends who lose money on your fight will still come after me."

"You said you didn't know what to do," I say, my volume increasing with each word. "But I do. Fucking call him, and I'll handle this situation."

Corbin hesitates for a long moment and turns his gaze to the parking lot. With each breath he calms himself until he finally pulls his cell phone out of his pocket and clicks on Justin's number.

The tense silence allows me to hear the other side of the conversation with perfect clarity. It rings twice before Justin picks up.

"Why are you calling me, Corbin?" Justin asks. "Nothing has changed."

After a forced swallow, Corbin says, "Where are you?"

"Why?"

"I want to see you. So we can talk about this."

"There's nothing to discuss."

"No… I want to talk about us."

Hearing Corbin say those words has me gritting my teeth.

"I tried to fuck you one last time before I left," Justin says with a laugh. "But you weren't very cooperative. It's too late to come begging for it now."

The cold sting of adrenaline sluices through my veins, tensing me beyond normal. Corbin doesn't look at me. That's fine. I don't blame him for Justin's lust. There's only one person to blame for all this.

"Please," Corbin says. "We've been through a lot together. Just one more chat."

"Fine," he says with a sigh. "I'll text you the address of the place I'm staying. As long as you promise I'll get to use that mouth of yours at the end of our little chat."

What a fucking scumbag. I'm seconds away from ripping the phone out of Corbin's hand and speaking to this animal myself, but I hold back. Corbin stares up at me through his eyelashes, not looking full on, a questioning look about him.

I reply with a curt nod.

Anything to get this guy to reveal his location.

"Sure," Corbin whispers.

"Good. Come around at ten tonight, got it? I have work to do before then."

"Sure. I'll see you then."

Corbin Friel

KEON HASN'T said much all day. Not while working out. Not while we drive. Not during dinner. Not even now, at 9:53 p.m., while we head to see Justin.

He's so cold and precise, like a razor-edged knife. I keep expecting him to yell or punch me or be upset with the situation. He never does. If anything, he gets irritated if I flinch or shy away from his touch. I'm surprised, since I consider this situation to be my fault. But Keon doesn't seem to think so.

We pull up to a quiet motel on the edge of Stockton. The patter of rain plays a chorus of gentle sounds throughout my otherwise silent car. I park in one of the crookedly marked spaces and turn off the engine. The overcast sky makes seeing the stars an impossibility.

The frigid darkness doesn't help my nerves.

Keon reaches for the passenger door handle. "What room is he in?"

"Room thirteen," I say.

"Wait here."

"But—" I grab his arm. "He'll probably have someone with him. What if Alfonz is there? Or what if there are ten other guys?"

"What of it?"

Keon's speech is just as cold as his demeanor. He can't allow anger to cloud his judgment. The consequences could be dire. If anyone should face that, it should be me.

"What if you get hurt?" I ask. "Those guys who jumped you in the gym were Justin's friends. Your fight is two days away, and your injuries won't be hidden like an infection in the leg. You might be forced to forfeit. It's not worth it."

"I told you. I'll handle this."

I rip open my glove box and withdraw my Taser. "Take this."

"I don't need it."

"I'd rather you have it as an option. Please."

After a short exhale, Keon takes the weapon. I release his arm, uncertain of what he plans to do. Will he talk to Justin and convince him to stop? I hope Keon doesn't try to fight a group of thugs. If he gets injured, I won't be able to live with myself.

Keon opens the passenger door and exits out into the rain.

The downpour has gotten stronger.

Keon Lynch

THE RAIN helps soothe the burning rage that lingers just below my skin—like a shark beneath the surface of the water, waiting for its chance to strike.

I place Corbin's Taser on top of his car, careful for him not to see the action. It's nice of him to think of me, but I don't want to walk into the meeting with a weapon in hand or one obviously in my pocket. I'll be civilized, like Corbin wants. I'll try talking first.

But this isn't going to end pretty, I already know. Even the weather wore black for this meeting.

Room thirteen has two sad brass numbers dangling from bent nails. The entire motel needs remodeling, but since there doesn't seem to be even a hint of a security guard around, I doubt they have the money. Or maybe this place doesn't want any attention. It looks like the type of place that wants to dwell in the shadow of society.

I knock on the door.

"It's open," someone shouts, an edge of anger in his voice.

I step in, soaked with the cold rain but hot from the slow burning anger smoldering in my gut. I shut the door behind me with a soft click.

It's a two-bed room with sheets that have seen better days and a TV straight from the '70s. Justin sits on one bed, and two guys sit on the other. Alfonz. And some other guy with an oily chin and far-set eyes—thin and not heavy on the muscle, but he could always have a handgun tucked away in his oversized jacket.

There are some lessons I'll never forget from the military. People hide firearms in all sorts of places.

Justin leaps off the end of the bed and sneers, his whole attitude and posture different than what I remember during our first meeting. He stomps over to me and stops a few feet away.

"I knew Corbin would do something stupid like this. Let me guess. He told you about me and wants you to take care of it?"

Alfonz stands and moves over to the front door, blocking the only exit. He cracks his knuckles, but I ignore the gesture.

"He told me everything," I say, almost surprised with how clear and calm my voice sounds, considering my turbulent insides.

"Heh." Justin shrugs and waves away the comment. "I had a backup plan just in case. How about we just give you a cut of the money to take the fall? How does ten thousand sound? I bet it's more than you make in a couple months. It's a pretty sweet paycheck for a single night's work."

3

3

3

I meet Justin's gaze, so he knows I'm serious. "I have a plan. How about you leave me and Corbin alone, and in return, I'll allow you to walk out of this motel with all your insides intact? I bet a guy like you doesn't have any medical insurance. It's a pretty sweet deal when you think of it like that."

Justin chuckles. "Oh, I don't think you want this to get serious, Grindr Whore. We're not gonna play by no regulation rules. We're gonna fuck you up, and then we'll keep fucking you up until you run away with your tail between your legs."

He glares at me, but his hands shake. Then he slams a palm into my shoulder and I take a step back from the blow. "You won't even know when the next beating will come, that's how much of a hell your life will become, cockbag."

Alfonz and the other guy are practically on the balls of their feet, coiled and ready.

I knew Justin wouldn't take the smart way out. Now we have to deal with this.

The battering of the rain against the window rings throughout the room.

Justin takes in a deep breath. I brush off my shirt.

"You remind me of my father," I say.

"So what, asshole? I'm not here for your daddy issues."

Alfonz steps toward me—I can hear it in the creak of the floor and notice the way Justin's eyes dart toward the movement. I spin around and strike Alfonz in the jaw with my elbow. He stumbles back, and my arm hurts from the hard strike to bone, but there's no holding back now.

"Frankie," Justin shouts. "Help him out!"

The creepster with the far-set eyes pulls out a switchblade. I breathe easier knowing he didn't come with a handgun, but my nerves crank back to ten when Frankie tosses the blade over to Alfonz. A weapon extends his potential reach.

Alfonz lunges. I jump back and hit the wall—the room is tiny and cluttered. When Alfonz slashes, I lean to the side and dodge. He holds the knife like he knows what he's doing and slashes a second time with an overhead blow.

I punch Alfonz straight in the lowest rib. Unlike the upper ribs, it isn't connected to anything—it just floats in front of the organs. A hard blow jabs it back, makes it easy to break. Alfonz doubles over and stumbles away.

Frankie grabs a lamp from the corner and throws it at me. I dodge underneath it, and it smashes into the wall, sending porcelain shards raining into the carpet.

Alfonz, recovering faster than I expected, kicks me in my shin. I half trip and almost fall onto the bed, but I correct myself. And nothing hurts. Corbin's medication really did fix the problem. And unlike in the gym, where the pain crippled me, I'm ready to go.

The sweet focus of fighting grips my mind, and I'm ready to tear everyone here apart.

I leap over the bed and corner Frankie. He's stunned—no doubt he thought I wasn't that fast, or I wasn't going to pick him—and I punch him across the face with a right hook, and then a left. His brow splits open, cascading blood down his eye as he sails to the ground, unconscious.

He had a glass jaw to go with his ugly face.

Alfonz leaps at me from the mattress. He wraps an arm around my neck, but I don't even bother blocking. Instead, I use his momentum and spin around to slam him into the wall. Then I elbow the same rib I punched, and he screams.

He slashes with his knife and catches my arm, slicing my skin from the elbow to the wrist. But he left his arm open in his attempt to reach me. I grab his hand and fall backward, taking him to the floor armfirst. Then I crank back and overextend the arm opposite the way it should normally bend.

Alfonz screams again as I torque the arm and break the bones—a textbook armbar. He must have dropped his blade in the panic of the situation, because he frantically yanks at his own mangled arm to wrestle it from my grip. I kick him in the side of the head and then jump to my feet.

Before Alfonz can get up, I deliver a twelve-to-six elbow—a powerful strike down, where the tip of my elbow hits the top of his fragile skull. It's illegal in MMA matches, and there's a reason. Alfonz takes the strike and spasms, rattled to his core but not unconscious. In his daze, I kick him in the face and render him helpless.

I stand up straight and inhale, enjoying the burst of energy from a clean breath.

Justin backs away, shaking so bad he might fall. I walk over to him, careful to step over Frankie's body. Justin pulls his own knife—some two-inch nonsense people use to open boxes.

I punch him square in the face, breaking his nose with a full-powered jab. He hits the floor and scrambles backward like a pathetic crab. I grab his leg and yank him back. He blubbers something—about letting him go or some shit—and I pick him up by the collar of his sweater and slam him into the wall.

Then I pin him there, my forearm across his neck.

"Y-you've made a b-big mistake," he stammers, blood getting in the way of his speech as it gushes from his twisted nose. "Even if you c-call the police, I s-still have friends who will g-go after you."

"I'm not going to call the cops," I say, cool and collected, despite my twitchy urge to continue punching Justin.

"B-but—"

"I don't need the police to protect me from you. *You* need police protection from *me*."

The statement drains the color from Justin's face. Or maybe it's his broken nose. Either way.

"Listen," I say, my volume getting lower and my tone shifting into a growl. "You're going to leave Corbin and his family alone. If you don't, I'm going to hunt you down as many times as it takes until the lesson sticks in your mind. And I'm not going to wait for the proof. If any of them get hurt—if even one of them so much as gets a goddamn paper cut—I'm going to assume you had a part to play in it and act accordingly."

Justin breathes through his mouth, blood mixing with the spittle at the edge of his lips.

I slam him against the wall a second time, and he yipes.

"Do you understand?" I ask.

"Y-yes," Justin says.

"I don't think you do."

Justin shakes his head and holds on to my arm. "I d-do. I swear. I'm not gonna do anything."

"Your friends better not do anything either."

"They won't."

I lift my forearm from Justin's throat and rotate my shoulder. "Good. Because, let's be honest, if we ever meet again, you're going to regret it. So don't bother talking to Corbin or visiting him at odd hours. I'll know about it."

"Okay."

Justin wipes at the blood on his face, his whole body trembling.

I turn and walk away, stepping over Frankie a second time to get to the front door.

Chapter 25
Amor Amplexu

Corbin Friel

THE STORM reflects my inner thoughts.

I shouldn't have waited in the car. I should've gone with him. What if something terrible happens? What if Justin threatens Keon? What if—

The passenger side door opens, and I jump in my seat, my heart beating out of control. Keon sits next to me and buckles himself in. His relaxed posture and easy breathing help me calm down, but my blood pressure rises once I spot the slash on his left forearm.

I reach over with an unsteady hand. "Oh God.... What happened?"

Keon holds out his arm to show me the cut. It's shallow, and the bleeding has washed away with the rivulets of rainwater. He should still disinfect it and cover the injury, but it's nothing terrible.

"We had a talk," Keon says. "And Justin understands he should leave you alone."

"And... what did he say?"

"He said that was a good idea."

I wait, with bated breath, but Keon doesn't elaborate. I place a hand on his knee. "Did he attack you? Were there other guys there?"

"Let's put it this way: I handled the situation. Justin won't be coming around anymore. And if he does, let me know, okay?"

"Okay."

Why bother arguing? Keon doesn't look like he's in the mood to recount the terrible story. I hope he's right. I hope Justin leaves me alone, and I really hope Lala doesn't get hurt because of my life's drama.

I start up the car, my pulse still quick. I drive out of the parking lot, but a bang on the trunk of my car startles me.

"What was that?" I ask, staring at the rearview mirror and seeing nothing.

Keon chuckles. "Your Taser. One sec. I'll get it."

I PARK the car at Keon's apartment.

The clouds hang low and heavy with water, but at least it isn't raining anymore. I doubt it'll last, considering this is California, and I'm thankful for that. I want this dreary part of my life to be over with, and the weather isn't helping much.

Keon walks with me in silence, all the way to the front door of his apartment. Is he upset? He still hasn't reprimanded me for the poor way I handled Justin. Maybe he needs to cool down from his fight to really unwind. Then he'll let me have it.

We step inside, and I realize I have no patience. Even as I grab the gauze and the antibiotic ointment, all I can dwell on is his silence. I wrap his sliced arm as quickly as possible before placing the medical supplies back on the counter.

"Are you upset with me?" I ask.

"Yeah," Keon replies.

His casual response stops me cold. I knew it.

"I apologize," I say.

Keon turns to face me, and I meet his dark gaze with a lifted eyebrow. He seems calmer than before. More at peace than he has been for a while.

"There's nothing to apologize for," he says. "Just don't let it happen again."

"I'm sure Justin won't be a problem if you handled the situation."

"I'm not talking about Justin. I mean—don't hide stuff like this from me ever again. I was worried about you. Worried sick for weeks. Every time I asked, you said you were fine, but it was a lie. Don't do it. Ever."

"Well—"

"There's only one correct answer, Corbin. Tell me you'll come to me with your problems. If we're a couple—if we're a team—I want to know about them. Always."

There's something tender about his tone that wasn't there before. I take a moment to mull over his words before I nod. "All right. I'll come to you when I have a problem."

"And I think we should get a place together."

"All right."

Now it's Keon's turn to hesitate. He stares into my eyes, searching for something I hope he finds.

"Really?" he asks. "Just like that?"

"I've never approved of this place, and I'm a fair distance from my school. But when you stay with me, you're a fair distance from your work and gym. Besides, my parents would be elated to hear I've found a roommate to cut down on costs."

"I'll pay for it."

"You have your sister to think about."

"That's true but—"

"Then let me worry about this, okay?"

Keon takes a moment to mull it over. I swallow hard, my mouth filling with the taste of cotton and twice as dry.

"Okay," he finally says.

Keon closes the distance between us and embraces me. I'm caught a little off guard, but I return the gesture, thankful to have this gap between us closed. I figured I would lose him over this, but now that it's over, I can't even imagine going a day without him in my life.

He kisses my neck and then my jaw and then my lips. Slow. Not rushed or lustful. He slides his tongue over mine, and I worship his mouth, my legs weak from the intimate contact. Keon's hands know right where to go to get me panting—his fingers at the edge of my pants, one hand running the length of my thigh. I'm hard, and my pants are entirely too tight.

Normally we mess around on his futon, but Keon takes me back to his room and shuts the door before stripping. I do the same—though it takes more effort for my clothes—and Keon waits at the edge of his bed. Once I fully remove my slacks, Keon takes my shoulders and pulls me into him.

I love the rock-hard sturdiness of his body and the way he breathes across my skin.

Keon sucks on my neck, caressing me with his tongue. I moan, probably too loud for the stage of our contact, but I can't help it. The relief of the evening has unshackled pent-up desires. I want to do this. I want to know, for sure, it's okay between us. Keon asked to live with me, sure, but his touch is what I want—what will tell me if we're going to make it.

We get onto the bed, and Keon lies underneath me, his physique a work of art. I run my hands over his muscled frame and back myself up until the cleft of my ass slides against his hard dick. He's leaking, and the bodily fluids slick up my skin, making the process easier.

Keon reaches over and pulls out a bottle of lubricant from one of his gym bags. He smears a handful over his palm before reaching down and prepping me and his dick. The way he stares at me while he does it—it's intense enough that I shudder.

I want to speak, but I can't. His gaze pierces me to my core, and I couldn't force out the words, even if I wanted to. I don't think he's ever looked at me this way before. I don't think *anyone* has ever looked at me this way before.

He reaches for my glasses, but I turn away. I'd rather see him and enjoy the sight than protect my eyewear.

Keon grabs my hips and guides me back. He doesn't force me on him or thrust hard into me. Instead, he allows me to dictate the pace, only stroking my thigh as though to encourage me. When he manages to enter past the ring of muscle, I moan again, just as loud as before, and Keon throws his head back.

"God," he mutters. "You're so fucking amazing."

I brace myself on his chest, my arms posted, sweat dripping off me and onto his abs. I shudder as I continue to sink onto him. Every inch becomes easier than the last, like my body is eager to take it all in. Once flush up against him, I lean forward and back, the piston motions drowning out all thought with pure pleasure. The mattress squeaks as Keon finally loses his self-control and bucks to meet my hips with each rock.

Keon stares up at me, and my heart stutters. Again, his gaze is something I've never seen before. He reaches up and pulls my head down.

Our lips connect, and his muffled moan mixes with the physical pleasure of his penetration, rubbing me at just the right spot.

Keon breathes heavy and hard and refuses to let me go. He was slow at first, but now he picks up his pace and growls into my ear with each pleasurable thrust.

I close my eyes, lost in the sensations. The moment Keon wraps his hand around my dick, I catch my breath and whimper something pleading, but I don't even know what I said. He pumps me in time with my movements, and I'm on the verge of collapsing atop him, my arms and legs weak.

"I love you," Keon says.

My heart stops, and my thoughts come back enough for me to comprehend the statement.

"I love you too," I mutter through shallow breaths.

The sensations build—not just my love for the man beneath me, but the physical reaction to the touch of his body. His eyes, the way he stares at me, it's enough to push me over the edge. I groan and coat his stomach with my semen, and Keon holds me close as he swells and does the same, releasing inside of me.

Gulping down air, I slide off of him and onto the mattress while my heart rate steadies. Keon rolls onto his side and lies with me, his own recovery a simple process.

Sticky and soiled. That's how I feel until I get another good look at Keon. Then I can't breathe, and I don't want to go anywhere else.

"I meant it," he says with the calm clarity that comes after an orgasm.

"So did I."

Every beat of my heart heats my already sweltering body. I want to go again, so we can have that intimate moment—and the closeness—that only comes with sex, but the body isn't always willing.

Keon strokes my hair with his knuckles. "I need you there for my fight."

"I already said I would be there."

"All my fights. From now until I retire. I'd be distracted if I didn't have you close."

I smile. I can't help it. Knowing he wants me wipes away all doubt.

"I'll be there for you. Always."

Keon Lynch

DAY OF the fight.

Last one before I can enter the UFC qualifier.

Alfonz *was* my opponent, but he dropped out yesterday. Of course he did. I broke his arm—no way he's in any condition to fight. And Justin lucked out. All previous bets will be off now that Alfonz isn't participating. Of course, it could have been bad for me if a new opponent wasn't found. Luckily, someone stepped up.

Hong Gil Dong.

I've never heard of the guy, and I don't have any time for research, so this is going to be a blind fight. It worries me, because he could know all about my fighting style and take advantage of that, but I can't do anything about it. I just have to be better than he is.

As I weigh in for the fight and as the photographers get everything they need in the way of poses, I spot Hong among the other competitors. He's solid with muscle, a guy with a good smile and a whole crew of people around him singing his praises. He thanks them all for coming and weighs in at exactly two hundred and five pounds.

For a brief second, our eyes meet, and I know he's appraising my ability from a glance as well.

He'll be a tough fight and a good sportsman. He has that aura about him.

Malala and Corbin wait for me on the sidelines. They wave once I'm finished, and I hustle over to them. I'm happy to see Malala without the splint on her leg, and her arm has a simple thin cast that she easily hides under a long-sleeved blouse.

To my surprise, Derek comes walking in through the door. Corbin stiffens his posture, but his sister practically turns into a bag of springs and Slinkys.

"Hello, Derek," she says with a wave. "You made it!"

He tucks his hands into his pockets and nods. "Yeah. Here I am."

They regard each other with an awkward silence, and it's weird seeing Malala keep her distance. Derek smiles, though, and Malala relaxes a bit. Is she still planning on speaking to him later tonight? I hope so. I'd hate it if they kept up this uneasy dance.

I tap Derek's shoulder with my knuckles. "I'm glad you could be here."

"Yeah. Sorry about ditching you like that."

"Don't worry about it."

"Thanks. You're the best, Keon."

I motion over to Hong. "I might legit need your help for this one. He's competent and confident."

"I'll be your corner man through and through. Trust me—no one has a perfect fighting stance, so if he has a weakness, I'll call it out for you."

"And I'll be there for support," Corbin chimes in.

Having my crew with me—I love it. I'm glad they could be here, together, even if some things aren't the same. I nod to each of them and smile. "Let's get something to eat. I need food to fuel my fight."

Chapter 26
What a Match

Keon Lynch

THE FAMILIAR pulse of a fight electrifies my nerves and gets me hyped.

Music rumbles the arena with a bass so heavy it could measure on the Richter scale. It flows up through the soles of my feet and straight to my spine. I hop around, trying to burn the excess energy before I get into the octagon. The announcer talks about Hong, so I need to wait until he introduces me.

"How are you feeling?" Derek asks.

With my mouth guard in, it's difficult to speak. I nod to him, and he understands. Derek gives me a thumbs-up.

But I'd be lying if I didn't admit the anxiety. It grips at the edges of my thoughts, taunting me with the possibility of failure. Will I arrive victorious? That's half the fun of a competition.

Proving to the world I can do it. I matter. I'll succeed. This is what I was made for—my talent and telos—the skill I've cultivated into an art.

Confidence is the fuel of the wise and the liquor of the fool. Which am I? We'll see by the end of the match.

The doors open, and I step out to the cheering of an excited crowd. The announcer says some things, no doubt about me and my undefeated record, but I don't care. I march up to the edge of the cage while he prattles on. Corbin and Derek give me one final set of nods before I head in.

Hong waits by the opposite side. He's in white shorts, exposing the tattoos of his wife and two children he has marked across his body. His hair is cut so short it almost looks bald in some spots, but that's practical. No chance it can get in the way, then.

A bell rings, and the announcer says something about the start of the match.

Hong holds up his glove so we can tap before the match. I walk over and return the gesture, and then we break apart before we fight. Hong is a good guy. He wants a clean fight, and I'm more than happy to give it to him.

Corbin Friel

I CAN'T watch. Already my heart is in my throat, threatening to leap out and cover my eyes for me. Keon and Hong approach each other in the middle of the cage, their arms up and their legs set apart in a wide stance. Derek sits next to me, rapt by the sight, but I keep glancing in every direction but right in front of me.

What if he loses?

I can still see the cut on his forearm from when he fought Justin. It didn't disqualify him from participating, but it reminds me that Keon can still be badly hurt. That would be worse than just losing—losing and being sent to the hospital immediately afterward.

Keon throws a punch, and Hong ducks away. Keon follows it up with a heavier, faster punch—I'd have been unconscious in a second— but Hong dodges that too. And then a third swing. And a fourth. Hong moves to the side or backs away, never getting hit.

"Press him," Derek yells. "He can't run forever!"

I wish Keon were faster. This Hong guy is practically running circles around him. And every punch Keon throws must wear down his stamina. He'll be tired by the time he gets Hong up against the fence. Can't Derek see that?

Keon does as Derek suggests and continues pummeling with all his might. Sure enough, when Hong gets near the fence, Keon is much slower than before. Hong notices. He jumps forward and does a roundhouse kick—so fast I'm surprised he doesn't spin up into the air—and his heel connects with Keon's jaw.

Keon staggers back, his eyes unfocused for a fleeting second.

With Keon on the ropes, Hong rushes forward again. He lifts his leg like he'll kick, but at the last second, he shoots a punch for Keon's gut. Keon—too slow to react to everything—had his arm up to block another roundhouse kick, leaving his abdomen exposed to the blow.

Hong is so much faster. And he's clever too. No wonder he's one of the guys competing to get into the UFC qualifier.

"Take him to the ground," Derek shouts. "Grapple him!"

Keon doesn't waste any time with his instructions. He lunges forward and grabs at Hong's legs, hoping to trip him. Hong twists and leaps out of Keon's grip in a true display of athleticism. Hong gives Keon a quick jab to the ribs for his efforts. With a grunt, Keon moves away.

I hadn't been paying attention to the crowd, but their roars reach a point they can no longer be ignored. Half the crowd cheers for Keon, while the other half screams incoherent nonsense about finishing the fight quickly. Hong has fans—his crew—but not many are here for him since he took the fight on late notice. I'm thankful, because I want Keon to have as much support as possible.

Before Derek can yell anything else, the bell rings, signaling the end of the first round. Keon and Hong retreat back to their corners, and the announcer opens the cage for coaches and medics. I follow Derek into the octagon and stand next to Keon. He's breathing heavy, but he doesn't take a seat or ask for any water.

"You okay?" Derek asks.

Keon replies with a curt nod.

"You need to land a few blows, man. He's going to chip you to death if this keeps up."

"He should pin him to the fence," I say, my voice almost lost to the raucous of the crowd. "Hong is too agile for anything else."

"You think so?" Derek asks, his expression serious.

I'm not that confident in my assessment. I don't know everything there is to know about fighting, and I've never trained for a fight myself, but it seems like a logical solution.

"I think it can work," I say. "The rules say you can push people against the fence, you just can't grab on to it." No putting their fingers through the slots and holding—that's the extent of the rule.

Derek pats Keon on the arm. "You might as well try."

Again, Keon nods.

The bell rings again, and I exit the octagon as quickly as possible. Staying in the ring too long after time could result in Keon getting penalty points.

Once everyone is clear, a woman in a tight black bikini walks around the octagon holding a sign with a giant number two. She winks and waves to the audience before taking a seat on the sideline, stretching out like she was on her own personal beachfront.

The bell rings again, and the second round begins.

Keon doesn't wait. He rushes forward and throws a few punches. Hong jumps back, and when his back hits the fence, Keon stops punching and football-tackles him against the chain-link edges of their cage.

Hong punishes him for the brash action. He punches Keon in the side, over and over, so hard I can hear the beat of hard knuckles against flesh. Keon winces each time, but he doesn't let go. Red marks appear on his battered body.

Move. Please. Get away from him. Anything but this.

Derek must be on the same wavelength because he shouts, "You've got to do something, Keon! Don't sit there and take it!"

I hold my breath. Keon continues to take the hits. Why? There must be some reason.

Then I spot it. He's moving his arms up around Hong's body, keeping his grip tight so Hong can't get away. Although he takes a number of strikes, it's not to his face or anywhere where he might be rendered unconscious. He just has to work through the pain. Once his grip is around Hong's lower ribs, Keon lifts his opponent.

Hong panics. He kicks and flails and twists in Keon's arms.

Keon leaps backward, arching his back like an upside-down U, and slams Hong's head straight into the mat.

The whole room collectively gasps.

Hong and Keon both get to their feet, but Hong stumbles, obviously in a daze. Keon throws one powerful right hook and connects with Hong's face.

In a split second, Hong falls to his knees and then forward, unconscious.

The blast of applause fills the arena.

"What a match!" the announcer screams. "Keon wins with a suplex throw to the ground, followed by a clean right hook! What a match, ladies and gentlemen. I can't say it enough! *What a match!*"

More roaring, more cheering—some people stomp their feet, as though they need to one-up their fellow MMA fans. I cover my ears and stick close to Derek, relief flooding my body.

I hate how a single fight can turn on a dime. One second a fighter can be losing, but all it takes is one good blow to get back into the running. It makes every second torture—there's no time to blink. I can only imagine how Keon feels.

At least he won.

WAITING FOR Keon is almost as painful as watching him fight.

I pace the back room and grit my teeth. Where is he? Other fighters have returned already. Are the medics testing him for drugs? Is he seriously injured? I want to hold him and congratulate him. Every person who does it before me actually gets me jealous. I should be the first person he runs to—or at least, I just want to be.

Derek pokes at his cell phone, his attention anywhere but here. I almost yell at him. Almost. How can he be so calm? Keon has worked so hard for this. Keon will finally be able to enter the UFC qualifier. He's doing it. He's becoming a famous fighter. People might know his name all around the world. Yet here Derek is, playing Candy Crush or some nonsense.

Or texting. He seems to type an awful lot.

I'm on the verge of asking him when he stands and walks off. We're the only two waiting for Keon—how can he get up and leave without telling me where he's going? And it's not like he's heading for the bathroom. He went straight for the back door out of the building.

I glance around. The other fighters hang with their groups, each with a table and a set of chairs all their own. It fascinates me that every arena has different accommodations for the fighters. Nothing is uniform. I shake my head and dispel the odd thoughts.

Derek should be here when Keon arrives. I should go get him.

With a huff and a sigh, I head for the back door. As Keon's manager, I'm allowed in the back room any time I want, so even if I get stuck outside, I can make it back. I exit out into the parking lot, confused when I find myself alone. The heavyweight fights are still in progress, so none of the audience has left yet.

But where is Derek?

I head for the corner of the building and stop when I hear voices. I recognize both of them.

Lala and Derek.

"—and I'll be able to fully remove the cast in about four weeks," Lala says.

"Cool," Derek replies, his uncomfortable posture traveling through his voice.

Did my sister text him and ask to meet? Why would she do that? He left her before—crushed her spirit and made her cry. I still can't believe it. My sister didn't deserve any of that, not while she needed to recover.

"So," my sister begins. "We should talk. I wrote out what I want to say, so I don't get confused or, you know, fumble with my thoughts."

"You don't have to do this, Malala."

"Let me finish?"

"Sure."

Lala clears her throat and then takes a deep breath. "You said you didn't want to hurt me, and I appreciate the sentiment, but I've known physical pain all my life. I'm sure I'll continue to have trips and falls. All people do."

"Malala"—Derek's voice is on the edge of breaking—"I love being with you, but all it takes is the wrong move. What if we're together, and then something happens, and you resent me forever? I don't know how I'd handle it."

"Derek," Lala says. "I'm not a liability. I'm a person. Maybe we can't do the things other people could, but we can have our own things. Every time you say you're too scared to be with me, it feels like you're saying, *Malala, you're not worth even trying to make it work*. It… it hurts more than the break or the medication. Like… I'm somehow less of a person, even though… even though I kn-know I'm not."

Every second of this conversation twists my insides. I wish I had the power to cure my sister of all diseases and ailments. That's what medicine is for, after all. Maybe someday, that's what I'll do.

S.A. Stovall

Derek exhales. "I don't think you're a liability."

"If I were… not like this… would you have stayed with me?"

Silence.

Perhaps Derek never wanted to be with her in the first place. Maybe he's just using this as an excuse to end his relationship and move one.

"Malala," he says. "I'm an idiot."

I almost laugh aloud, but I stifle the reaction.

"No, you're not," she says.

"I am. I know it. I… I'm so sorry. Ever since I left you in the clinic, you're all I could think about. You were smiling before I spoke to you, and then I did what I said I was trying to avoid—I made you cry. The guilt ate at me. I didn't call or return your texts because I figured you hated me for it. That I was an idiot for thinking I could be with you."

"You don't have to worry about me. I'll be like this whether I'm with you or not. The real question is… and I won't be angry no matter what you say… but…."

"I want to be with you," Derek injects. "That is, as long as you want to be together. And you're able to forgive me."

"Really?"

"Yeah. Life is better when you're around. Trust me. These few weeks have been awful without you."

"Derek… I knew the moment we met you were someone I'd want to keep close."

"When you won those backstage passes?" he asks with a laugh.

"No," Lala replies, a hint of seriousness to her tone. "When you helped me in second grade."

I hold my breath, waiting for the final reply. How can he turn her away now? But nothing happens. No words exchanged. Curiosity destroys my willpower and I chance a glance around the corner of the building.

Derek and Lala hold each other tight, lost in their embrace, their eyes not even open.

I duck back around the building.

"I have to meet Keon," Derek mutters.

"Okay," Lala says. "I'll go make us reservations so we can celebrate."

"Sounds great."

They break apart, and I breathe easy. I'm glad this worked out. Maybe Derek isn't the best man to be with my sister, but he's everything my sister seems to want, which is what really matters. When Derek walks around the building and spots me, he freezes up, a perplexed look on his face.

"Hey," he says. "How long have you—"

"You better be good to my sister," I snap.

Derek rubs the back of his neck and smiles. "Don't worry. I will."

"I expect nothing less."

"You saying you'll kick my ass if I don't?"

"No. Doctors don't hurt people. I'll have Keon kick your ass."

With a laugh, Derek grabs my shoulder and pulls me into a quick hug. He pats my back a few times, hard enough to wind me.

"You're a good brother. I'm glad you're looking out for Malala, but you can pass the torch on, got it? I'll be there for her."

I return his hug, awkward in every regard. He has a physique like Keon, which means I'm patting rock hidden under skin, and he squeezes a little too tight.

I hope he's there for Lala. I hope they make it—that they're happy. I don't want to see my sister upset like that ever again.

"Let's get inside," Derek says. "Before Keon wonders where we are."

He breaks the embrace, and we make our way back into the fighter waiting room. Keon stands around in the far corner, and my urge to hug him increases tenfold. I jog to him and throw my arms around his torso.

"*Tsk*," he says as he sucks in his breath. "Watch the side."

"Sorry." I loosen my grip, but I don't let go.

Keon strokes my back. "This is it. I'm on my way."

"I know. The UFC qualifier is right around the corner."

"Five weeks."

"I'll be here for you."

Keon lifts my head and lightly kisses me. "Good. I wouldn't want to go through with it unless I had my biggest fan."

I flush. "I love you."

"And I you."

Chapter 27
UFC Qualifier

Keon Lynch

TRAINING CONSUMES me. Time passes by with a phantom speed. One minute it's Monday, and the next time I check, it's Friday. My hands shake when I lift my weights or when I go for my run. There's no better time to be alive than right now, on the edge of achieving everything I've worked for.

I lift the forty-pound hand weight with one arm seven times. I need to focus. The fight is right around the corner. Two weeks now. Only two, but I'm sure that'll melt away like an ice cube in the desert.

Corbin sits next to me, reading over his medical books. When I glance his way, he straightens his glasses and returns the look. Then we return to our separate activities, and I'm comforted knowing he's here. Training would be torture without him at his point. I've come to rely on his support like a drug addict relies on a quick hit to get out of bed every morning.

"I don't want to add any stress," Corbin says, breaking my chain of thoughts, "but do you know who your opponent will be yet?"

"I do."

"Who is it?"

"Some guy named Odo Rieffel."

"How do you plan to beat him?"

"He's a couple inches shorter than I am," I say.

Corbin lifts an eyebrow. "And?"

"And that's enough to make the difference."

"A few inches gives you a significant advantage? You're not more worried about this?"

I switch arms and do another seven reps, curling the weight all the way up to my shoulder. The burn helps, and I can't wait to get to the steam room after this.

"I have a pretty good kick," I say. "I haven't used it since I found out I had an infection in my shin. I doubt Odo will be expecting it, especially if he's watched my previous videos. I wasn't heavy on the kicking then, so it might not be in his strategy to guard for that. Every little advantage will help me win."

Corbin mulls over the information before returning his gaze to his books. For another couple minutes, we resume our standard procedure, but Corbin once again stops. He looks at me, and then back to the page, and then to me again.

"What is it?" I ask.

"I have a present for you," he says.

"Okay. Where is it?"

"Well, it's a surprise. It should be at our apartment the day of the fight. In the morning."

"I don't need anything, Corbin. Having your support is good enough."

"I… think you'll like this."

"Is it sex?" I ask with a half a smile. "Because if it isn't, you wasted money."

"It's not sex." Corbin huffs and glares down at his anatomy book. "I just wanted to warn you about the present before it arrived."

Warn me? This doesn't sound good. What could he possibly be talking about? I'm half tempted to demand the answer from him, but I hold off. There's no need to fight. If it's a present, I'm sure I'll enjoy it no matter what. And as long as Corbin is with me at the fight, that's all that matters.

"Hey!"

I jerk my attention up and see Harvey marching over toward my station. I set the weight down on the ground and stand. I'm on the verge of saluting—some habits never die—until Harvey crosses his arms and frowns.

"Is it true you went to another gym and flirted with the idea of joining?" he asks.

How did he even hear about the Hideki guys?

I sigh. "Yeah."

"They have a better gym than me?"

I nod.

"And better trainers and workout equipment?"

"Yeah."

"Then what're you still doing here?" Harvey asks. He motions to a treadmill that's been out of order since I moved to California. "You've got to get the best trainin' possible if you're gonna beat those assholes in the qualifier. Don't hold yourself back on my account."

"But—"

"You just let me put my logo on everything you wear once you're huge," Harvey says, ignoring me the entire time. "Free advertisement. Maybe even say I was the one that helped you out."

"You were."

"Good. Yeah. Sell it."

I run a hand over my face and shake my head. "They also wouldn't let me train with Corbin around, so this was the best spot for me still."

Harvey glances to Corbin. Corbin replies with a short wave.

"Hey," Harvey says, returning his attention to me. "What I'm tryin' to say is—I know I haven't been there for you every inch of the way."

"You've helped me a lot, Harvey. More than most friends. You don't need to do me any additional favors."

"No. I do. You've got drive and talent, and I'm some shmuck who buys and sells properties. I should be helpin' you out whenever possible. Besides, we were in the same battalion and even went overseas together. You've got to succeed."

Harvey is a good guy. This is why I stuck with his gym even when I could've gone with the Hideki guys. I don't want to betray his faith and loyalty in me, and I want to remember my roots, so to speak. It can't be like this forever, but it can be for right now.

"Thank you, Harvey."

"Hey, if you need any extra bags or water or training equipment, just let me know. I'll see what I can do for ya. Oh, and I'm going to be there for your fight, so this better not be the one you lose, got it?"

"I won't lose."

Harvey pats my shoulders and hustles off, no doubt checking the property and counting the new memberships for the month.

"I like Harvey," Corbin says, his attention focused on his book.

"Me too."

DAY OF the fight.

How is it here already? I can't remember half of the stuff that has happened in the last month. I've stuck to my schedule, I've kept to my diet—there's nothing left. We're going to drive to San Francisco and be at the weigh-ins by 1200 hours.

By tomorrow morning I'll either be a UFC fighter or a… a guy who didn't make it.

Where is Corbin? He left early in the morning, before the sun even rose, and he hasn't returned since. He says he has something for me, but I don't want him to be late over a stupid gift. Maybe I should call his sister. Malala can always talk some sense into him.

The front door to our apartment opens and closes. I splash my face from the water of our bathroom faucet and stare at myself in the mirror. Anxious energy keeps me keen and focused. I'm already packed and ready to go. Corbin and I should head out soon.

I exit the bathroom and walk through our new bedroom. It's a much better apartment than either of us had previously. Corbin's rent was ridiculous because he lived in Sacramento, which meant he had a small place. This apartment, nestled between Stockton and Sacramento, might be twice as large. We have a walk-in closet, a proper living room, two bathrooms, and a nice kitchen. What more could we want for the time being?

I enter the living room and stop dead in my tracks, my last breath caught in my throat.

Corbin stands by the door, a sheepish look on his face, and my sister, Alisha, stands at his side.

I… haven't seen her in years. Her long dark hair has been cut pixie-short, and her clothes are appropriate for colder weather than California, but I'd recognize her no matter the slight changes to appearance.

Alisha offers me a forced smile.

"Keon," Corbin begins. "I spoke with your sister on the phone and asked her to come out for your fight. She knows everything. I told her about the trust fund and what you've been doing. Please don't be upset, but I figured she would want to know what's going on in her brother's life."

He steps back and motions for Alisha to take over.

I still can't seem to breathe. We didn't part on good terms last we saw each other.

"Corbin has nothing but good things to say about you," Alisha says, a nervousness to her voice. "He gushed the entire drive back from the airport hotel about how you've won each of your professional fights."

"I'm glad to hear it."

"Keon." She takes a deep breath and steps closer. Alisha has always reminded me of our mother. They share the same facial shape and expressions. "I had no idea you were looking out for me."

I don't know what to say to that. Maybe Corbin shouldn't have said anything.

"I thought you moved to California to escape your problems, but that's just not the case. Corbin said you were working as an exterminator, and pro fighting on the side, sending all your spare cash to help me pay for med school…. It's a completely different picture than what I had thought for years."

"I didn't try very hard to explain," I say. "I'm sorry about that."

"I'm the one who should be apologizing. I took all my frustration about our father out on you."

I take two breaths that soothe my nerves. "It was rough back then."

"No. That's no excuse. I should've realized. We should've been there for each other—I should've been there for you—and we could have grown as a family who survived domestic violence. Truly, Keon. I'm sorry."

She says each word with perfect precision, no waver in her voice, but her eyes glaze over, and tears run the length of her face. I remember this look. Always putting on a brave face. Her steel will would never let her give in to sadness.

"I've long forgiven you," I say. "I didn't handle it the best either. That doesn't matter. It's in the past. I'm just… shocked you're even here. Thank you."

Alisha wipes away the tears from her face and smiles—a genuine smile this time. "Corbin says you're about to enter an important fight?"

"Yeah."

"I'm glad you're using your talents for something constructive. I never imagined you would take to sports. But now that I think of it... this is what you were meant to do."

"You're not bothered by the fact I'm fighting?"

"I'd rather you were a tennis player," she says with a laugh. "But you should follow your heart. If this means a lot to you, then it means a lot to me. I want to be part of your life again, and I don't want to start our new relationship by insulting your choice of sports."

Wow. Corbin must've really talked to her. I never thought she would understand my choice. I figured she would've criticized it and claimed I did it only for the violence.

As if Alisha can read my mind, she smiles. "Corbin showed me the videos of your fights, and told me about everything you've done to get here. I'm proud of you, Keon. I really am."

The last of my doubt melts away. I grab Alisha and we embrace, her tears returning. We did survive a lot together, and I can't imagine what my life would've been like if she hadn't been there when we were kids. I'm thankful she came to see my fight, and I'm eternally grateful to Corbin for making this happen.

I give him a quick look, and he smiles.

He's made this day perfect—now all I have to do is deliver.

Corbin Friel

THE SAN Francisco arena is unlike any that came before it.

Huge. Sprawling. The crowds are three times the size they were at the pro events and there are live camera feeds to broadcast the fights all over the world. The motto of the qualifier seems to be *Go big or go home*. Whereas the smaller fight nights had one or two sexy girls holding signs, this qualifier has five. Whereas the smaller fight nights had a single announcer and three judges per fight, this qualifier has two commentators, an in-cage referee, and five judges on the panel—two of which are UFC fighters themselves.

And there are big-screen televisions all around the arena, showcasing the event so that even the people in the boonies can see the blood splatter.

Everyone who wins their match gets a UFC contract to fight with them in the big leagues.

The scope reminds me this is a massively popular sport, even if I didn't care for it a year ago.

Keon and Derek wait in the official fighter's room. They don't allow managers or agents or even low-level coaches with the fighters, only corner men and the lead coach. I sit in the front row with Lala and Alisha, my heart pounding so hard it drowns out all other noise. The glare of the high-powered lights is enough to bake a frog. Luckily we sit just at the edge, hidden in the darkness of the arena, waiting for the middleweight fighters to finish their bout.

After that is the light heavyweight division. Keon's fight.

"Have you ever been to a fight night before?" Lala asks as she shakes Alisha's arm.

"No," Alisha says, no doubt thrown off by Lala's never-ending enthusiasm.

"Okay, I'll show you everything we need to do. First, I brought this banner. You should help me hold it. It has Keon's name on this side and hearts on the other side."

"O-okay."

"And we need to scream and cheer for him when he wins. As loud as possible!"

"*If* he wins. We should be prepared to support him if—"

"*When* he wins! He's going to do it. I can tell."

That's what she said about Derek's fight.

When the middleweight fight ends—I wasn't even watching, I just know from the massive amount of cheering and epic levels of applause—the main announcer steps into the octagon. The two commentators quiet themselves for the introductions, and my chest tightens with each second before the fight.

"Fighting out of the blue corner," he shouts, showmanship in his voice and mannerisms as he flails his arms and drags out each word, "a mixed martial artist holding a professional record of seventeen wins and two losses, he stands five feet, eleven inches, weighing in at an ideal weight of two hundred and five pounds, and representing Oakland, California, I present to you *Odo 'the Guillotine' Rieffel*!"

Odo jumps into the octagon to a wave of cheering.

The announcer continues, regardless of the audience, his microphone on a whole new level. "This fight is brought to you by Bud Light—*here you go*! And MetroPCS 4G LTE, *a network for all*!"

Odo slams himself on the chain-link fence of the cage, his arms in the air. He has a scruffy beard, much like Derek, and his hair is braided into cornrows.

"And now, fighting out of the red corner, this man has an undefeated professional record of seven wins, each match ending before the third round, standing six feet, two inches, and also weighing in at two hundred and five pounds, and representing Stockton, California, I present to you *Keon 'the Watchman' Lynch*!"

Through the myriad of shouts and screams, Alisha smiles wide and says, "The Watchman? Oh gosh, that was our mom's favorite cop show growing up. I can't believe he chose that nickname...."

"Go, the Watchman," Lala cheers. She jumps up and down, and I grit my teeth, worrying about her. "You can do it!"

"Steve Franklin will be our referee for the match," the announcer continues. "And without further ado, let the first round begin!"

The bell that sounds is practically a siren. In one quick burst, it heralds the start of the match. Keon and Odo leap for the center of the octagon, but neither strikes. They feint back and throw a few punches, but nothing lands.

The crowd hushes, a low murmur of white noise filling the arena. Alisha grabs Lala's arm and grips tight. "Is it always this tense?"

"Yeah," Lala says. "That's the beauty of the fight."

I'm still struggling to watch. Odo and Keon circle each other, their eyes set and their hands up in tight fists.

"It's going to be an entertaining match," one commentator says, their voice booming over the speaker system. "Odo Rieffel has won all seventeen of his victories with a total knockout. One powerful jab to the face. That's right. He has sheer power behind those fists."

"His new nickname should be rocket fist," the second commentator says.

"Yes! I love it. Rocket Fist is a perfect name for Odo."

No wonder Keon keeps his distance. Both he and Odo dance around, circling more times than carrion birds. Whenever they get within a few feet, they both throw out another round of warning punches. The crowd grows restless with each tense second. Some stand from their seats, and others cheer for action.

The referee walks along the edge of the octagon, keeping an eye on the bout with narrowed eyes.

"Looks like both fighters might be suffering from nerves," Commentator One says.

Commentator Two whistles. "I bet that's the case. This is the ultimate league, and hundreds of thousands of people are watching. You have to be careful not to choke."

"Indeed."

I close my eyes. I can't take it. I've seen Keon go through thick and thin—he's gone to bat for his dream, and now he wants to claim it. What if he loses? I know the answer. He won't give up. Even if he fails here, he'll try again, even if it'll cost him, even if he'll never get another chance. And I'll be there for him. I'll help him any way I can. And so will Lala. And Harvey. And Derek. And Alisha.

I open my eyes, and the two fighters have stopped their circling. They inch closer and closer, their stances wide as the gap between them narrows.

No matter what, Keon will be a UFC fighter. I know it. I have to believe it.

"It's do-or-die time," Commentator-One shouts. "I want to see some blood!"

Commentator Two bangs his hand on the desk. "The crowd is restless. Where's that round-ending punch from Odo?"

"You can do it, Keon!" I shout.

Lala and Alisha jump, their eyes wide. But then they both get to their feet as well.

"Yeah," Lala says, joining in. "Go Keon! Go Keon!"

"Go Keon," Alisha repeats.

To my surprise, the chant spreads through the audience. I remember when Keon wasn't liked at all—when he used his cocky bravado to rile the crowds since he was a nobody—but now he's a somebody. People can recognize him, and his winning streak has made him famous. People want to see him win.

I know I do.

Commentator One chuckles. "Seems the crowd has a favorite for this fight, and it *isn't* the guy with seventeen wins. Interesting."

"Keon has an undefeated victory streak," the other comments. "And he served his country for eight years."

"Not only that, but his sponsor seems to be a workout gym. That's no certified fighting academy—this guy is self-made."

"Unbelievable. The guy's got talent."

Keon lunges, and the crowd collectively gasps.

Odo jumps away, but he takes a few punches to the face. While Keon throws another overhand, Odo kicks at his leg and trips Keon.

"Here we go," Commentator One says. "Time for some ground 'n' pound!"

Keon hits the mat on his back and then rolls to his side and jumps to his feet before Odo even has a chance to scratch him. He's so much faster than Odo that he lands a few more punches and forces the guy back.

"We only have thirty seconds before the end of the round," Commentator Two says. "Will they make it? Or will one of them get knocked out?"

Odo does it—he throws his heavy punches. People in the arena stand, with bated breath.

Keon dodges, but he has to block his face with his forearms. Blow after blow rocks him, his own arms slamming into cheek and ear.

Alisha can't breathe, and Lala holds her close.

I relax.

Something about the way Keon is moving—I've seen it before in his other matches. It's a confidence he has when he has a plan. He moves differently then. He acts differently. Odo throws punch after punch, but Keon's biding his time.

Odo's too slow.

He's already lost.

Sure enough, the moment Odo takes the time for a deep breath, Keon brings his leg up—his once-infected leg—and kicks Odo hard in the side of the head, right above the temple. The man is unconscious before he even hits the mat.

The shock and awe of the blow sends ripples through the crowd. The big screens replay the kick over and over, showing Odo's eyes rolling back into his skull.

The commentators go berserk.

"Fantastic!"

"Perfectly executed knockout from Keon! His new name should be *The Undying*! He just can't lose!"

I'm on my feet, clapping as hard as I can. Keon circles around, his hands in the air, waving to the crowd. But then he stops and turns his gaze to my portion of the audience. Although I'm shrouded in the darkness, I know he's looking to me, Lala, and Alisha.

"He did it," his sister says. "He really won!"

Lala shakes her again. "Of course he did! I told you so!"

I take in a few shallow breaths, excitement coursing through my veins and arteries.

This is it. The moment our lives begin.

Both of us living our dream.

S.A. STOVALL grew up in California's central valley with a single mother and little brother. Despite no one in her family having a degree higher than a GED, she put herself through college (earning a BA in History), and then continued on to law school where she obtained her Juris Doctorate.

As a child, Stovall's favorite novel was *Island of the Blue Dolphins* by Scott O'Dell. The adventure on a deserted island opened her mind to ideas and realities she had never given thought before—and it was the moment Stovall realized that storytelling (specifically fiction) became her passion. Anything that told a story, be it a movie, book, video game, or comic, she had to experience. Now as a professor and author, Stovall wants to add her voice to the myriad of stories in the world, and she hopes you enjoy.

You can contact her at the following addresses:
Twitter: @GameOverStation
Email: s.adelle.s@gmail.com

WORLD
OF LOVE

THE
DUSK
PARLOR

S.A. STOVALL

Former soldier Hugh Harris is a "hāfu"—half-Japanese, half-American—and, after his father's death, he returns to Kobe, Japan, in order to connect with his mother and her family. Confused and feeling out of place, Hugh finds work as a waiter at an upscale nightclub. The other employees, an odd and eclectic bunch, quickly make him feel at home, especially the bartender, Ren, and the club host, Kaito.

But the tranquility doesn't last forever. As Hugh gets deeper into his relationships with both men, he finds they may have dubious connections with the yakuza in town… and when the local street leaders send their enforcers to the Dusk Parlor, Hugh, Ren, and Kaito may be in for a storm of trouble.

www.dreampsinnerpress.com

www.ingramcontent.com/pod-product-compliance
Lightning Source LLC
Chambersburg PA
CBHW051635260626
47170CB00004B/1188